Lost on the Edge of Eternity

Lost on the Edge of Eternity

Jonathan Floyd

Wild Ideas

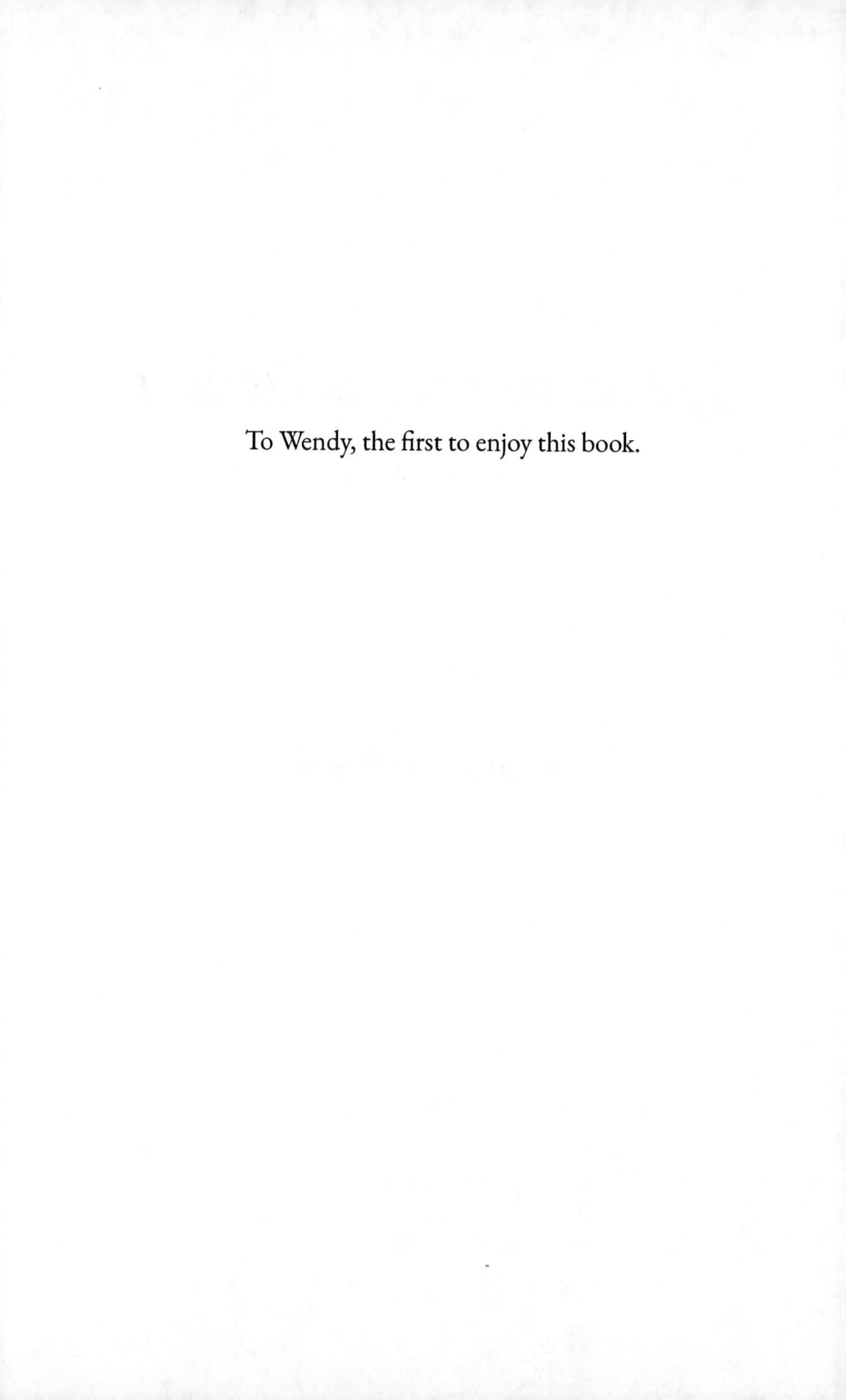

To Wendy, the first to enjoy this book.

ISBN 978-0-9620031-7-2

Published by:
Wild Ideas

https://jfloyd203.wixsite.com/mysite

Praise for *Lost on the Edge of Eternity*

"A brilliant paranormal novel . . . expertly written, [Floyd] has created a delightfully poignant story that leaves the reader with a good feeling." – *Readers' Favorite*

"A thought-provoking and unpredictable story of hope and second chances . . . This novel is thematically strong, with well-developed characters and an original premise that will appeal to a YA audience, but also boasts plenty of wisdom for older readers." – *Self-Publishing Review*

"*Lost on the Edge of Eternity* is a well-written page turner, with a clever plot and many intriguing twists." – Elizabeth Graham, author of *Jacintha Point* (commenting on the 2001 edition)

"I enjoyed *Lost on the Edge of Eternity* very much."
– Donald Hamilton, creator of the Matt Helm adventure series (commenting on the 2001 edition).

"A poignant look at life and regrets . . . ideal for anyone wanting a feel-good story." – *Online Book Club*

"A refreshing ghost story delivering more psychology and good will than horror." – *Kirkus Reviews*

"*Lost on the Edge of Eternity* is a crazy delightful story. . . Well-done voice and style that will suck in YA readers, not to mention their parents, too. We need more books out there like this. Poignant and memorable.." – C. Hope Clark, author of *The Edisto Island Mysteries* and *The Carolina Slade Mysteries*.

"Floyd's fluid, dreamlike narrative takes the reader through motley political climates, social zeitgeists, and musical tastes during . . . Floyd's highly entertaining ghost story gone wild." – *US Review of Books*

"An excellent, multifaceted story about life's meaning . . . recommended reading for mature teen to adult readers." – D. Donovan, Senior Reviewer, *Midwest Book Review*

"*Lost on the Edge of Eternity* is an unbridled look at life, death, peer pressure, fitting in, bullying, society prejudices and second chances. I highly recommend this book to Young Adults and older." – *Reader Views*

"Jonathan Floyd's *Lost on the Edge of Eternity*, a story of regret laced with otherworldly vibes, is an enrapturing and playful piece of fiction that achieves a combination of wit and wisdom, along with enjoyable, easy-to-read charm." – *IndieReader*

"Floyd is a smart, accomplished writer." -- The Booklife Prize

Awards

Finalist for 2021 Chanticleer International Book Awards for Paranormal Fiction

Winner, 2024 International Impact Book Awards for Young Adult

1

only caught a glimpse of him that first time, so I can't say for sure whether I recognized him right off or it dawned on me later that he looked like somebody I once knew. He was standing at the corner of the east wing hall, just down from my office, with his foot propped up against a locker like he owned the place. It's unusual to see that kind of posture in a new student. Usually they have that scared, disoriented look, always wondering where to go next, even in a school as small as Brownville High.

But not this kid.

He didn't care where he went next, and he wasn't in a hurry to get there.

I was just getting in from a miserable spring testing workshop at the district office, and as luck would have it, my arrival coincided with the beginning of first lunch. That meant I nearly got trampled by the herd of ninth grade buffalo that stampeded out of Miss Quaid's Algebra I class (having been spooked by the 11:30 bell) so they could huddle in the lunch line before the seniors started cutting in.

But even in the chaos of changing classes, I spotted the new kid right off. Since Parkland, the universal school rule has been to never let a stranger in the hall go unquestioned. Besides, as guidance counselor,

I was responsible for registering and orienting new students, so I started over to introduce myself. But before I got as far as the water cooler, Shelly Brice shoved a transcript request in my hand, and when I looked up, the new kid was gone.

"How was your meeting?" asked Sandra Burnsides, the school secretary. She was a pixieish brunette who looked like she had just graduated from college. The male students still flirted with her, and Larry Ringer claimed the reason he got sent out of Mrs. Brehmer's class twice a week was so he'd have an excuse to look at her on the way to Mr. Jacobs's office. It was only after you saw the efficient way she operated that you realized she had almost a dozen years' experience.

"Don't ask," I replied.

"That bad, huh?"

I took the mail out of my cubbyhole and thumbed through it. "Let's just say it started out so-so and went downhill."

She laughed.

I tore open an envelope. "Anything interesting happen while I was gone?"

She turned from her computer. "Let's see. Bennie Norris was suspended."

"Again? What did he do this time?"

"He got in a shoving match with Ted Kass. When Mrs. Wilson tried to break it up, he hit her. Broke her glasses."

I shook my head. "I just had a long talk with Bennie yesterday. It's nice to know everything I said went in one ear and out the other."

"I doubt it even went in one ear."

"Probably not."

"Mr. Jacobs is going to take Bennie before the board for expulsion. I'm typing up the papers now."

"I guess we've done all we could," I muttered, hoping that was true. I paused on my way out. "By the way, Sandra, who's the new student?"

"What new student?"

"Well, I assumed he was a new student. I saw this kid standing in the hall. I don't believe I've seen him around before."

"What did he look like?"

"Medium height. Dark, shaggy hair. Sharp nose. I believe he wore jeans and a fatigue shirt."

"I don't know who he could have been."

"Maybe he wasn't a student."

"Or maybe Mr. Jacobs enrolled him while I was gone to the bank."

"I'll ask him."

Before the school board's consolidation vote in mid-February, Mr. Jacobs had been a hard man to find. He had an uncanny way of knowing when trouble was about to come his way, and he could always make himself scarce just before it hit. It was remarkable how quickly he could disappear in a school as small as Brownville High.

But lately you could always find him in his office, with his feet up on his desk, working the daily crossword puzzle or just doodling on his notepad. He no longer seemed to care whether trouble found him. He was what is known in political circles as a lame duck. The local L. B. Brown textile mill, Brownville's only source of employment, had closed its doors for good in January after eighty years of operation, thanks to cheap textile imports and management's failure to modernize. Without the mill, Brownville High's projected enrollment would not be sufficient to keep its doors open. The school board had faced the situation with uncharacteristic decisiveness by voting to close down Brownville High at the end of the current school year, making the class of 2010 the school's last graduating class. The student body would be consolidated with the two thousand-student high school in the county seat seventeen miles down the road. The town of Brownville had fought stubbornly to keep its school open, and Principal Stanley Jacobs, a 1979 graduate of Brownville High, had led the bitter but unsuccessful fight.

Now Jacobs whiled away his last days as principal like a defeated Confederate general waiting in the shade for Reconstruction. He was depressed and irritable when I found him.

He didn't bother to remove his feet from his desk when I entered his office. He cut me a sharp look, the kind he reserved for students sent out of Mrs. Brehmer's class for shooting spitballs.

"What-choo need, Fellars?"

"I saw a new kid in the hall today. I was wondering if you enrolled anybody while I was gone."

He rubbed his bald scalp as if he still had enough hair there to push out of his eyes. "No. What'd he look like?"

"Dark complexion. Sharp nose. Shaggy hair. You know, now that I think about it, he looked a lot like Randy Galphin."

"Randy Galphin? Hot dang, Bill. You need a vacation worse than I do."

I was going over the testing schedule I had picked up at the district office, trying to figure out how I was going to come up with enough monitors for eight classrooms, when the new kid sauntered into the guidance office.

I gave him a hard stare and saw right off that he wasn't, in fact, a new kid after all.

"Randy? Randy Galphin?"

He gave me a grin I hadn't seen in a long time. He walked over and sat on the ledge of my window like he always had, propping his foot on the radiator.

"Hello, Mr. Fellars. You busy?"

I don't think I even answered him.

He turned and looked out the window at the faculty parking lot. He was watching two girls walk from the band house to the girls' restroom, which was right below my office. He cracked the window a few inches, and I thought he was going to yell at them. I made ready to scold him if he did. That's one of my pet peeves, kids yelling out my window.

But he didn't. He closed the window and turned back to face me.

I was still staring at him.

"Randy, I thought you were dead."

"I am," he said.

2

༄

Randy Galphin was a good kid. They're all good kids in my book, even the troublemakers. Bennie Norris might slit your tires, but he never failed to speak to you on the street.

But Randy Galphin was no Bennie Norris. I don't think he got in a lick of trouble the three years he was at Brownville High. He may have had to pull detention hall three or four times a year, but that's small potatoes at Brownville High. Well within the norm.

Randy came from one of those family situations where you would expect him to be the school's worst hellion. Alcoholic father. Neurotic mother. An unbearable marriage that had ended in the father's murder by a jealous husband, leaving the mother to raise seven kids in abject poverty. The word around Brownville was that the Galphins had worse luck than the Kennedys, without the luxury of all their wealth. What I admired most about them was that they never let poverty and hardship become an excuse for turning into thugs.

Randy was the oldest child, and when he turned seventeen, he dropped out of school and went to work in the local textile mill, becoming the major breadwinner of the family. When he got his girlfriend pregnant, he did the honorable thing and married her. She moved into the Galphin household, adding to their financial strain.

The year he dropped out, his junior year, I believe, he'd had study hall second period. Now, when I went to high school, we did our homework in study hall, or at least copied somebody else's. But at Brownville High, the kids don't do their homework for the most part, and in study hall, they sit there and get yelled at for talking, or the ones who can read bury themselves in sci-fi stories or manga graphic novels. Randy wasn't a reader, so to avoid getting yelled at, he would come up to my office second period to shoot the breeze.

I usually reserved second period as my planning period, so I seldom scheduled any appointments then. If a kid did come up to talk, Randy would politely leave and wait in my outer office. Sometimes he'd help me file away my mail. But mostly he'd sit on my window ledge with his feet propped up on my radiator, and we'd talk.

He seldom talked much about his problems. He would talk about hunting and fishing, or about drag racing on the back roads with Neddy Walker, or about a cock fight he'd gone to over on Little Goose Creek. Whenever I would nudge the conversation around to his home life, Randy was always evasive. If I tried to get him to talk about his feelings or tried for insight into his problems, he'd cut me off cold by changing the subject or finding an excuse to leave. I figured he wasn't ready to talk about it.

A couple of years after he quit school, Randy got in what the *Brownville Courier* called an "altercation in the workplace." He got into a major dispute with a coworker named Carl Shayne, who had a reputation as the second-shift jerk; there seems to be one in every workplace. I never learned the details, except that it started over practically nothing and escalated into a verbal war of one-upmanship. Randy's temper flared to the point that he went out to his truck and retrieved a pistol from the glove compartment. He returned to the spinning room with murder in his heart. Shaking with rage, he trained his gun on Shayne. The argument continued until, at the last second, Randy turned the gun on himself and put a bullet in his own head.

After that happened, I often wondered if there was something I could have done to make him open up to me.

"I see you've had your tonsils out," Randy Galphin said wryly.

I became aware that my jaw was slack. I closed my mouth.

"This has got to be a joke. I. . . " The sentence died in my throat.

He turned his crestfallen face so that his eyes avoided mine and stared painfully at the floor. "If it's a joke, I ain't laughing. I could pull up my hair and show you the exit wound where the bullet came out the back of my head. It's stuffed with mortician's wax. But I got to warn you, it ain't pretty."

I had no desire to view his exit wound. Instead, I leaned over my desk and touched his hand. It was cold. I jerked my hand away.

His pale face brightened a shade, and I figured he knew I was taking him at his word.

"I'm not going to bite you," he said with a shy grin. "Can we talk?"

His voice was so warm I found myself grinning back. Dead or not, he was the same good old boy he always was.

I eased back into my chair. "Sure."

It was a moment before he spoke again. He tapped his foot absently against the side of my radiator. "It's a crying shame about the school."

"It sure is," I agreed, somewhat awed at how easily I could talk to him.

"Every one of them board members ought to be tarred and feathered and boiled in oil."

"Do you think it's fair to blame them, Randy? With the mill situation the way it is?"

"We could have still kept the school. A lot of people in Brownville work out of town."

That's all he wanted to talk about. They should have kept the school open. The town was dead without its school. It was the rich people on the other side of the county, the farmers along the Upper Green Valley and the industrialists in the county seat, who had always looked down on the mill town of Brownville, and now who had finally gotten a chance to strangle the town and rob it of its community spirit.

He was distraught. I'd never seen him so bitter before. There were so many things I wanted to ask him, but I couldn't get past his obsession with the school closing.

There was no arguing with him. No chance that I could show him the other side of the issue. I could only sympathize. *Yeah, Randy, I'm upset about it too. I don't have a job for next year, Randy. They'll try to place us within the district, but maybe they won't be able to. It's a scary feeling, Randy.*

There was a knock on my door.

"Let me see who that is," I said, excusing myself.

It was Bonnie Griffin. She stared into the room behind me. "Are you busy, Mr. Fellars? I thought I heard you talking to somebody."

"Well, I was just . . ."

I turned around. Randy Galphin was gone.

3

◠◡◠

The next day, another strange kid walked into my office. He wore faded jeans and sneakers, and his hair was down below his shoulders, a style that had been out of vogue at Brownville High since the late nineties.

"G'mornin', Mr. Fellars. I'm Tony Cunningham."

He looked so vaguely familiar that I said with a frown, "Forgive my memory, Tony, but have we met before?"

"No. I'm a friend of Randy Galphin's."

I immediately placed him. I had seen his picture in the 1999-2000 school yearbook, which was dedicated to him. He had been killed in an automobile accident in 1999, the summer before I came to Brownville High. He'd had a carload of kids with him, and they were all stoned on pot. Tony had died at the wheel, a hero since he didn't take any of the other kids with him. During the fall of 1999, you could often see a kid or two sitting by his grave.

"What do you want?" I asked, somewhat apprehensively.

"I need to talk. Randy said you're a good listener."

I nodded. "Sit down."

He did so.

"I feel like I know you, Tony, even if we never met," I said, breaking

13

the ice. "A lot of kids were upset when you died. They came by here that fall in droves. They all spoke well of you."

He looked down at his hands. "I let a lot of people down."

"You're saying you feel guilty for getting killed?"

"Yeah. I was just sixteen. I wasn't ready to go."

"You're still not, obviously."

"No."

"You've been hanging around since 1999?"

"Yeah."

"Doing what?"

"Just watching. Hanging out. Like I did when I was alive."

"Don't you feel it's time to rest?"

His face clouded over. "I can't rest. I got cheated out of sixty years of living."

Unlike Randy Galphin, he was opening up. I decided to bring out his feelings. "I hear anger in your voice. And resentment. Am I right?"

"Why shouldn't I be angry? I made one little mistake and I got cut off from it all. I can't even feel it when I scratch my nose."

"It seems like death is always more tragic when it comes to a young person," I observed lamely.

He nodded. "Any way you cut it, being dead's a real drag."

I leaned back and folded my hands. "Okay, Tony, where do you want to go from here?"

"I don't know."

"You obviously can't come back."

"No."

"So the way I see it, you either have to cross over to wherever it is you're supposed to go, or you just keep hanging around."

"I'm scared to cross over."

"That leaves hanging around, for now."

"I can't do that much longer."

"Why not?"

"The mill's closing down. The school too. The town's going to dry up. By next September, there'll be tumbleweeds blowing up Main Street."

"That's an exaggeration, but not too far off the mark."

"We gotta be near people. When the people leave, we gotta cross over. That's just the way it is. We can't follow the people. If we stay on this side, we gotta stay close to where we lived."

I stroked my chin. "Randy was upset about the school's closing. Now I see why."

"We're all upset about it," he said.

I raised my brow. "How many of you are there?"

"Quite a few. Can you help us?"

I considered. I wanted to say no very badly. "I can only spare one session. I'll meet you here tonight at seven o'clock. I'll get the key from Mr. Jacobs. Bring the others with you."

4

かたく

I knew almost every one of them when they filed into my office that night. I'd spent the afternoon in the media center poring over old yearbooks, and I knew who to look for.

George Baucom and Linda Sue Boyle came in holding hands. They had been high school sweethearts until George drowned in Indian Lake the same summer Tony Cunningham had his wreck. Linda Sue went through a bad marriage and was struck by lightning at the age of twenty-one. She and George had got back together after they died.

Automobile wrecks accounted for several of them being there. Sharon Summer, a dropout, was killed on Little Gypsy Road three years previously. Barbara Fields lost control of the new Camaro her father had just bought for her sixteenth birthday. Mike Sanders was killed on the way home from Army Guard camp. Will Masters and Charlie Green had brought it on themselves by drag racing up Lover's Lane one night while loaded. They were stopped by an oncoming semi.

Steve Hall was electrocuted while putting up his grandmother's television antenna. Chadwick Corley, butt of a lifetime of jokes, was accidentally killed during a hazing incident at band camp. Johnny Brown fell off a hay truck and rolled under its wheels.

Melissa King was probably the most tragic one there. She was five years old and had been killed trying to snatch her cocker spaniel puppy out of the path of Rev. Malcolm Grady's beat-up Oldsmobile. Rev. Grady was the Presbyterian minister, and I never once saw him smile after that. Melissa skipped into my office behind the others, her dead spaniel in tow. She was so beautiful it made you want to cry.

Four of them I didn't know, but I knew of them. One was Sally Brock, the town lawyer's daughter, who had attended Brownville High well before my time. She had dropped dead during her junior year in college, the victim of some strange thirteen-letter illness that nobody could pronounce. They still talked about her in the teacher's lounge, about how much potential she'd had. Another was Freddy Seaton, still in his Army dress uniform. Freddy was killed at Pleiku in 1967. At age twenty-five, he was the oldest among them. A third was Sammy Tribble, who was lynched by rogue Klan members in late 1953. He still had rope burns on his neck. And finally, there was Laval Crenshaw, a child of the eighties who'd died of AIDS.

I hugged them all when they came in, even the ones I didn't know.

I had no idea where I would go with them. Usually when I encounter a problem clearly out of my league, I refer it to the school psychologist or the psychiatrist at the county seat. This problem was out of my league, but if I referred it, they would put *me* away. Like Dr. James Harvey, the therapist to the dead in the movie *Casper*, I was going to have to operate in psychological territory that was off the map. Unlike the whimsical Dr. Harvey, I had enough sense to keep my mouth shut about it.

I sat on the corner of my desk. "I'll begin by summarizing the situation as I see it. You all died young, before your time. You have unfulfilled dreams and ambitions. You feel you were cheated out of what should have been a long and prosperous life. Because you weren't ready, you haven't crossed over to what we'll call the state of eternal rest. You've managed to stay behind, at least in limbo, though not on this side either.

"Some of you have been in this in-between state for many years. Now you come to a crisis point. The closing of the school and the mill indicate the town is drying up. When the people move out of Brownville, you'll no longer have the warmth of the living to sustain you, and you'll have to cross over. This frightens you. I want to focus in on this fear. Who wants to talk about it?"

I had no takers. They were circled around my desk. Some sat on my window ledge.

I looked at Randy Galphin. "Randy?"

He started on the school closing again. It was the same diatribe he had delivered the last time. They ought to skin the board members.

After five minutes, Barbara Fields cut him off. "You don't have a right to complain. You chose to die. You killed yourself. The rest of us didn't ask for it."

Randy flinched. "I didn't ask for it either. You think if I could undo it, I wouldn't?"

I looked at Barbara. Her hair was beautiful and full, still retaining the coiffure the beautician had given her in the morgue.

"You seem angry because Randy had a choice and you didn't," I told her.

She looked back at me with ice in her eyes. "And what are you going to do, Moses? Lead us over?"

I shook my head. "I can't do that. I'd have to die."

"Well . . . ?"

"It's not my time."

"It wasn't my time either."

"Could it be that you're angry with me because I still have my life and you don't?"

She softened. "I guess so."

That's the way the first session went. I chipped away at their emotions—fear, anger, guilt—until I brought them out. But despite my intentions, we didn't finish that night. Nor the next week.

Nor the next month.

5

I've always felt that you die when it's your time to go, but the lost souls who filled my office that evening had sent that philosophy back to committee for further debate. You couldn't look at them and not feel that, the mysterious and inevitable dictates of Fate notwithstanding, they were all too young to die.

I found myself wanting to know more about them. By haunting the school newspaper morgue in the media center, studying obscure group shots in old yearbooks, picking the brains of the veterans on the faculty, and even combing my own memory, I was able to come up with a list of who their friends had been.

I set about seeking them out, inventing an array of pretexts that related to school business but always managing to interject the long-dead friend into the conversation in an incidental way.

Randy Galphin I figured I knew well enough.

Tony Cunningham, who'd sought me out on the heels of Randy's visit, was a nonperson as far as his teachers were concerned. "He never caused any problem in my class," his history teacher told me. "In fact, he slept through the American Revolution, World War II, and everything in between. He would have snoozed his way through Korea and Vietnam, but we never made it that far."

In talking to Ted Simmons, Tony's running buddy, I found out why. Tony had worked third shift, from 10:00 p.m. to 6:00 a.m., at $7.25 an hour to pay for a red Buick Regal GS. "He would sit in the back of the room with his head on his desk while the rest of us cut the fool. We didn't learn any more than he did, but we had more fun.

"Tony was just like the rest of us back then. All he cared about was riding around town and showing off that red Buick. It was an extension of his personality. He was convinced he was nobody without it. And he was probably right. He always had a carload of girls, and they probably wouldn't have given him the time of day without that car. The only time I ever saw him get upset was when Marshall Grant backed out of Li'l Cricket and put a dent in it.

"Tony never got in any trouble, except the time he shot Langston Marsh's cow. We'd been deer hunting that morning, and we spent five hours in thirty-degree rain in a deer stand without even hearing a twig snap. We were on the way home, trudging through the swamp with our socks wet, when out of the woods pops one of Langston Marsh's Holsteins.

"'Blast her, Tony, I can't. My fingers are numb,' Billy Wilcox says. The rest of us egged him on. 'Yeah, Tony, we got to have something to show for our trouble.' So Tony blasted her, just because we told him to."

When I worked Ted around to the wreck, I found it was the same story. The wreck was not easy for Ted to talk about, because he'd been one of the survivors, the limp in his left leg serving as a daily reminder. "It wouldn't have happened if it hadn't been for Billy Wilcox. He's the one that got us the pot. And he's the one that kept telling Tony to open it up, even when he was pushing ninety on the straightaway. I don't blame Billy, though. We was all crazy back then.

"So what you could say about Tony Cunningham is that he wanted to be liked. He shot a man's cow, bought a red car, and drove it like a maniac just so he could be liked. That red car was his undoing. It's just as well it died with him."

George Baucom and Linda Sue Boyle were a hot item for as long as anyone could remember, and you never saw one without the other. In the social structure of high school, when the average life span of a fling was two months and trying to keep track of the love lives of students could drive you up the wall, George and Linda Sue were "the old married couple."

George Baucom's quiet strength, easy good humor, and striking looks made him popular with both sexes. Girls envied his sandy locks and warmed to his shy smile and deep blue eyes that twinkled when he made one of his frequent witty quips. He was lean and muscular and quick enough to be talked about all over town as Friday night football games were replayed on Saturday mornings in barbershops and truck stops and shops along Main Street. Although his name and impressive yardage stats were a regular fixture in the sports section of *The Greenville News*, George was a source of frustration to his coaches, who had to tell visiting college scouts that George had no plans for college.

He was particularly weak in math, and marginal in the other two Rs, but he was good with his hands. His mentor was Bobby Graham, the shop teacher who hated to read (and never used a textbook in his classes) but hadn't let that stop him from developing a reputation as somebody who could do anything he set his mind to. George had worked for Bobby in the contracting business he ran on the side.

Bobby's voice still softened when he talked about George. "He was always talking about how much I taught him, but I'll never forget the lesson he taught me," Bobby told me on bus duty one morning, then shared the following story.

Cynthia Ferguson was the school loser of her day. There's one in every school generation (later it would be Chadwick Corley, who was the butt of everybody's joke), just like there's a school bully and a class clown and a football hero and the girl everybody knows is destined to be prom queen in every group. Cynthia was grossly overweight, odd enough to be from another planet, and hysterical enough in her reaction to hazing to bring out the worst in otherwise decent kids.

Bobby Graham's biggest fault as a teacher was that he was often as bad as the kids in ridiculing the oddballs. Cynthia Ferguson caught her share of snide remarks from him.

Cynthia always sat apart from the others at lunch, always at the same table in the corner of the cafeteria. One day a handful of students who were supposed to be running errands for the lunchroom staff decided to "sabotage" Cynthia's table. The cafeteria had folding rectangular tables back then, and the students released the catches on one end of the table so that it would collapse under the slightest pressure. All this was done with a snickering audience of cafeteria staff.

By the time the big moment came, the word had gone around school, and all eyes were on Cynthia as she waddled with her tray over to her table. Students poked each other to stifle their giggles lest somebody let the cat out of the bag.

Cynthia didn't disappoint anybody. She placed her tray on her table without incident, but as soon as she plopped down in her chair and wriggled it forward, the right end of the table collapsed. Cynthia's tray went sliding toward the floor. She instinctively grabbed for the tray and tumbled out of her chair, spilling tea all over her lap. She found herself sitting on the floor, dress pulled up to her waist, exposing her huge white thighs, with her food in streaks and lumps all over the floor.

The students went wild, erupting in an orgy of screams, laughter, and catcalls. Bobby Graham slapped his knees and joined the laughter.

Out of the bedlam walked George Baucom. He strode calmly over to Cynthia, set his tray on a nearby table, and proceeded to help her up. He brushed off her dress with a wad of napkins. He picked up the end of the collapsed table, kicked the legs securely into place, and brushed aside the spilled food. He pulled her chair out for her to sit down and offered her his tray, and when she declined, he escorted her from the cafeteria.

George's unexpected chivalry dumbfounded the students into silence and made a lasting impression on his mentor. "He put me to shame that day," Bobby told me with a sad grin.

As it turned out, Linda Sue Boyle had taught me as valuable a lesson as the one George taught Bobby. George and Linda Sue had decided to take senior English in summer school so they could have a slack senior year. Linda Sue finished out the course, but George didn't. He drowned one Sunday afternoon in July while trying to swim across Indian Lake and back.

The following fall was my rookie year at Brownville High. I was taking a counseling course that met once a week at the University of South Carolina, and my instructor expected me to bring in a tape of counseling sessions each week for him to critique. I was doing my initial interviews with seniors, and when Linda Sue came in for her appointment, I secured her permission to tape the session.

She was uptight from the start, which made me uptight, because I could tell it would not be a good session. I had to drag everything out of her. Somewhere in the first five minutes, she broke down, pointed to the tape recorder, and pleaded, "Turn it off."

She proceeded to tell me about George, about how they had gone to summer school together and how, following the drowning, she'd had to sit in class every day and look at his empty desk. She was upset because there was a strain between the Baucoms and her family. George's parents blamed Linda Sue's brother, who was the last one to see George alive, for letting him try to swim across the lake by himself.

In my concern for producing a tape for my class, and in my ignorance of how my efforts to get her to focus on her future without George were affecting her, I had completely misread Linda Sue. She taught me early in my career that after I punched that time clock, the students' needs came first, and taking care of my own needs came when I could get around to them.

Linda Sue told me that day that she'd felt she and George were destined for each other. As if to prove it, she later botched her one chance at matrimony before death, in the form of a lightning bolt in her front yard, claimed her.

Freddy Seaton, who graduated from Brownville High in 1960, was a child of the fifties. He had watched the birth of television and rock and roll (he was going into the ninth grade when Elvis made his first Sullivan appearance) and the McDonald's hamburger chain, and he had gotten his driver's license back when cars had fins and the center of teen social life was the drive-in theater. The other dead youth held him in awe because he had been there at the dawn of time as far as they were concerned, there being no life to speak of before television and rock and roll and fast food. Freddy made them feel close to the things they had loved in life and lost in death.

The Seatons were part of Brownville's upper crust, such as it was. The family had moved to Brownville just after World War II, when James Seaton bought the local Ford franchise. The business prospered, and Seaton began branching out, opening a trailer park the locals referred to as "Tornado Alley," after the jet stream began dumping twisters into the South, and launching a chain of laundromats that reached out to surrounding counties. James Seaton also dabbled in local politics, serving stints on the town and county councils and becoming a permanent fixture on the school board.

Freddy Seaton was blessed with a memory that allowed him to absorb enough in class that he could maintain top grades without studying, much to the envy of his peers in the college prep track, who often pretended not to study but did so in secret for fear of being branded "bookworms." That Freddy was able to absorb anything in class often amazed his teachers because, as one of them put it, "he was always into tomfoolery."

Freddy's mischievous streak made him a regular in detention hall, which he often skipped. He tried to rely on his father's political clout to save him, but Vernon Preston, Brownville High's principal at the time, was stubborn enough to go out of his way to avoid any appearance of favoritism, and James Seaton was wise enough not to interfere.

Nevertheless, Freddy was good at charming his way out of trouble. He was always late to school, and his eleventh-grade homeroom teacher, Mary Reed, actually found herself looking forward to the outlandish excuses he would proffer each day. Her favorite: "I left my mother out in the yard in an iron lung. It looks like rain, so I had to run back home and get her in so she won't rust."

Other teachers resented what they considered Freddy's snobbish attitude, as did a healthy number of students from the wrong side of the tracks.

Today we get kids in school who have a juvenile record and a probation officer for violations like beating up their grandmothers, trafficking in drugs, and petty larceny. In the 1950s, the worst thing kids did was skip school and drink a couple of beers, and that's exactly what Freddy did. He cut school one day and drove out to the airport with a case of Pabst and Alfreda Mills, who had the reputation of being "everybody's girl." This escapade earned him a three-day suspension and cost him the respect of the faculty. It also thoroughly scandalized his parents. It did wonders for his reputation among the student body, however, and Freddy soared to new heights of popularity.

Freddy graduated with honors, went to The Citadel, and suddenly grew up. "He walked into the town café one June day with his father and spotted four or five of us teachers having lunch at a corner table," recalled retired science teacher Dusty Foreman. "Freddy walked over and shook our hands. He really looked like a leader, and it wasn't just the military crew cut. His grip was firm and he spoke with confidence, and he was as polite as any Southern gentleman you ever met. We couldn't get over it."

After Freddy was commissioned into the infantry, he spent a year in graduate school, then volunteered for Vietnam. He won the Bronze Star during his first tour and made captain during his second. In May of 1967, the country was still largely behind the war—Daniel Ellsberg, the Tet Offensive, Woodstock, Kent State, the Chicago Democratic Convention riot, the King and second Kennedy assassinations were knocking at the door but were still somewhere out there in the future. However, the war was just starting to turn sour, and Freddy, in step with the pulse of the nation, could sense the winds of change.

Freddy died at Pleiku during a predawn mortar attack. He related the experience to me one evening as we sat under an oak tree at the edge of the golf course. I can't tell you how bizarre it was listening to a man describe his own death.

Freddy had been through the rain of fire many times, but this time he had a bad feeling as soon as he heard the *thonk thonk* of NVA rounds being dropped into the tubes from somewhere out beyond the wire. He screamed for his men to take cover, then ran for the nearest bunker as he heard the whistle of incoming. The rounds walked in closer and closer until he could feel his teeth rattle. He called out for his radioman but was unable to hear above the shouts that erupted every time a weapons depot or fuel tank exploded. Freddy had time to fire off a prayer before the end came.

They shipped his shrapnel-riddled body home in a bag, and the whole town turned out for his funeral, his indiscretion with Alfreda Mills and high school pranks long forgiven. They buried him with full military honors and proudly hung his portrait and burial flag in Town Hall, but Freddy found no peace.

had a fair idea of what little Melissa King would have looked like as a young woman had the Grim Reaper not snatched her life at the tender age of five. Her sister Kayla had graduated from Brownville High a couple of years back, and Kayla was a proud parent's dream—tanned and leggy, with a thick mane of golden locks she liked to toss about wildly on the dance floor or on the cheering line, big eyes that were made for flirting, and a figure that deserved a second glance. I realize siblings can be as different as night and day, but the King sisters' baby pictures showed enough resemblance to let you see Melissa's lost promise. She would have been gorgeous.

Shonda King's second pregnancy was a particularly troubling one. At six weeks, she began to hemorrhage and had to take two weeks off work under doctor's orders. She was bedridden, leaving her husband, Joel, to cook and tend to Kayla, then six years old. She spotted throughout the first trimester and almost miscarried twice more. Melissa was two months premature and had to begin life in an incubator. Her fight for life early on added a bitter twist to Shonda King's grief when Melissa was killed five years later. "It's devastating to have gone through that much pain, only to lose her now," she confessed to a neighbor.

Melissa wasn't a bad child, but she was always getting scolded, thanks to an insatiable curiosity that caused her to experiment, or in her mother's words, "meddle." She wondered what the cold cream would look like smeared all over the bathroom mirror, or what the dog's tail would look like with a rubber band wrapped as tightly around as you could get it, or what the brick column on the carport would look like with blue shutter paint streaked on it, or how high in the air she could throw the cat. She set out to answer these and other questions for herself, causing her father to voice the belated conclusion, "I'm too old to have children."

Joel King was a third-shift floor manager at the L. B. Brown textile mill. The night shift left him feeling bone-tired all the time, and he seldom got to see his children during the week, but he resisted his wife's requests that he switch to first shift. "The top brass aren't always breathing down your neck at night. I like to be left alone to do my job," was his answer.

Joel's decision to remain on third shift carried with it an enormous debt of guilt after Melissa's death. He realized with painful regret that too many memories consisted of spanking her for what amounted to acting like a child. Even on weekends, he generally started off the day by scolding her for making too much noise while he was trying to sleep late.

Melissa received a terrier-spaniel crossbreed for her fifth birthday. She named the dog Scuttles and would often ride the dog around in her Barbie stroller. She slept with Scuttles until it became evident that the dog wasn't housebroken. Scuttles was banished to the backyard, and when she began wandering into the street, causing horns to honk, Joel King tied her to a leash.

That's when Melissa began to lobby for a dog pen. Joel promised to build one for her the next weekend. However, on the appointed weekend, it rained, and Joel deferred his promise until the next weekend. That weekend his plant manager invited him to a golf game, so he again deferred the promise. The next weekend, his brother wanted him to pick him up from the Atlanta airport. The weekend after that, he decided that the paint job on the deck couldn't wait any longer. The weekend after that, he told himself he was just too tired to dig postholes.

Joel King was asleep on the couch the day Melissa died. Shonda had gone shopping and left Joel to watch the kids. He heard them playing in Kayla's room as he dozed off.

The long screech of braking tires jerked him awake. It was followed immediately by a high-pitched scream.

He ran down his driveway, thinking Kayla had been hurt because she was jumping up and down and screaming hysterically. Rev. Grady was standing beside his car, saying over and over to her, "I'm so sorry. I'm so sorry."

Then Joel saw Melissa and her dog lying in the ditch. The dog was dead and Melissa was in bad shape, but not too far gone to be concerned about her dog. "Scuttles ran in the road. I tried to save her," she said.

Joel cradled her in his arms and, out of frustration or habit, scolded her for the last time. "Didn't I tell you not to let Scuttles off her leash when me and Mom were inside the house?"

Melissa looked at her dead dog and, seemingly oblivious to her own impending death, gave her father a belated lesson in priorities by saying, "She doesn't need her pen now, Daddy."

6

Randy Galphin walked into my office and claimed his perch on my window ledge. He came during second period, just like seven years ago. It was amazing how quickly I got used to him again.

He propped his foot up on my radiator and gave me his big grin. "Hello, Mr. Fellars. You busy?"

I shoved aside the schedule request forms I was sorting. "No, Randy. I was just shuffling papers. You wouldn't believe how my load of paperwork has grown since we used to talk."

"I can come back some other time."

"That's all right. How you been?"

"Pretty good for a dead boy."

He grinned and I chuckled politely. You know you're talking to a good-natured fellow when he jokes about his shortcomings.

I was hoping he wouldn't start railing against the school board again. As a preemptive measure, I asked a question I hadn't got to ask the last time.

"What's it like being dead?"

"It ain't like nothing."

"Do you eat? I hope you don't mind me asking—"

"Ain't no need to eat. I can't taste nothing. Can't feel nothing. I never thought I'd miss taking a crap."

I smiled. "You don't feel a thing?"

"You know how your arm goes to sleep when you lay on it?"

"Yeah."

"It's like my whole body went to sleep. It ain't s'posed to be this way."

"Not supposed to be what way?"

"I ain't s'posed to know nothing. Or I'm s'posed to be up in heaven. I ain't s'posed to be stuck here."

"Do you feel pain? Not with your body, but on the inside?"

His face crumbled. "I don't feel nothing but pain on the inside."

I leaned forward. "What are some things that cause you pain? On the inside?"

His voice was tense. "I tore my family up. They was already in a bad way, but when I cut out, it tore them all to pieces. You seen how they was at the funeral."

"Yes." My voice was a whisper.

Mother wailing. Brothers hugging. Sisters quaking with sobs. One sister fainting and being carried out of the chapel.

He must have watched the scene from wherever he was. He covered his face with his hands. "I wished I hadn't done it as soon as I pulled the trigger. I lost my head. I was so mad at Carl, I almost shot him."

"Well, you did one thing right, Randy."

"What's that?"

"Look at it this way. You were mad enough to kill somebody. You took the bullet yourself to spare Carl. When you get down to it, you sacrificed your life to save his."

"That don't make up for what I did to my family." He removed his hands from his face and looked at me. "Mr. Fellars?"

"Yeah, Randy."

"Can you tell them I'm sorry?"

I pushed myself back away from my desk. "Randy, they know

you're sorry. They all loved you." I immediately regretted using the past tense. "I'm sure they've forgiven you."

"They still blame Carl. They never even spoke to the Shayne family after I cut out."

"You must have watched your family. To see how they acted toward the Shayne family."

He nodded. "I used to watch them, especially Christie and little Ben, but I ain't visited them in a long time. Christie's remarried, you know."

"Is that right?"

His voice took on a bitter edge. "It ain't no fun sitting around watching somebody else living with your wife. Raising up your kid."

I visualized my own kid living with her mother and stepdad and thought, *Tell me about it.* "I suppose not."

He gave me a big grin again. "I seen Ben a couple of times at school, on the playground. He'd be in the second grade now. If he didn't flunk, like I did."

"You've seen your family, but have they seen you? Have you appeared to anybody besides me?"

"Nobody's seen any of us but you. And Sadie Dennis."

My jaw dropped. "Sadie Dennis?"

Sadie Dennis was Brownville's representative on the school board. Although she cast the sole opposing vote on the consolidation issue, the town still held a grudge against her and claimed she hadn't done enough to prevent the closing of Brownville High. She had recently left town for an extended stay with her sister in Oklahoma. She'd left to escape the wrath of her constituents, the town had it.

"Gordon Wallace paid her a visit. He tried to give her a heart attack. He's as mean as he was when he was alive."

A lump of cold ice settled in my chest. "He wasn't with the rest of you on Wednesday night," I said. I hadn't even missed him.

Randy shook his head. "He wouldn't come. He tried to talk the rest of us out of it."

The lump of coldness sank into my stomach. Gordon Wallace was not a person I wanted as an enemy, dead or alive. Especially dead. He and Gary Norris, Bennie Norris's brother, who was on death row, had terrorized Brownville High almost a decade ago, during the early days of my tenure.

"Is Gordon the only one who didn't come?" I asked.

"Todd Grant. They're the only two."

"That figures." Todd had been Gordon's shadow. It was rumored that Gordon, Todd, and Gary Norris had been in the other car drag racing with Will Masters and Charlie Green the night they got killed. Gordon and Todd didn't live six months past that fatal night.

Randy's dead eyes glazed over. "I'm scared of Gordon Wallace. I stay out of his way."

"I can't say I blame you."

"I'm glad he didn't show up the other night."

I nodded. We were on the same wavelength. "Why do you suppose he didn't?"

"He don't act like he's scared to cross over. He don't act like he's scared of nothing."

"That sounds like a cover-up. If he wasn't just as scared as the rest of you, he wouldn't be hanging around."

Randy's face furrowed. "I think he's hanging around to get us."

"What?"

"It's like he knows he's going to hell, and maybe he thinks he can rack up brownie points with the devil if he leads the rest of us there too."

"I'll bet that's what he wants you to think," I said, hoping I sounded more confident than I felt. "Is that the way the others feel about him too?"

"We're all scared of him."

"And you're all scared to cross over. I think that's what we need to talk about. What are the things that are holding you here?"

He looked down at his hands. "Lots of things."

"Let's sort them out. Name one."

His hollow face looked pinched, his eyes searching. "I'm scared to leave my brothers and sisters without nobody being able to provide for them right. They've got a bad life."

"You had six brothers and sisters, right?"

"Yeah."

"Three of them have already made it on their own. The other three will make it out too," I assured him.

He nodded. "It was hard on them."

"Of course it was," I agreed. "Your mother had her hands full with seven kids to raise. She did the best job she knew how to do. I know they had it rough for a lot of years. But you know what?"

He looked expectantly. "What?"

"I know every one of your brothers and sisters. You all turned out to be good people."

He smiled. Whatever he thought of that, he kept it to himself.

"What else is holding you here?" I probed.

He considered, then prefaced his answer with a sigh. "I don't want to leave without telling them I'm sorry I hurt them."

"What's to stop you?"

"I don't know how."

"Have you considered appearing to them, the way you came to my office?"

He had. "I don't know how they'd take it. I don't want to hurt them again."

"I see."

He hesitated. "I was hoping you'd give them a message for me."

It was the second time he'd made the request. I'd sidestepped it the first time. "I can't do that, Randy. If I tell them I've talked to you, they'll think I'm crazy."

His face fell, then he nodded. "I reckon you're right."

"I will check on your brothers and sisters from time to time. And I'll even find a way to visit Ben over at the elementary school."

The session was beginning to die. I didn't know if I would get another chance to reach Randy. I stood and walked around to the edge of the desk. I sat on a corner by my in-basket, facing him. "Now then, Randy, let's cut this problem to the bone. I want you to think for a minute. Then I want you to tell me the biggest reason you don't want to cross over. What scares you the most?"

He struggled with his thoughts. Then his face withered and he buried it in his hands again. His body was racked with sobs, hopeless moans of despair. "I killed myself. I'm scared I'll go to hell."

I reached out and put my hand on his hand. It was cold, but this time I did not pull away.

"Randy, you're not going to hell."

"How do you know?" he asked from behind his hands.

I had no answer for that. The truth was, I had no idea what awaited him on the other side.

7

"A few ground rules," I said to them. They were clustered about my office, sitting anywhere they could find space. It was the second session. "First of all, don't ask me to contact living relatives with messages. I'm not willing to share this with anybody else yet. And second, I want you to be very careful about showing up at school during school hours. The people here are upset enough about the closing of the school. It's not fair to impose your problems on them. Agreed?"

They nodded and mumbled assent as I circled the room with my eyes.

I was sitting on the edge of my desk, my folded hands cradling my knee. "Would anyone here care to define the problem we have?"

"We're all dead as doornails," Tony Cunningham said cheerfully. Sharon Summer and Barbara Fields cut him a look of disapproval.

"No, we're the Undead," Will Masters corrected him. His stringy brown hair looked greasy, like it hadn't been washed in years. Which, of course, it hadn't. But that was a moot point, since they had all been preserved in their physical appearance at the time of their deaths.

"We're the living dead," Charlie Green added.

"My favorite show is *Saturday Night Dead* on NBC."

"Why don't you guys grow up?" Barbara Fields cut in.

Her comment brought to mind a quote from cop novelist Joseph Wambaugh. I'm paraphrasing it here. *Females are sawed-off women at age two, while men are still little boys at age eighty.*

"We can't grow up. We're sixteen forever," Tony Cunningham said.

"Yeah. We're into permanent adolescence," observed Chadwick Corley.

"Chad, you're a permanent idiot," somebody said. They still picked on him, even in death.

Sharon Summer sighed. "What did we do to deserve being stuck with permanent adolescents?"

"My ex would argue that all men are permanent adolescents," I said, then regretted saying it. Like they needed me to add my baggage to the load.

"At least we're harmless, even if we are dead," Mike Sanders remarked. He and Freddy Seaton were both still in uniform.

"Except for Gordon Wallace," somebody else said.

"Gordon's a real ghoul," offered Freddy Seaton.

"At least he tried to do something about keeping the school open," Will Masters said. "What have any of you done?"

That did it. I was very uneasy about any comment that turned Gordon Wallace into a hero. I seized the floor. "School consolidation is a problem for the living. It's not your problem. Your problem, as one of you pointed out, is that you're all dead. Well, no, that isn't the problem. Your problem, and this is what we have to work on, is that you haven't accepted your deaths."

"We haven't found our eternal resting place," Tony Cunningham observed, still cheerful. I liked him and regretted that I had never known him in life.

"Or gone on to our just reward," added Barbara Fields sarcastically.

"Or to eternal damnation," said Will Masters.

Linda Sue Boyle flinched. She was sitting with her back against my filing cabinet, holding George Baucom's hand. Little Melissa King sat in her lap, humming to her spaniel. Linda Sue stared at Will. "Do you have to be so pessimistic?"

Will came back at her. "If you're not pessimistic, why are you still hanging around?"

"She knows she's going to heaven, but she's not so sure about George."

"I'm not sure about George either."

"With good reason."

George smiled. "At least I won't be by myself."

Linda Sue didn't smile. Her pale cheeks would have flushed if she'd had any blood in her veins. "You guys are upsetting me."

"Too late to fret now, girl," Will said. "Preacher man says you have to make amends before you die."

"Yeah. Jesus don't accept apologies from dead people," Tony Cunningham added helpfully.

That may or may not have been sound theology, but it was nothing we could change one way or the other, so I didn't see any point in continuing down that rabbit hole.

I took the floor again. "You've expressed the same fears that every person who ever lived on this planet has faced. It's human nature to fear death, to fear the unknown. But we can't change the fact that you're all dead. We can't change the fact that when the town dies, you can't follow the living. You'll have to cross over within a few months now."

Will Masters shifted his position on the corner of my desk. "Maybe we can change the fact that the town's dying."

"Maybe Gordon can persuade them to open up the mill again."

I was beginning to realize that Gordon Wallace would become my adversary in my attempts to send them over. I tried to redirect the conversation.

"You're still not facing up to your situation. Whether the town dies or not, you are all eventually going to have to cross over."

"At least there wouldn't be any hurry about it if the mill and the school were kept open," Will Masters argued.

"All right," I nodded. "Let's examine your situation. This half-living, half-dead state you're all stuck in. Is anyone really pleased with it? Are you satisfied being the way you are?"

"It's not so bad," Will Masters declared. He was becoming their spokesman.

"It's better than nothing," Johnny Brown echoed.

"That's not true at all," countered Barbara Fields. Her eyes glistened. "It's lonely."

A gloom of silence settled over the room. The playfulness went out of the clowns who had been making light of their condition.

Freddy Seaton nodded. "There's a certain . . . anxiety that goes with it."

"It's more like torment," added Sally Brock.

I glanced around the room. "What else?"

"Hopelessness."

"Hopelessness. What else?"

The answers came quickly from all corners of the room.

"You're worried all the time, but you don't know why."

"I cry a lot."

"Me too."

"I stay depressed all the time."

"Sometimes I wish I could kill myself, but I'm already dead."

I kept my eyes moving. "What are some things that make you depressed?"

Barbara Fields let out a hollow cackle and fixed her big blue eyes on me. "Are you for real? Wouldn't you be depressed if you were dead?"

I flushed. "You'll have to excuse me. I'm used to counseling the living. Sometimes we have to ask stupid questions just to move the session along. I realize that wasn't an appropriate question, so let's back up. In the context of being dead, what makes you depressed?"

"Having to stand around and watch people our age have fun."

"Doing things we missed out on."

"What do you miss most about being alive?"

"Sex," came the quick answer from Tony Cunningham.

"At least you got plenty before you died. I was a virgin," admitted Barbara Fields.

"Then you don't know what you missed."

"I should have gotten the opportunity. I feel like I was cheated."

"It's not just sex," observed Sally Brock. "It's watching people we went to school with get married and raise families."

"And open businesses and run for public office," said Freddy Seaton, who had been groomed to take over his family's chain of businesses.

"And stuff themselves at Thanksgiving and Christmas parties."

"I wanted my life to count for something. I didn't get to make my mark."

"Me too. When you die at fifteen, what's the point of it all?"

"I couldn'ta made my mark noway. A Black man don't got a chance to get ahead," said Sammy Tribble, the teen who'd been lynched.

"That's 'cause you're stuck in the fifties. My old man lost out on a promotion because of affirmative action," put in Charlie Green.

Tribble bristled. "It didn't do me no good, though, did it?"

Sharon Summer took the conversation into a new direction. "I used to hang with Bob Goodman. It should have been me he ended up with instead of Gail Hill."

"You would have made him a lot happier. She treats him like a dog."

"She looks like a dog."

"If I could just taste a hamburger right now."

"Remember how Cokes used to taste?"

"God, this is depressing."

"I miss touching things," Sally Brock said wistfully. "I was a very physical person. Just to hold somebody's hand and feel it. I see now why demons possess people. I'd do it if I knew how."

"That's cute, Sally. You could possess Cameron Mason. He'd strut down the hall and nobody would know the difference."

"He's the only guy I know with a seductive walk."

"Seductive to you, maybe."

"You guys don't have any right to make fun of somebody's sexual preference. After all, there's a lot of prejudice out there against dead people." That came from Laval Crenshaw, the AIDS victim who had spent what little adult life he'd had fending off jokes about his homosexuality. The disease had left him gaunt and frail, and somehow he looked more dead than the others. His stricture brought quiet to the room.

I cut in again. "All right, what I hear you saying, gang, is that this state you're in is not satisfactory to you. The question is, how do we come to terms with it?"

"That's what we came to you for, Moses," Barbara Fields informed me. I liked her too. She had spunk.

I smiled at her. "You're in luck. I think I can help you."

That got their attention. They sat on the edges of their seats in anticipation.

I paused for effect, then continued, "Here's my theory. I think if I can help each of you do something you missed out on, or help you do something that will add meaning to your life, maybe you can find the peace you deserve. We don't have much time. I can't give you a lifetime of accomplishments. But maybe I can help you do something important, make some significant contribution, do something you got cheated out of doing in the time you have left.

"I want to hear about your hopes and dreams. Specific things you wanted to do before you died. Somebody said you wanted to make your life count for something. How would you do that? Who wants to start?"

No one spoke.

I looked at Linda Sue Boyle. "Linda Sue, what was your big dream?"

Linda Sue Boyle pushed her long blonde strands out of her eyes. She still had freckles on her dead face. "Nothing special. I just wanted a happy marriage. I botched the one chance I had."

I looked at George Baucom, who was still holding her hand. "George?"

"I don't know. I just wanted to settle down. Raise a family." He was soft-spoken.

"I believe you were dating Linda Sue when you died."

"Yeah."

"Were you going to marry her?"

He grinned shyly. "If she'd have had me."

"Linda Sue, would you have had him?"

She beamed but remained coy. "Maybe."

"Well, I'll leave it to you two to figure out how I can help you achieve your dream. I want to hear from the rest of you. You each get one wish, so choose carefully. Talk to me."

I had to drag it out of them, but I heard from each one. Because death strips away the flesh and the wants of the flesh, their last requests were simple and basic for the most part, void of the materialism that would appeal to the living, with a focus of priorities that the prospect of longevity often distorts.

Tony Cunningham wanted to find a way to warn other kids not to walk in his footsteps. Sharon Summer wanted to find a way to turn her little sister's life around. Barbara Fields just wanted to tell her parents she loved them. Mike Sanders wanted to get rid of the stepdad who abused his mom. On the other hand, Johnny Brown wanted to help his widowed mother find a new dad for his little brother. Will Masters and Charlie Green wanted nothing more than one last party. Freddy Seaton wanted people to appreciate his sacrifice in Vietnam.

Laval Crenshaw wanted to do something for animals but wasn't sure what. Sally Brock had always wanted to pen a novel. Sammy Tribble wanted to put out a jazz album. Randy Galphin wanted to find a way to make sure his family was taken care of. Steve Hall wanted to do something heroic. Chadwick Corley wanted to get even with the town for heaping years of ridicule on him. I made a mental note to try to channel him away from that one. Little Melissa King wasn't able to say what she wanted.

"No promises," I told them, "but I'll do what I can."

8

I caught Bennie Norris waiting for the bus to the alternative school the next time I had morning bus duty. Mr. Jacobs had put him up for expulsion, but the district discipline committee had assigned him to the alternative school in the county seat seventeen miles away. The alternative school required students to wear a uniform, khaki trousers and a blue chambray shirt neatly tucked into the trousers. Bennie seemed shamed by the attire, like a lion that had just had its mane sheared off. He was sitting on a bench near the bus port with a hang-dog look. Normally he would be strutting around the school with his pants sagging, his shirttail out, and cap on backward.

"Hello, Bennie."

He mumbled something.

"You ready for your new adventure today?" I asked.

He looked up at me like I had just repeated one of the insults the eighth graders are always hurling at each other. He had a hatchet face pocked with craters and a scar on his forehead from when his older brother had slammed his head against a brick wall in the alley behind Willard's Pharmacy. Bennie had tattled on his brother for shoplifting. He was just five at the time and didn't know any better. His brown eyes locked on mine.

"You trying to be funny?"

"No. I didn't mean to offend you."

A bus pulled up and disgorged students, who walked by Bennie. Several of them spoke to me. They ignored Bennie like he wasn't even there.

"This whole place offends me," Bennie said.

I spared him the lecture about how a change in attitude would do wonders for his well-being. I'm not one to waste my breath.

"Well, I just want to wish you luck in your new school," I said.

"I'll be back. All I got to do is suck up and be a White Uncle Tom for a few weeks. If I keep my nose clean and don't get any demerits, they'll send me back here before school is out. I know how the system works."

I was wondering why he would be so eager to come back to a school where he found everything offensive when the bus to the alternative school pulled up. When Bennie stood, his five-foot-four frame was dwarfed by the other students approaching the bus. Bennie turned to me just before he got on.

"You heard it here, Mr. Fellars. I'll be back. Then I'm going to settle some scores."

I shook my head. No chance for a change in attitude there. I realized Bennie was right. He would work his way back from the alternative school, and when he returned to regular school, he would have a whole new bag of tricks he had learned from other misfits at the alternative school, and he would have enhanced his reputation as the school renegade.

A wave of depression washed over me. I was dealing with the dead students, full of remorse and despair, who had come to me for help, while in the land of the living, I had to watch Bennie Norris throw his life away.

What a crummy job I have, I told myself.

I moseyed on over to the computer lab, where I had to configure the computers so that they would interface with the computers at the nearby technical college. A representative from that school was due at Brownville High the following morning to assist seniors in filling out admissions applications.

I received an error message on the first computer I booted up. I tried another computer. Same error message.

I walked into the school library, which was adjacent to the computer lab. I approached the circulation desk, where Ms. Noble, the school librarian, had her nose to her computer.

"Can you help me with the computers?"

She turned and looked at me like I had just interrupted the conversation she was having with herself in her head.

"What's the problem?"

"I got an error message."

"What was the message?"

"I don't remember exactly."

"Didn't you write it down?"

"No."

"That's just great. I have to know the message to be able to call it in."

"I thought maybe you could come and look at the computers."

"I don't have time to look at the computers. Bring me the message if you want me to call it in."

She dismissed me and turned back to her computer.

Helen Noble didn't like me, as you can probably discern from that conversation. I guess she had her reasons. Helen Noble ran a tight ship. She didn't brook foolishness in her library. Once when Tommy Grimes was written up for horseplay, I interceded on his behalf and got Mr. Jacobs to reduce his detention to a warning. That's the way Mr. Jacobs was. He would cave to pressure. It was easy for me to talk him out of punishing Tommy, because he didn't want to have to deal with Tommy's parents. I had my reasons for going to bat for Tommy, not least of which was his rotten home life. But Helen Noble had never had much use for me after that.

I get that reaction a lot from teachers. There's an inherent conflict in our roles. While the teacher has to look out for the welfare of the entire class, the counselor's focus is on the individual. Sometimes teachers resent it when I end up taking the student's side. It's an occupational hazard.

I walked back into the computer lab and copied down the error message. I returned to the circulation desk and gave the error message to Her Highness.

9

George Baucom and Linda Sue Boyle came to me after school one day and announced that they wanted to get married. Linda Sue held out her hand and beamed a 100-watt smile. "See what George gave me?"

A diamond sparkled under my florescent light.

I whistled. "That's got to be at least a karat."

"Two," she said.

I looked at George. "Where'd you pick that up?"

"I stole it from Thompson's Jewelers."

I raised my brow.

"We're just borrowing it," Linda Sue said. "Randy Galphin promised to return it after George and I cross over."

I no longer wanted to risk meeting at school at night, so I picked them up at the garbage dump one evening after dark and we rode around the outskirts of town in my car and planned the wedding. I asked them to bring Freddy Seaton with them. At twenty-five, Freddy was the most mature among them, and I needed his level head.

The first problem was how to obtain a marriage license.

"I know of a publishing company called Loompanics that operates out of Port Townsend, Washington," I announced. "They take the first amendment very seriously and publish a lot of underground work. One of their top titles is *Fake ID*. If I can get a copy, we can use it to get a phony license."

"It has to be real," George announced from the back seat. "We have to have a real wedding, which means it has to be registered in the courthouse. That means a real license."

That was just as well. I later learned that Loompanics went out of business in 2006.

"It's going to be near to impossible to do that," I protested.

"Then you're wasting your time," said Freddy, riding shotgun. He wore his dress greens with a chest full of battle ribbons. "If this is going to work, everything you do for us has to be real. They have to feel really married if you're going to send them over."

I maneuvered my Mazda onto Little Gypsy Road and accelerated.

"Okay, I'll trust your instinct when it comes to the rules of the afterlife." I looked in my rearview mirror. "George, that means you and Linda Sue will have to go to Elmwood."

"No way," Linda Sue said. She was sitting beside George, directly behind me.

"Besides, I'm only seventeen," George added. "When we give our birth dates, we'd be in our late twenties. There's no way I could pass for almost thirty."

I looked at Freddy. He nodded agreement.

I studied the ribbon of road ahead while I turned the matter over in my head.

"Then I'll have to get the license for you," I said reluctantly. "I'll have to be George Baucom."

"Can you pass for thirty?" George asked. "We'll have to iron out some of those wrinkles."

I cut to the rearview. He had an impish grin on his face.

"I'll let that remark pass."

"Who's going to go with you and pretend to be me?" Linda Sue asked.

Her question unsettled me. It looked like I was going to have to recruit a female accomplice if I was going to keep my commitment to them.

"I don't know," I replied. "I'll work on it."

"We need somebody to marry us," George observed.

"Will you settle for a notary public?"

"I want a preacher. And a church wedding," Linda Sue said firmly.

I frowned. "And I suppose you want to invite all your aunts and cousins."

"I know I can't do that. But I won't feel married without a preacher or a church wedding."

We came to the curve in the road where Sharon Summer had died. I dimmed for an oncoming car.

"That's risky," I replied. "We obviously can't hold the ceremony out of town. And the preachers in town all know you."

"Not necessarily," Linda Sue argued.

Freddy came to my defense. "Mr. Fellars is right on this one. Even if we pick a preacher who came to town after we all died, sooner or later they'll tell a member of their congregation that they married George Baucom and Linda Sue Boyle. You can imagine what the town will do with that one."

"It's not fair to put a preacher in that kind of spot," I agreed. "And if I coordinate the wedding, I'll be the one who has to answer questions."

"The best thing to do," Freddy continued, "is to try to get an evangelist visiting Elmwood or Deep Valley. Somebody just passing through, with no connections to Brownville."

I nodded. "I'll check the papers for revivals."

"We still need a church," Linda Sue said.

"We don't have any leeway on that one," I replied. "We'll just have to rent a local church for a private ceremony."

"And try to keep it quiet," Freddy agreed.

"We'll set it up on very short notice, before word has a chance to spread," I added.

"Knowing Brownville, we'd better have rented it yesterday," George cracked.

"So what's our first step?" Linda Sue wanted to know.

Freddy shifted in his seat and looked back at her. "The marriage license." He turned to face me. "What do we need to do to get one?"

I turned off of Little Gypsy Road onto Victorian Drive.

"Birth certificates, I think. Lucky for us, South Carolina is one of the few states where you don't need a blood test."

Freddy nodded. "Birth certificates should be no problem to come by. I don't see why George and Linda Sue can't just write and ask for them."

"We can't have them sent to our addresses, though. Our parents would get them."

I cut my eyes to the rearview. "I'll have them mailed to my post office box in Elmwood."

"Are we ready to set a date?" Linda Sue's voice was bubbly.

"Let's see if we can get the license first," I cautioned. "That's going to be the biggest hurdle. I don't see how I'm going to be able to set this wedding up without a woman's help. You don't know any ghosts in Elmwood, do you?"

George chuckled. "Sorry. I'm afraid our social life is kind of stale."

"Do you have any friends who will help you, no questions asked?" Freddy wanted to know.

I shook my head. "Definitely not. I'm going to have to share this with somebody. That's going to be hard."

Freddy nodded sympathetically. "We know. It was hard for us to come to you."

"Randy was the first one to break the ice and come to you because he was closest to you when we were on this side," George offered. "After Randy led the way, Tony got up enough nerve to visit you. If you hadn't sent for the rest of us, we may not have come to you for help at all."

"I'm going to need some of that nerve Tony found."

"Maybe we can help you," Linda Sue's voice came out of the dark behind me. "We can appear to them the way Randy came to you."

The offer was very appealing. I had no idea how I would approach anyone with this preposterous story. The easiest way to convince them would be to let the dead students approach them. But intuition told me I needed to keep this situation under my control.

"I prefer to solicit my own hired help, but I don't have a clue how to do it. I may have to take you up on your offer. Let me sleep on it."

10

༄

Helen Noble, the school librarian who didn't like me very much, was proud of her mixed ancestry. Her mother was Mexican and her father European, which gave her a dark complexion and stunning features. She would joke that she was a melting pot, just like America, and that would invite an argument from Coach West. Coach West taught American history and claimed that America wasn't really a melting pot but instead a patchwork of different cultures. Despite a youthful face, Helen could wilt students making too much noise in the stacks with a flash of her dark eyes. She belied the stereotype of the spinster librarian in several respects.

Her love for the outdoors was stained on her bronze skin. According to the writeup the *Brownville Courier* did on her when she came to Brownville High three years ago, she was into fishing and skeet shooting, as well as Romantic and Victorian poetry, and she allegedly rode a Harley-Davidson, though I'd never seen her on it. When the town council had wanted to cut down hundred-year-old trees to widen Elm Street two years ago, she led a successful battle to save the trees that landed her on the six o'clock news. Helen Noble had a heart. At least, that was what I was counting on. I just had to figure out how to melt it.

We had our faculty meetings in the media center every Wednesday after school. Mr. Jacobs always arranged the chairs in a circle, because when the faculty sat at tables, the coaches always clustered at a corner table and had a field day passing notes and cracking jokes to each other. That's one thing about teachers. They're as bad as students when it comes to getting them to pay attention in a meeting.

Unfortunately, when the meeting was over, everybody made a hasty exit out of the media center, Mr. Jacobs included, leaving it up to Helen to move the chairs back to their tables.

This time I lingered behind to help her.

"Helen, I need a favor," I said as I slid the last two chairs in place at their table.

She cut me a look. "What kind of favor?"

I looked over my shoulder to make sure no one else had entered the media center. I could hear Coach Wood in the hall laughing with Mrs. Rice.

"I need you to go to Elmwood with me and get a marriage license."

She looked at me suspiciously over the top of her glasses. "Don't you think we should have a few dates first?"

"It's for a couple of friends of mine."

She cocked her head. "You just lost me."

"I have these two friends who want to get married, but they can't go to the courthouse. I'm going to go to Elmwood and pretend to be my friend. I need for you to pretend to be his fiancée so we can get them a marriage license."

She wasn't about to humor me without an explanation. "Why can't they get their own license?"

"They have a problem," I said evasively.

"I'm afraid to ask, but what kind of problem?"

"Come up to my office and I'll explain. How about bringing the 2000 and 2004 yearbooks with you?"

She looked a little alarmed when I locked the door behind her in my outer office. Before she could dwell on it, I ushered her into my inner office. George Baucom and Linda Sue Boyle were waiting on us.

I made quick introductions, then plowed into what was not going to be an easy task no matter how I did it. "George and Linda Sue want to get married, but they can't leave the place where they live, so they can't go to Elmwood to get a license. Before I explain any more, I want you to look on page three of the 2000 yearbook. Then look on page nine of the 2004 yearbook. Tell me what you see."

She opened the 2000 yearbook first. It was dedicated to Tony Cunningham and George Baucom. George's smiling school photo was captioned, *In Loving Memory, George Baucom. April 15, 1982 - July 11, 1999*. It was flanked by photos of George on his motorcycle, George hamming it up at the Brownville-Whitmire football game with his friends, George holding hands with Linda Sue, his high school sweetheart.

It took a moment for the situation to register. Helen looked from one photograph to the other. Then it was like her features took on weight until they began to sag, her brow furrowing, her jaw beginning to drop, and when she looked up from the yearbook to gape at George, her head seemed to move with great difficulty.

She managed to maintain her composure and picked up the 2004 yearbook.

"What was the other page number you said?" she asked evenly.

"Nine."

She opened the book and found the page. It contained a single photo of Linda Sue in her prom dress. The caption said:

In Memory

Linda Sue Boyle

None knew her but to love her

Nor named her but to praise

Helen looked up again with no less difficulty and stared at the couple before her. She looked down at the yearbook again. Then she turned to me.

"Bill, what's going on here?"

"Just what it looks like. There was no other way I could explain it to you. A picture is worth a thousand words, as the old cliché goes. Seeing is believing, to quote another. Thank God for old clichés."

She shook her head. "I don't understand."

"All right, Helen, you tell me what you think you see."

"It looks like two dead people are sitting in your office."

I nodded. "What do you think would happen if you went downstairs and reported what you think you see to anybody else on the faculty?"

"They would think I was nuts."

"Precisely. Now you can appreciate my difficulty in conveying to you what happened to me. If I'd told you downstairs that I'm trying to help two people who are—I won't call them dead, they're kind of stuck between this side and the other side . . . lost on the edge of eternity—you'd have laughed me out of the library. I really hate to drag you into this, Helen, but I'm trying to help them, and I can't do it by myself."

She looked totally disoriented for a long moment, then she managed to wander her way out of the wilderness. She stood up and laughed.

"Bill, I don't know how you pulled this, but I'm not biting. It's good, though. They look just like the people in the yearbook."

I looked at George. "Who's the last one who died?"

"Johnny Brown."

I turned to Helen. "Do you remember Johnny Brown? Got killed when he fell off a hay truck?"

She nodded. "Yes. It was my first year here. I caught him sneaking one of my *Hot Rod* magazines out of the library once."

I turned back to George. "See if you can get Johnny up here."

"Okay."

Helen had been edging toward the door, but this interchange caused her to take a step back toward us. Curiosity reeled her in like a rock bass.

George walked over to my closet and opened the door. Johnny walked out like he'd been hiding there all along. It was as simple as that.

He was a little guy with freckles all over his face and cowlicked sandy hair. You couldn't tell his face had been flattened by a ton and a half of hay-supporting tire rolling over it. Maybe the undertaker had fixed him up. I don't know. I hadn't attended his funeral.

Dumbstruck, Helen gaped at him.

"Hello, Miz Noble," Johnny said. "Sorry about that magazine you were talking about. There's no excuse for me taking it. I guess that's what people remember you for, the things you did wrong. I was hoping you'd remember when I used to help you push the COW back from Miz Tucker's room."

The COW, or Computer on Wheels, was a workstation of computers that could be pushed from classroom to classroom.

She smiled nervously. "I do remember, Johnny. And I appreciated it."

Her words seemed to shock her. By talking to the dead boy I had conjured up, she was admitting that she accepted the ridiculous situation in which I had placed her. She looked at me helplessly.

"Are you ready to listen to me now?" I asked.

She sat back down. "Yes."

I told her the whole story. How Randy Galphin had showed up in my office a couple of weeks ago. Followed by Tony Cunningham. Then the first two sessions. About how the town's dying had placed the dead children of Brownville in a crisis. About my theory that if I could help each of them do something significant in the time we had left, I could help them cross over.

She listened attentively with respectful suspension of disbelief, as the writers who populated her library called it.

When I'd finished making my case, it was Linda Sue who cinched it.

"Will you help us, Miss Noble?" she asked. Her voice teetered between sincerity and desperation.

Helen nodded. "I'll help you. God help me."

11

∽

The birth certificates arrived the next Monday, and on Tuesday, Helen and I rode to Elmwood together. I stopped at Phil's BP station just outside of Elmwood and got my overnight bag out of the trunk of my Mazda, then disappeared into the men's room.

When I came out ten minutes later, I was wearing sunglasses and my hair was dyed blonde.

"How do I look?" I asked Helen.

She gave me the once-over. "What have you done to your hair?"

"My cousin's wife works in the tax assessor's office. I don't want her to recognize me."

Helen rolled her eyes. "Oh, this is just great!"

"Why do I feel like I'm committing a crime?" Helen asked as we walked up the stone steps of the imposing courthouse building in the town square.

"Because we are. Quit complaining."

"At least we're not robbing a bank."

"Not this time. I don't know where all this is going to lead."

"Oh, this is just great."

I espied my cousin's wife as we sailed past the tax assessor's office

60

on our way to the probate judge's office. She was stuffing her face with Bojangles carryout chicken and laughing with a coworker. I probably hadn't needed the dye job after all.

We stopped at a door that said

Judge of Probate

102

Marriage Licenses

I winked at Helen. "We're here."

She smiled back. "After you."

The sign on the counter said *Please be seated. Someone will be with you shortly.*

Helen and I sat in two uncomfortable plastic chairs.

Shortly, a woman emerged from an adjacent room and stepped up to the other side of the counter. She looked like she didn't have long to wait for retirement. "Can I help you?"

Helen and I stood. "We'd like to get a marriage license."

"I'll need your birth certificates."

I fished them out of my shirt pocket and handed them over.

She copied them on the copier and handed the originals back to me. She sat behind an Acer computer and pulled up a form.

"Groom's full name?"

"Baucom, George Henry."

"Spell Baucom."

"B-A-U-C-O-M."

She hunted and pecked with her index fingers.

"Birth date?"

"April 15, 1982."

"Address?"

"704 Brent Circle, Brownville."

"Previous marriages?"

"None."

"Bride's full name?"

"Boyle," Helen said. "B-O-Y-L-E. Linda Sue."

"Date of birth?"

"September 12, 1982"

"Address?"

"134 Harris Lane, Brownville."

"Previous marriages?"

"None."

"One," I interrupted.

Helen started. The woman at the computer jerked her head up and stared at us.

I turned to Helen. "You've got to be honest with her, dear." I turned back to the woman at the computer. "Linda Sue is sensitive about her previous marriage."

"That's right," Helen stammered. "I . . . forgot. This is my second marriage."

The woman at the computer shook her head and continued typing.

She printed off the document and took it into the next room to have the probate judge sign it. Then she took our ten dollars and we left. That's all there was to it.

"I can't believe I did that!" Helen fumed as we descended the steps outside. "I'm sorry, I was so nervous, I—"

"You did great," I said.

I opened the car door for her. "Helen?"

"What?"

"Thanks."

I kissed her on the cheek. I think she started liking me after that.

12

W e held the wedding in the First Baptist Church in Brownville at 9:00 p.m. on a Saturday night. It followed a week of whirlwind activity that had included hasty arrangements, a bachelor party at Helen's apartment on her night out, and a wedding shower.

I didn't attend the shower, during which I understand the girls presented Linda Sue with an array of gifts purloined from houses and businesses in Brownville—some of Mable Whitaker's finest china, Martha Driggers's heirloom necklace, and an antique clock from Coleman's Treasures, among other things. As with Linda Sue's ring, the others promised to return the gifts after George and Linda Sue crossed over.

I did attend the bachelor party. I risked my reputation by renting four naughty movies from the back room of Video Showplace in Elmwood. This store was on its last leg and destined to go out of business a year later. In keeping with tradition, I also sneaked in a belly dancer from Spartanburg. I would have thought the whole affair would have been depressing for the guys, like having a diabetic at a banquet of pastries and cakes that were strictly off the diet. But they whooped it up with catcalls and lewd comments and guzzled down two cases of beer that I knew they couldn't taste. I suppose it's like a middle-aged man watching Sharon Stone in a movie; he knows she's off limits, but he can still appreciate her legs. When I thought about it later, I decided that they had gotten drunk on camaraderie.

At 8:30 on the night of the wedding, Rev. Howell, the pastor of First Baptist, who had opened the church up for us half an hour earlier, was still piddling around in the basement.

"Is there a problem, sir?" I called down to him.

I was eager to get rid of him before the evangelist showed up. I didn't want them to compare notes on who was getting married.

He ascended the stairs. "I can't get the boiler on. It's going to be like the Arctic in here."

It was just our luck that a cold snap happened to occur on Linda Sue's wedding day.

"Don't worry about the heat. We're going to be in and out of here in twenty minutes. If you think it's going to be a problem tomorrow morning, why don't you call Ted Simmons and tell him to come over at 9:30 and take a look at it. We'll be out of here by then."

"Are you sure?"

"I'm positive."

He issued a couple more apologies, then mercifully left.

The evangelist arrived twenty minutes later. His name was Eddie Campbell, and he was finishing up a revival at the First Wesleyan Church in Elmwood. He was a reformed motorcycle gang leader, and he used his past as his calling card. He hadn't removed the tattoos that protruded from his shirtsleeves, and he wore a big cowboy hat, with shoulder-length hair spilling out from under it. In his sermons, he often mentioned the healed scars of track marks that dotted the undersides of his arms.

At my request, he had brought along his organist, an overweight, matronly woman with glasses, too much perfume, and thinning hair like a man's.

I think after he left the service that night, Rev. Campbell must have had a lingering suspicion that something was a shade off-kilter with this wedding. For one thing, Helen's and mine were the only two cars in the church parking lot. Besides Freddy Seaton, Laval Crenshaw and Sally Brock, we were the only two past the teenage years on the guest list. Little Melissa King was there without a parent. One of the guys, Tony Cunningham, had refused to dress up, opting instead for the jeans in which he was buried. There was the way Linda Sue's eyes had widened at the phrase "until death do us part," and the way both Linda Sue and George had amended the phrase to "for all eternity."

There was a feeling that the coldness in the room belonged there, and it wasn't just from the furnace malfunction. And there was the odd fact that, when he looked at the birth dates on the marriage license to make sure that the youthful couple were at the age of responsibility, he saw that the bride and groom, who looked like teen-agers (despite the frosted dye jobs and mascara that had darkened George's sideburns), were actually approaching thirty.

I'm not into weddings, but I have to say it was a touching cere-mony. George and Linda Sue held hands throughout the service, and when they spoke their vows, they looked into each other's eyes as if they were the only ones in the room. Maybe it was Bach's "Prelude in G" at the hands of an organist with no other claim to beauty, or Sammy Tribble's sad voice as he wailed "Prelude to a Kiss"; maybe it was hearing the quiet sobs of Barbara Fields and Sharon Summer; maybe it was watching little Melissa King hold Linda Sue's bridal train and knowing she would never grow up; maybe it was watching a couple of kids finally get to squeeze out a fleeting moment of happi-ness life had cheated them out of, or maybe it was all that together.

For whatever reason, I couldn't stop the tears from welling up in my eyes.

13

꧁꧂

I was sitting at my desk, dreading having to start tackling the report the district office wanted on handicapped enrollment, when my extension buzzed.

"Mr. Fellars, there's a couple here in the office to see you," Sandra said.

"Send them on up."

I met them at the door. They looked like they wanted to spit nails. When you've been in this business a while, you learn to spot a couple of irate parents a mile away. I found myself wondering what I had done to offend anybody lately.

"Mr. Fellars, I'm Tim Boyle. This is my wife, Charlene."

Linda Sue's parents. My stomach tied itself into a knot.

They were both in their mid-fifties. Mr. Boyle had a full head of graying hair and bushy brows. He was an insurance salesman, but he'd left at home the glad hand and smile that had preceded many policy signings with the residents of Brownville. Linda Sue had gotten her looks from her mother. She was somewhat shorter than Linda Sue, but she had kept her figure. You could visualize her in one of those mother-daughter beauty commercials. But not with the angry expression she was giving me now.

"Nice to meet you," I said politely as I stuck out my hand.

Neither of them bothered to shake it. I noticed that Mr. Boyle was cradling a folded newspaper under his arm.

"I don't know whether it's nice to meet you or not," he said. "You've got some explaining to do."

I played dumb. "Oh?"

He slapped the newspaper down on the edge of my desk. "What's the meaning of this?"

A headline jumped off the middle of the first column and yanked another loop in the knot in my stomach.

Boyle-Baucom Wedding:
Brownville Couple Exchanges Vows

I fought the urge to look up. I quickly read the article.

George Baucom and Linda Sue Boyle were married Saturday evening at the First Baptist Church in Brownville. The private ceremony was followed by a luncheon in the church reception hall. The bride was given in marriage by Mr. Freddy Seaton of Brownville. Flower girls were Melissa King, Sally Brock, Sharon Summer, and Barbara Fields. A vocal rendition of "Prelude to a Kiss" was performed by Sammy Tribble.

George is the son of Kathie and the late Stanley Baucom of Brownville. Linda Sue is the daughter of Mr. and Mrs. Tim Boyle.

The couple will reside on Cemetery Drive in Brownville.

I turned the newspaper over and looked at the masthead. It was the *Pineville Chronicle*.

I looked up from the newspaper, searching for something to say. I didn't find it.

"Can you tell me why my daughter, who has been dead for seven years, is written up in the *Pineville Chronicle* as marrying a boy who has been dead eleven years?" Mr. Boyle demanded.

"I have no idea how that got in the paper."

"No? I talked to Reverend Howell. He says you rented the church for a wedding Saturday."

"That's right."

"Who got married?"

"Well, it was a private ceremony."

"You can't tell me who got married?"

"You wouldn't believe me."

"Mr. Fellars, this looks like a cruel hoax. You owe us an explanation."

"Mr. Boyle, I don't have an explanation."

Charlene Boyle exploded. "You don't have an explanation? If that's the best you can do, we'll see you in court."

Mr. Boyle nodded. He picked up the newspaper and folded it back under his arm. "We're suing you; we're suing the newspaper; we're suing the First Baptist Church. I wanted to talk to Mr. Jacobs, but he's not here. I guess I'll have to go to the school board to find out why they have a sadist in our schools. But first, I'm going to see the sheriff."

Helen Noble took one look at me and said, "What's wrong?"

I pulled her back into her corner office and shut the door.

"Linda Sue's parents were just here to see me. Somebody put a writeup on the wedding in the *Pineville Chronicle*."

Her eyes widened. "Good Lord! Who would do that?"

"I don't know."

"What did you tell Linda Sue's parents?"

"Nothing. But they know I rented the church for a wedding on Saturday. They think I'm behind a hoax. They're ready to hang me."

She grimaced. "This is just great. Did they say anything about me?"

"They evidently don't know about you—yet. But they're on their way to see the sheriff about me."

She placed her hand on my arm. "Oh, Bill!"

I took her hand. "Helen, I'm sorry I got you into this—"

She cut me off. "It's too late for that now. We need to talk to Linda Sue and George. How do we find them?"

I shrugged. "I don't know. Let's try the cemetery."

14

We drove out to the cemetery at the far end of Cemetery Drive. I walked across the grass until I came to Linda Sue's grave, across from the Molesworths' plot. Her tombstone still sparkled because her mother came twice a week to wipe it down. The flowers were purple and looked top of the line.

Helen followed along behind me.

I cupped my hand out in the direction of the magnolia tree not far from Linda Sue's grave.

"Linda Sue! George! I need to talk to you. Paging Linda Sue Boyle, I mean, Baucom. Come here, girl!"

I saw Helen stop to look at two kids who had stopped their bicycles along the road to look at us. Helen stared them down, and they moved on.

She turned back to me. "I don't think you need to shout so loud."

I watched the two kids pedaling toward town. "I see what you mean. Why aren't those kids in school?"

I turned back to Linda Sue's grave. "Linda Sue," I said conversationally, "if you can hear me, please show up. I really need to talk to you."

I waited, kicking rocks aside as I paced. Helen stood by with her arms crossed.

After several minutes, I said, "This is stupid."

I started back to the car.

"It was worth a try," Helen said, following me.

I was looking down, watching my feet make their way through the grass, feeling my shoulders slump and not fighting it, when I heard Helen say, "Somebody's sitting in your car."

It was George and Linda Sue, sitting in the back seat, with Melissa King sitting between them, her puppy in her lap. Helen and I sat in the front seat.

I turned to face them.

"Before you say anything, could we please get out of here?" George said. "This place gives me the willies." He looked extremely uncomfortable.

I drove to the end of Cemetery Drive and pulled over.

"I figured I'd find you guys at the cemetery," I said.

"I figured we'd find you guys there," George replied. "That's not a good place to look for us. That's the last place I want to be."

"Look what I've got," Melissa said as she held up a Barbie doll dressed in a nurse's uniform. It was tattered and dingy, and I later learned she had pilfered it from her room years ago. It had been her favorite toy when she was alive. "I was going to be a nurse when I grew up. George says I'll never grow up because I stunted my growth smoking. Isn't he silly?"

"Yes," Helen laughed. "That sounds just like something George would say."

"Sorry to interrupt your honeymoon, kids, but we have a problem." I looked at Linda Sue. "Your parents came to see me this afternoon."

She nodded. "We know. Randy saw them pull up in front of the school, and he followed them to your office."

"Then you know they think I'm a sadist. Guys, how did your writeup get in the *Pineville Chronicle*?"

"I've got a doctor's kit at home," Melissa said. "I can take your blood pressure. Do you have a blood pressure?"

Helen smiled at her. "Yes."

"I don't have a blood pressure. Neither do George and Linda Sue. Did you know you don't have a blood pressure when you're dead? Can I take your blood pressure next time I see you?"

Linda Sue shushed her. "Honey, you'll have to be quiet while we talk to Mr. Fellars." She looked back at me. "I have no idea how our writeup got in the *Pineville Chronicle.*"

"Who could have done it?"

"I wouldn't put it past Gordon Wallace," George offered.

"Did he know about the wedding?"

"He heard us planning it," Linda Sue said.

"At least it didn't get in the *Brownville Courier.*"

"The *Brownville Courier* wouldn't have printed it," Linda Sue observed. "They would have remembered all the names in the writeup and known we were all dead. Pineville is two counties over. They wouldn't know us at the paper. One of the readers must have known me and sent a copy of the paper to my parents. Or whoever put the article in the paper sent them a copy."

Melissa's puppy began chewing on her doll, and she scolded her. "Bad dog, Scuttles." She looked at Helen and grinned, revealing a gap where one of her teeth had gone to the tooth fairy. Helen grinned back at her.

"Whoever did it put me in an awkward jam," I said to Linda Sue. "Your parents are ready to lynch me."

"We've already fixed it," George assured me.

Linda Sue nodded. "We just talked to my parents. They understand everything."

I started. "You made contact with your parents?"

"We more or less had to. It was the only way we could undo the damage."

"And they're not going to have me arrested?"

"Dad never made it to the sheriff's office. But he did talk to Bubba Wilson before we could get to him. He called Bubba before we left and told him it was all a misunderstanding."

Bubba Wilson was a town cop on the take. As far as I was concerned, he was the worst person Tim Boyle could have talked to.

Helen patted me on the arm. "Do you feel better now?"

"Yeah. But Bubba Wilson makes me nervous. He's got a grudge against me. I had to report him for child abuse a couple of years ago. If he goes digging into this, he can make trouble. We broke the law getting that marriage license."

"You worry too much," Helen said. "You dyed your hair, remember? The records clerk looked like she was recruited from a nursing home. She'll never be able to identify you."

"Suppose they question the evangelist?"

Helen laughed. "Once he starts describing who was on the guest list, he's not going to have any credibility. I don't think you'll hear a peep out of Bubba Wilson."

"Let's hope not."

"I really hate this happened," Linda Sue said. "But at least now my parents know we're happy."

I smiled at her. "Are you happy enough to cross over?"

She and George looked at each other.

"We're not quite ready yet," George said.

"We have another request," Linda Sue added.

I frowned. "The deal was only one wish, remember? I've got the others to work on."

"It's not for us," George said. "It's for Melissa."

Linda Sue looked down at her. "Remember when you asked us what we wanted to do in the time we had left? Melissa didn't know what she wanted. Now she does."

"She wants us to adopt her."

Helen grabbed my arm. "Bill, isn't that sweet?"

"Yeah," I sighed. "I suppose it has to be legal."

Linda Sue nodded. "Of course. Otherwise she won't feel like she really belongs to us."

15

I sat in my car in front of the Li'l Cricket on Shade Street in Elmwood and watched Vince Echols emerge with a paper bag in his arms. I had followed him from Brownville on a hunch. It was 9:20 p.m.

I rolled down my window and called to him, "What you got in the bag, Vince?"

He looked like the proverbial cat with its paw in the canary cage.

"Hello, Mr. Fellars." He looked at the bag in his hand. "I had to pick up some Listerine for my mom."

He was wearing a baseball cap, a T-shirt with an eagle and Harley-Davidson slogan on it, and ragged jeans.

"Vince, how did you convince that girl to sell you some beer?"

He was underage, and he knew I knew it. He had dropped out of Brownville High last fall.

He walked over to my car. "Aw, don't bust me, Mr. Fellars."

"I'm not going to bust you, Vince. Get in."

He sat on my passenger's side.

"Now, you didn't answer my question."

He sighed. "I have a fake ID."

"Let me see it."

I examined it under the light from the store. I pulled out my own driver's license and compared them. "It's good. Where did you get it?"

"I'd rather not say."

I handed him back his fake driver's license. "Maybe I'd better explain where I'm coming from here. I need one of these. For a friend. Can you help me get one?"

He cocked his head. "I guess so. But I don't get it. You're old enough to buy beer for your friend."

"I don't want it to buy beer. My friend is older than I am."

"So why does he need a fake ID?"

"I'd rather not say."

He grinned. "I can dig that."

"Good. Now let's start over. Where do we get one of these?"

"A dude at Elmwood College makes them. In his dorm room."

"In his dorm room?"

"Yeah."

"How does he do it?"

"On his computer. He's got special software."

"Can you introduce me to him?"

"Sure."

I followed Vince Echols up to the second-floor hallway of Elmwood College's Copeland Hall to room 216. Tim Boyle tagged behind us. Tim Boyle and I had made our peace over the stricture he and his wife had heaped on me in my office by ignoring the incident, and he was now my ally.

Vince gave the secret knock at the door.

"Come in."

The room smelled of stale cigarette smoke. The desk in the corner was littered with candy wrappers and empty Miller cans. There was a Dell Inspiron computer, plastic card printer, scanner, and small laminator on a table beside the desk. Beside the printer were stacks of

Teslin paper and plastic laminate pouches. Four playmate centerfolds lined the wall at the foot of the bunk beds.

A guy in plaid shorts and a crew cut was fooling with a digital camera on a tripod in front of the computer setup when we walked in. He looked at us from behind black horn-rimmed glasses, and he clearly didn't like what he saw.

"Here's the new business I was telling you about," Vince said by way of introduction.

We were older than his normal clientele, and our age put him off.

"What do they need this for?" he asked suspiciously.

Tim Boyle pulled out his wallet. "Son, there's an extra hundred in this if you don't ask questions. I don't like doing this, but I'm in a jam. We're not here to bust you."

Vince looked at me. "They're okay. He's my high school guidance counselor."

I winced.

The young man shrugged, evidently figuring he had nothing to lose. "Whatever you say." He pointed to a spot in front of the desk that had been marked with masking tape. "Step up to the X and look at the birdie."

Sometime back, the state of South Carolina had altered its driver's license format to make counterfeiting more difficult, but the young man in room 216 had software that circumvented the state's efforts, including the ability to add holograms to both sides of the license. He opened his computer screen to a file that contained a perfect replica of a South Carolina license. At the top of the screen was the caption, South Carolina Driver's License, flanked by a small red map of the palmetto state. Below this was a red line that stretched across the image. In the center of the screen was the pale blue emblem of a palmetto tree and quarter moon. On the left side of the screen was a light blue inset where a photo would be inserted. There was a smaller inset at the lower right corner, above the signature of the governor of the state. Between the insets was a column for the usual identifying information.

He looked at Tim Boyle. "Your name?" he said.

Tim took a deep breath and said, "Baucom, George Henry."

The problem that had led Tim Boyle and me to Copeland Hall was how to get the family court system to allow George and Linda Sue Baucom to adopt Melissa King. In my line of work, I've noticed that grandparents frequently end up raising their grandchildren, a fact which causes me no end of headaches when it comes to sorting out who to put down on financial aid forms for college.

We decided that the easiest way to accomplish our goal was to have Linda Sue's parents impersonate George and Linda Sue Baucom and claim to be Melissa King's grandparents. Helen Noble and I would impersonate Joel and Shonda King. Helen would also have to claim to be the daughter of "the Baucoms." We would then petition the court to let Melissa's "grandparents" adopt her. This entirely fabricated family constellation would give us paperwork legalizing adoption of Melissa King by George and Linda Sue Baucom, and it would give the court a presentable set of circumstances with which to work.

The maze of authentic paperwork needed to carry out this deception had us stumped until Freddy Seaton pointed out that only the final document, the court decree granting the adoption, had to be legal. The trail of paperwork that led us to the genuine article could be "as phony as Joe Murray's hairpiece."

It was on that premise that we constructed our family facade.

Tim Boyle took the fake driver's license to Charleston, where his brother was a hospital administrator, and opened up a bank account at Bank of America in the name of George Baucom. He used a check drawn on the account to pay a Charleston attorney to initiate adoption proceedings for Melissa King on behalf of George and Linda Sue Baucom. Helen and I went along as Joel and Shonda King, requesting that our child be given over to the Baucoms because Shonda had a terminal illness and wouldn't be able to care for her, and Joel was a traveling salesman who would not be there for her either.

To establish Charleston residency, Tim rented a two-story antebellum home near the Battery, which cost him an arm and a leg, in George Baucom's name.

Tim Boyle had summoned John Boyle, his brother and the chief administrator of St. Mary's Hospital in North Charleston, to Brownville and gotten him knee-walking drunk. When John was sufficiently inebriated, Tim reacquainted him with his dead niece. Then he introduced him to the real George Baucom and Melissa King. He presented him with the problem of finding a way for George and Linda Sue to adopt Melissa. Like Helen and me, John Boyle had not been able to say no when asked to help. It didn't take much to fall in love with Melissa King, snaggle-tooth, Scuttles, Barbie doll, and all.

The next morning, Tim entered the guest room, where his brother was nursing a hangover.

"I'm sorry about your hangover, but I had to get you drunk to ask you the favor I needed," he said.

"Just what did happen here last night?" John wanted to know like he didn't really want to know.

Tim paused a beat, wondering how much of the previous evening his brother remembered. "I can get them back to talk to you."

His brother apparently remembered quite a lot. "No, don't do that."

"You promised to help."

"I'll help. But I don't think I need to see them again."

John's help came through his acquaintance with Milton Nessler, a Charleston family court judge and longtime golfing buddy. John bent the judge's ear with a character reference for "George Baucom," who the judge learned was John's stepbrother (because of the different last names). John proceeded to persuade the judge to rush through the adoption proceedings on the strength of Shonda's fabricated terminal illness. Hopefully, we wouldn't need to document the illness, but if we did, John would have to pull some strings at the hospital. We also hoped that the strength of John's character reference, along with the prestigious address near the Battery, would eliminate the need for the judge to burden overworked welfare workers by having them investigate conditions in the "Baucom" household before granting the adoption.

According to the petition the attorney filed, the Baucoms wanted to change Melissa's name from King to Baucom. Joel King, according to the petition, gave his blessing to this request.

The entire transaction took place in the judge's chambers. The only hitch came when the judge noticed that the name of Melissa's mother on her birth certificate was Shonda Deal. Since she was supposed to be George and Linda Sue Baucom's daughter, the names didn't match. It was a detail we had overlooked.

Helen thought fast on her feet this time. "Joel and I weren't married when Melissa was born. I was married to a Deal at the time. The nurse at the hospital got confused and put down Deal as my maiden name. I was too embarrassed to tell her any different. I never got around to straightening it out. It doesn't matter now."

The judge was taken in by Helen's impromptu performance, and we were home free.

16

The dead youth who made up my alternate universe began to worm their way into my thoughts during my daily counseling sessions with the living. The day I realized this fact was when I got a referral on Larry Ringer for disruptive behavior in Mrs. Brehmer's math class. I had been counseling work-shy students for years, but my sudden exposure to students who had had their lives cut short robbed me of any tolerance for anyone on this side of the grave who was throwing his life away.

"I've seen your record, Larry. You're so smart. Why aren't you applying yourself?"

"Why should I?"

His answer stumped me.

"Why should you? Are you serious?"

He didn't answer. He gave me a look, and I realized he was.

Larry Ringer was a big, hulking teddy bear of a boy with sandy hair and pale skin who laughed his way through life. School was a joke, church was a joke, responsibility was a joke, and any serious question called for a flippant response. He had a 130 IQ. Schools don't give IQ tests anymore unless a kid gets referred to the school psychologist. In elementary school, Larry's performance was so poor that he had been suspected of having a learning disability, which led to his being tested and his genius being documented in his school record. He sat across my desk smacking a wad of Bazooka.

"Tell me something, Larry. What are your plans for the future?" I asked.

"To let it happen."

That's the kind of answer you got when you asked Larry a serious question. I was going to have to dig to get anything meaningful out of him.

"Okay, let's go five years down the road. How do you see yourself?"

He blew out a bubble of Bazooka and let it pop. "A beach bum."

"A beach bum. And how will you support yourself?"

"Like I'm doing now. Leech off my mom."

"And what happens when your mom is gone?"

He smacked his gum. "By then automation will put everybody out of work, and the government will have to support us."

"Where did you get that idea?"

"I read a lot."

"That's a good habit."

He stopped chewing his gum and gave me a serious look. "You ever hear of the technological singularity?"

"Can't say that I have."

"It's when technology explodes to the point that machines are smarter than humans, and we no longer control the way things work. You ever read Verner Vinge?"

"No."

"He writes science fiction. Good stuff. But I read a nonfiction article he wrote in an old issue of *Whole Earth Review*. 'The Coming Technological Singularity,' or something like that."

"Yeah?"

"Vinge says machines may become so smart they figure they don't need humans anymore. Even if they don't kill us, they'll put us out of work."

"That's unsettling," I said. "What do you think we would all do in a world where humans didn't work?"

He began popping his gum with renewed vigor. "We'd get our kicks doing drugs and playing video games. The government will have to pay us to not work."

"You think you could be happy sitting around all day playing video games, not contributing anything worthwhile to society?"

He grinned. "Works for me so far."

During my freshman year at Clemson, I'd had a roommate who ran with a pack that spent their time cutting class, playing pool, going to movies, flying model airplanes, picking up girls, attending concerts, playing tennis, getting drunk, raising the devil, and having an all-around good time while flunking out. It seemed like that schedule would get old by the time they were my age.

I gave Larry one more shot. "Even if Vinge's vision for the future comes about, not all humans will be put out of work. You're smart enough to be one that controls the machines."

"If I apply myself."

"Yes, if you apply yourself."

He dismissed that idea.

"A waste of time. Most of what kids learn in school today will be obsolete by the time they are your age."

I shook my head. "Larry, I don't know what I'm going to do with you. I hate to see someone with your ability get left behind."

"I'm not going to be left behind. I'm ahead of my time. I'm practicing to be part of the useless generation."

Larry was indeed ahead of his time. His ideas would be echoed five years after our conversation took place, in a groundbreaking book by Israeli historian Yuval Noah Harari, entitled *Homo Deus: A Brief History of Tomorrow*. According to Harari, in the near future, machines will displace many humans, who will not only be unemployed, but will be unemployable. Harari refers to them as the useless class.

Larry Ringer left my office that day as entrenched in apathy as he had been when he entered, also leaving me feeling like a total failure. I found myself fantasizing about having my dead friends lecture him on missed opportunities. As it was, I didn't dare share my Larry Ringer experience with them. Counseling sessions are supposed to be confidential—but I could have convinced myself that that restriction doesn't apply when it comes to dead people. The truth was, I knew my dead teenagers would be highly upset over Larry's priorities in life.

My thanks to Verner Vinge for unwittingly giving Larry Ringer the philosophical underpinning to justify being shiftless in his schoolwork and aimless in his ambition.

17

"You live with your mom?" Helen asked, without masking her surprise.

We were eating lunch alone in her corner office, and I was telling her about the family farm.

I chewed a mouthful of bologna cheese and swallowed. "I moved in after my divorce five years ago to take care of her. She's seventy-two now."

"Oh? How long were you married?"

"Twelve years."

"Any children?"

"I have a sixteen-year-old daughter. Pamela."

"Do you see her often?"

"About three or four times a year."

She started. "What?"

"We're not on very good terms."

"That's a shame. Why not? I hope I'm not being too nosy."

I took another mouthful, then dug a chip of gristle out of the corner of my mouth with my napkin, trying not to gross her out. "Lots of reasons. But it boils down to the fact that Pamela never forgave me for leaving her mom. She won't come down to see me. I used to go up and visit her on Sunday afternoons, but when kids get to be teenagers, you lose them. They get their own friends. Pamela's never there on Sundays anymore. What about you? Were you ever married?"

She shook her head. "No. I'm still waiting for Mr. Right. I'm very picky."

"Well, I hope you get to try it someday. I think everybody should go through at least one marriage, just for the education."

She laughed, politely, because it wasn't really that funny. "I'm afraid the closest I've come is when we went to Elmwood to get the marriage license. Do you have any pictures of your daughter?"

I started to reach for my wallet but realized I didn't. I was suddenly ashamed of myself. "At home on my dresser," I said.

"Bring it to school. I'd like to see it."

I noticed she had small dimples at the corners of her smile and a cute little mole on her neck.

"I've got a better idea. Come to my house for dinner on Sunday and I'll show it to you. My mom's a master chef when she has a guest to feed."

M om was putting on the tablecloth when we walked in. She had on the Sunday dress she used to go to church in when Dad was alive. For years she hadn't been able to get into it, but diabetes had shed pounds that years of diets and pills hadn't been able to burn off. She had been to the beautician the day before, and her hair showed it. She seldom dressed up, because I seldom brought home guests, but that Sunday she made me proud.

Her greeting was warm. "Helen, I'm so glad to meet you. Bill says you're the school librarian."

"That's right. My official job title is library media specialist, because I deal with a lot more than just books. I'm the go-to person whenever there's a problem with technology. But yes, I'm the school librarian."

"I think I need to take you to the Elmwood Library with me

and have you show me how to find books. I never got used to the computer system they have. I have to ramble through the aisles and see what's on the shelves."

Helen nodded sympathetically. "Actually, Mrs. Fellars, once you get used to computers, you wonder how you ever got along without them."

"That's what Bill says. But I'm like an old dog. I don't think I can learn any new tricks."

Helen smiled. "Now, Mrs. Fellars, you look like a quick study to me. If you're serious about wanting me to walk you through the computer system, I'll be glad to."

"I might just take you up on that."

"I might want a favor in return," Helen said with a twinkle in her eye. "Bill told me you were into azaleas and orchids. I never can get flowers to bloom. Maybe you can show me what I'm doing wrong."

Mom seemed pleased with the horse trade. "That sounds like a fair bargain." She reached for an apron draped across the back of a chair and put it over her Sunday dress. "I'm sorry I'm late for dinner. I forgot to thaw the pork chops. It'll be ready in half an hour."

She walked to the china cabinet and reached for her crystal goblets.

"Let me help you set the table," Helen offered.

She began placing the goblets. "Bill will tell you that I don't have many rules, but one of them is that I don't let guests set the table. Another is that I don't let them wash the dishes. Thanks for offering, though."

"I'll show you that picture you wanted to see," I said to Helen.

Helen had formed an opinion of my mother based on that short encounter.

"She's a very nice lady," she said when we got to my room. "I was surprised when you said you lived with your mother, because I couldn't wait to get away from mine. She still tries to run my life from seventy miles away. But your mom isn't like mine at all."

I smiled at her. "She likes you too. She doesn't set out her crystal goblets for just anybody."

"Are you sure she's seventy-two? She looks like she's in her fifties."

"She looks young now, but when she's been working in the yard all day long, she looks her age. Sometimes I'll come home from work and see her in her recliner, and she'll be pale as chalk, breathing so shallow you can't detect it, and I'll have to watch her for a couple of minutes to make sure she isn't dead."

She gave me the evil eye. "Bill, you're terrible."

"I'm serious. When she lived alone and I checked on her twice a week, my biggest fear was that one day I'd walk in and find her gone. Not just dead, but good and dead, three days ripe, bloated with a stink that would knock me over coming up the walk."

She swatted me on the arm. "You're worse than terrible. You're a dog. Is that your daughter?"

I turned to the portrait on my dresser. "That's her."

"Do you have any pictures of your wife?"

"My ex-wife. Yes and no."

"Do you always talk in riddles?"

"I don't have any pictures of Karen," I explained, "but if you see Pamela, you see Karen. They look just alike."

"Maybe that's another reason you don't get along with Pamela."

"Psychiatrist Noble," I said sarcastically.

She gave my room the once-over. "I hate to say it, Bill, but your room sure is messy." Her eyes settled on my closet. "At least you press your clothes."

"My mom does it," I confessed.

"Aha. You said you moved in to take care of her. But I'll bet she's the one who takes care of you."

Her insight was keen.

"She won't let me do anything for her," I said defensively.

"I saw that already when I offered to set the table. Your room really looks like a little boy's. Are you into comic books?"

I looked at the mess that spilled across my chest of drawers. "I've got *Conan* comics because I'm a Robert E. Howard fan. He really knew how to give readers their money's worth. You've got a point about the room, though. It's an eerie feeling to find yourself forty years old and sleeping in the same bed you slept in when you were ten, being called to dinner with a reminder to wash your hands, having your mom laundering your dirty clothes and hinting for you to clean up your room. But in a way, it helps me relate to the kids at school."

"How's that?"

"They all live with their parents, too, and are dependent on them. I think they pick up on the fact that I share that experience with them. I think it actually forms a bond between us."

"That's a nice way of looking at it," she said.

"You know, I actually tried to relive my adolescence a couple of years ago. I reread the same books I read in high school—Bradbury's *Something Wicked This Way Comes*, Steinbeck's *East of Eden*, Wolfe's *Look Homeward, Angel*, Burrough's *Land that Time Forgot*, Bloch's *The Dead Beat*, Salinger's *Catcher in the Rye*, and of course, Robert E. Howard. I guess the idea was that if I could revert to adolescence, maybe once I got through it again, a new life would be waiting for me and I could start over again."

"Did it help?" she asked.

"No. My second adolescence was much like my first. Lonely and depressing. Just like this conversation is getting. My apologies. Let's step outside. I'll show you the farm."

She shadowed me while I did my daily chores. I fed the beagles. They danced, climbed the sides of their pen, raced to their trough, and nuzzled each other out of the way, reminding me of the kids at school fighting their way into the lunch line. Then I fed the cows, which wasn't strictly necessary, since they had plenty of grazing land, but when your fences had deteriorated as badly as ours had since my dad died, you had to keep the cows tame enough to follow you with a bucket of feed when they got out.

We'd never made the farm pay for itself. I ran a dozen or so cows on the place and sold calves to pay the taxes. But it seemed like every year the tractor would break down, and getting it fixed would eat up everything I'd cleared on the calves. The farm was more like a hobby—a very expensive hobby—to me. It gave me a chance to walk in my dad's footsteps for a while, mending fences he'd strung, plowing across furrows he'd plowed, running his beagles through the woods. Sometimes I could feel his soul moving about the river bottoms.

Helen and I walked the pastures until we heard the dinner bell ring.

18

What I remembered most about Mike Sanders was seeing him lying in that coffin the year before he died on his way home from monthly Guard training. That Halloween, the Willards went a little overboard on seasonal festivities and borrowed a coffin from the prop room of the Elmwood Little Theater, where John Willard served as stage manager. They placed it on their front porch to impress the trick-or-treaters. Mike was visiting Tim Willard that evening, and they took a photo of Mike lying in that coffin, dressed in an ill-fitting coat he had borrowed from Tim. That photo flashed through my mind the day I attended Mike's funeral, giving me a firsthand appreciation of the concept of *déjà vu*.

Another thing I remembered about Mike was how big his feet were. The first-block vocational bus would arrive back at Brownville High right in the middle of third period, and you could hear Mike stomping his way down the hall in his size twelve work boots, then noisily slamming his locker door. It's funny what kids will do to get attention. Mrs. Dill, whose French class was right across the hall from his locker, would open the door and scold him, or sometimes give him the evil eye. Mike always seemed disappointed when she had a sub who didn't care about his racket (because of all the racket in the classroom).

91

Mike had enough redneck in him to get into a fight four or five times a year. His mother always took his side, even when she knew he was in the wrong. When I went to school, if you got in trouble at school, you got a double dose when you got home, but parents play by different rules today. It got to where we hated seeing Nancy Sanders coming through the door.

It's ironic, but one of the reasons Mike got into fights was because of his mother. By the time he got to high school, she had shown her hind quarters on his behalf so frequently that kids had begun calling him "mama's boy." That usually resulted in another fight, after which Nancy Sanders would storm into the school for another bloodletting with the administration.

The older Mike got, the more embarrassment his mother's meddling on his behalf caused him, but he was unable to call her off. "It's for your own good, Mikey," she'd say, causing him to grit his teeth. Sometimes during parent conferences, she would let her guard down and say just enough to reveal that she knew she was doing him wrong, as overprotective mothers know in their hearts, but she was unable to help herself. Sometimes parents can love their children too much.

Mike tried to become the man of the house when his dad died during his senior year, but his mother was determined to continue to mother him to death. When he'd had all he could stomach, Mike moved out on his own.

His first act of rebellion was to defer going to college in favor of a job so he could enjoy life for a while. He joined the National Guard to sock away educational benefits for the day when he would resume his schooling. First, he had to get his head together and decide what he wanted to do.

Two years later, it seemed that everything was finally going his way. He had a good job, a new car, a girlfriend, and plans to join the Brownville police force as soon as he finished his evening classes in criminal justice at technical college. Unfortunately, he fell asleep at the wheel on his way home from weekend Guard training and never woke up this side of the grave.

Carl Riley was a two-timing leech, according to Mike Sanders. Nancy Riley, who had been Nancy Sanders during Mike's lifetime, supported Carl Riley and her eight-year-old son, Teddy Sanders, by working as a secretary at the Duke Power office on Main Street.

She had married Carl Riley because, as a widow who had lost her husband in a hunting accident two years before Mike's death and who had a toddler to raise, she had felt she needed a man in her life. Carl Riley had wined and dined her and bought her gifts in a whirlwind romance that added color to her life and lifted her out of her depression, and she soon found herself hopelessly dependent on him.

But it was an old story I have seen played out many times over the years. As soon as the ink dried on the marriage license, the thoughtful, considerate, fun-loving suitor changed colors and turned into a different person. He went through the motions of trying to get a job but always managed to find an excuse to avoid work. Her relatives would use their pull to get him a job, but he seemed to feel he was too good to be loading fertilizer bags onto trucks at Helen's Greenhouse or to be unloading lumber at McKinley's Hardware, and his surly tongue would get him fired. It was two years before Nancy Riley realized her husband had no intention of holding down a job.

Carl Riley spent his days loafing at Neal's grocery and his evenings bumming drinks at Butch's Bar. He attracted a steady string of women with lies about how his old lady mistreated him at home and cramped his style, and women were easily taken by his charm and seemed to want to mother him. Nancy Riley had suffered the indignity of his various affairs, but she always forgave him and took him back. Even when he came home drunk and ended up beating her once or twice a week. The need for a man at all costs was too great.

While he felt he had the privilege of coming and going as he pleased, Carl Riley expected his wife to be there waiting for him when he needed her. A night on the town with the girls was out of the question. He would grill her about who she saw at work, and if he suspected she had been the recipient of male attention, he was quick to make a federal case out of it. He liked to toy with her. If he sent her out for a chicken dinner at the truck stop, he would swear he had asked for a hamburger steak, and likely as not, he would throw the chicken dinner against the wall and make her clean it up. Then he would send her back out for his hamburger steak.

All this bothered Mike, who had watched over the years as his mother's life seemed to seep away until she wasn't much more alive than he was. But what really distressed him was the way Carl Riley treated his younger brother, Teddy. Having Carl Riley for a stepdad was like being in boot camp. Whatever you did was wrong, and any action—or inaction—would bring a scolding. Carl would belittle Teddy by calling him stupid whenever he sprayed gravel into the flower bed when doing wheelies on his bike, or when he bumped the paddle against the boat and scared the fish away, or when he was too slow bringing Carl a beer during the Friday night football highlights. Sometimes when Carl beat his mom, Teddy would try to take up for her and end up deflecting the beating from her onto himself.

Mike Sanders wanted more than anything to get Carl Riley out of the house where he had grown up. And he figured he owed his mom big-time. She'd interfered in his life "for his own good" when he was alive to the point that, God help him, he'd wanted to smack her. So he figured it was high time to return the favor and do a little interfering in her life.

For her own good.

Legrand Warfield was Brownville's answer to Al Capone. He lived with his wife and four kids in a two-story log house at the edge of the swamp on four hundred acres of what had once been his father's family farm approximately three miles outside of Brownville. When the dairy business went from small one-man operations to big agribusiness in the sixties, Legrand Warfield's grandfather had been squeezed out of business and had turned to moon-shine for his livelihood, an enterprise he'd handed down to his son and grandson.

Legrand could still make some of the best corn mash in the southeast, if you believe local lore, but had turned to importing and wholesaling illegal drugs to make his fortune. The town had it that his drug connections extended to South America.

The county sheriff had privately vowed to put him behind bars, and Warfield had publicly boasted in Butch's Bar that he would never serve time. Warfield often boasted about his gun collection, which was reported to be an arsenal that could fend off the local National Guard unit. The sheriff's efforts to incarcerate him had so far been frustrated by the fact that all the Brownville police and several county deputies were allegedly on Warfield's Dixie Mafia payroll. I don't know how true that is, but I do know that whenever law enforcement officials make "surprise" visits to Brownville High to have the county drug dog sniff out student lockers, the word goes around school before they arrive, and they have never found so much as a marijuana reefer on school property.

I knew a lot about what went on in the Warfield household, because his son Seth was a regular client in my guidance office. Seth had a brother in the fifth grade, who'd also shared his troubled life with the counselor at Brownville Elementary. When Warfield learned his youngest son had been talking to a school counselor, he had gone to the elementary school and threatened to fit the principal and counselor with cement shoes. The counselor had stopped talking to the student out of fear for her life. Fortunately, I had received no such threats, because Warfield never learned that I had counseled his son. When kids reach high school age, they usually learn not to tattle on each other or go home and reveal the secrets they've disclosed to their school counselor.

Mike Sanders and Randy Galphin came to me together one day during my lunch hour. I usually ate with Helen in the school library, but on this particular day she was off to a grant-writing workshop, and I had decided to eat in my office.

Mike was a tall kid, still wearing the crew cut he had received at Fort Bragg five years before. The ruddy complexion he had when he was alive had been bleached out by death, but he was still a nice-looking boy. He wore his Army fatigues.

Mike sat on the edge of my desk. "We're working together on our project."

Randy Galphin claimed his seat on my window ledge. "When you asked what we wanted to accomplish during the time we had left, I said I wanted to see that my family was provided for. I've found a way."

I put my BLT sandwich back in the wrapper and leaned back in my chair. "Oh? Let's hear it."

"We know where Legrand Warfield's drug money is hid," Mike announced.

"It's buried in the swamp. We're going to dig it up and give it to my mom."

Mike grinned. "Most of it."

"We're going to give a wad of it to Carl Riley."

I cocked my head. "You're going to give money to your stepdad?"

"Yeah. And when he starts flashing it around town, Legrand Warfield will think he's the one that stole it."

I frowned. "That could get your stepdad killed."

"No, it won't. At the first hint of trouble, he'll run. And my mom will be rid of him."

I looked at Randy. "What makes you think your family won't attract attention flashing money around town?"

"We want you to hold onto it and send them a little bit every month. Just enough to live off of. And when it comes time to put the kids through school, you can send it to the college for them. Otherwise, they're just like me. They would go through it in a month."

I heaved a deep sigh. "I don't like it. Stealing is wrong."

"Stealing from a crook ain't regular stealing," Randy argued.

"We're taxing him," Mike rationalized. "We're taking money he owes the government and using it to help feed and educate the needy. Just like the government does."

"It's still against the law, Mike."

"He's got the law in his pocket," Randy said.

"Randy and I need you to help us dig up the money. We can do it ourselves, but I don't know how long it'll take. It's a lot harder to move things around after you're dead."

"And we need you to dole out the money for several years. I won't be around to do it," Randy said. When I didn't answer, he continued, with an edge of desperation in his voice, "Besides, they were counting on me to feed them when I cut out on them. I let them down, and this is the only way I can make it up to them."

I looked at them for a long moment. "Just whose idea was this?"

"Mine," Mike grinned proudly. "Pretty good, ain't it?"

He still needed approval, I thought. He'd stomped down the hall of Brownville High in those heavy boots to get noticed, and he was wanting me to brag on his scheme.

But I couldn't. "Mike, I didn't realize you were that devious," I said.

He took it as a compliment. "I am, ain't I?"

"Surely there's a better way to get what you want."

Randy issued me a challenge. "All right. If you can think of a better way, we'll do it your way."

I couldn't, of course. Sometimes the laws of this world hurt those they're not supposed to hurt and protect those they're not supposed to protect. The more I thought about it, the clearer it became that a higher justice was served in stealing Legrand Warfield's drug money and giving it to the Galphins.

I gave in. "Make sure Gordon Wallace doesn't get wind of this."

"We've already gotten the word," Randy assured me.

19

I parked my car off the side of an old logging road off Highway 21 late that Saturday night and walked the barbed wire fence of the Warfield property to the edge of the swamp. There was very little moonlight, but I didn't dare risk a flashlight. I walked gingerly, cringing at every twig that snapped under my rubber boots. I carried a shovel, a box of plastic garbage bags, a pulley, and some rope.

I met Mike Sanders and Randy Galphin at Cane Creek. They gestured for me to follow them. We crossed the fence and walked the edge of Legrand Warfield's south pasture to the power line that crossed the swamp. The air smelled of cow manure. A chorus of tree frogs and crickets spilled out from the swamp.

We crossed the fence again and walked down the power line to where the solid ground turned to mush. They stopped and pulled back the brush to reveal a wheelbarrow they had scrounged from Legrand Warfield's shed the night before. It had taken the entire gang to move it, including George and Linda Sue and Melissa Baucom, who hadn't crossed over yet because they were still waiting on Melissa's adoption papers to arrive.

We sloshed our way through the bog the length of two power line towers. Then we broke off into the woods and made for the heart of the swamp. At some point, the water ran over the tops of my boots and soaked my socks. Briars shredded my clothing, and mosquitoes swarmed about me. The odor of stagnant water rode on the wind.

At last we came to a mound of high ground. According to Seth Warfield, in the early nineteenth century, Cane Creek had been dammed up to provide power for a grist mill that served settlers in the area that would later become Brownville. The mound of high ground was all that remained of the old dam.

I heard the branches snap, and I turned to see Steve Hall leading Warfield's mule out of the bush. Steve had been electrocuted putting up his grandmother's television antenna, and he was terrified at the sight of electrical wires. It had taken a tremendous act of courage for him to cross the power line that traversed Legrand Warfield's property.

Steve had had trouble putting the collar and blinders on Warfield's mule, and he was leading her with a rope. The collar and bridle were strapped across the mule's back.

"What's the mule for?" I whispered.

"The treasure's under the millstone," Randy answered. "Warfield raises it with the mule."

They led me to the millstone, which lay under a huge oak tree. Laval Crenshaw, the animal lover who had died of AIDS, was there, and I saw that he had managed to muzzle Warfield's Doberman and chain it to a tree. Normally the animal had the run of the swamp. When the dog saw me, it began lunging for me, but the chain held it in check. The dog snorted and fought the muzzle with its front paws, but Laval sweet-talked the dog into behaving.

"Do you know how to harness a mule?" Randy asked me.

I looked at the strings of leather dangling from the mule's neck. "I can probably figure it out."

In ten minutes, I had the reins hopelessly tangled and was turning the halter inside out trying to untangle it. I was rescued by Sammy Tribble, who'd drifted across the dam.

Sammy Tribble had followed a mule and plow across many a furrow in the late 1940s as he'd helped his father try to scratch out a living on the patch of rock he was sharecropping. Sammy was tall and lanky, unlike Steve Hall, who was small for his age. I figured he would give me grief for having knotted up the harness, but he started on Laval Crenshaw instead as he went about pulling apart the mess I'd made.

"Hey, Laval, check out this low-tech winch. I bet you can't raise this millstone with no Apple."

"Shut up or I'll turn this dog on you. You died before Selma, so you missed out on Bull Conner, but I can make it up to you."

The exchange referred to Laval Crenshaw's obsession with anything high-tech. Unfortunately for Laval, the dead youth were all stuck in the technology of their time and were unable to progress to anything that came after their life spans had ended. Personal computers had been just coming of age when he died, which in his aborted lifetime amounted to the Apple IIe. By lingering behind after he should have moved on, Laval had witnessed the advent of Windows, the internet, digital cameras, cell phones, and the unveiling of the iPad three months previously, but he neither understood them nor was able to operate them. He could only watch the world of technology unfold with envy. The others used his frustration with developing technology to toy with him when the opportunity presented itself.

Randy Galphin climbed the oak tree and rigged up a block and tackle with the rope and pulley I'd brought.

Sammy looked at the block and tackle. "Hey, Laval, how about come over here and help us download this rope."

"Why don't you slip it around your neck and dangle from it? We need a counterbalance."

The play flushed out of Sammy's face. He had been hanged by Klan members, and he had the same fear of the rope that Steve Hall had of electrical wires.

Sammy stared at Laval as I tied the end of the rope to the mule.

After fuming for a moment, he said, "That was uncalled for, homo boy."

Laval stiffened. "No need to get personal."

"No need for you to get hateful," Sammy said.

"What? Your comment wasn't hateful?"

"He was just joking with you, Sammy. Lighten up," Randy said, looking down from the tree limb.

That's the way they were. They would gang up on Laval and toy with him, but when the ribbing got out of hand, they would come to his rescue.

Sammy looked up at Randy. "Lighten up? You gonna say that to a Black man?"

"Come on, Sammy. No need to play the race card," Steve Hall said.

Sammy glowered at him, like he considered that remark coming from another Black man a sign of betrayal.

"Come on, all of you," I said. "We've got a job to do. You guys can insult each other after we're finished here."

Anger and hurt feelings floated about the swamp for a moment. Then Mike said, "You guys are clowns when you're chafed. You really were funny."

Sammy Tribble broke into a laugh that spread to Steve Hall, then to Randy and Mike. When Sammy Tribble smiled, his dark skin framed his white teeth like a picture. It was a smile that would have charmed concert audiences all over the world if Sammy had gotten the chance to follow his dream of becoming a jazz pianist.

Laval laughed with them, and the shared laughter signaled that this round of ridicule was over.

The mule was used to doing her job, and she had the millstone up in short order. Once it was up, I rolled it out of the way and let it drop to the ground.

Sammy tied the mule to a branch. Laval stayed with me and

stroked the Doberman while the others left to move about the swamp and watch for trouble. I took the shovel and started to dig.

Evidently, Warfield added to his cache regularly, because the ground was soft and easy on the shovel. It wasn't long until I struck metal.

I pulled out fifteen metal military ammunition boxes. Each box contained four bundles of twenties, five hundred notes to a bundle, wrapped in plastic. I made a mental calculation and determined that the take was close to $600,000.

Once I struck paydirt, Mike, Randy, Steve, and Sammy materialized out of the swamp and surveyed the boxes. Randy took a bundle out of the plastic and fanned the bills. He stuck the bundle under my nose. "Smell it for me, Mr. Fellars. Tell me how it smells." He was grinning ear to ear.

I sniffed. "It smells like money."

I had to rent eight safe deposit boxes in eight different banks to hold all the bills. I picked three banks in Columbia, three banks in Greenville, and two in Spartanburg.

I went to the Columbia post office and mailed two items. One was an envelope with $1,000 to Mary Galphin. The other was a package with $20,000 to Carl Riley. Neither package had a return address.

Randy was watching the day his mom got the money.

She was sitting on the porch of the two-story shack they were renting when the mailman pulled up. She sat on the porch often this time of the year (on the end that hadn't caved in) and enjoyed the sunshine, because the family had just suffered through a particularly harsh winter. The plywood covering the front window had not kept the cold out, and the cracks in the wall hadn't helped either. Summers were no picnic without screens on the windows or doors, but she could suffer the bugs better than the bite of winter.

Ragged and barefoot, the three kids she still had living at home raced down the pathway toward the highway to see who could get to the mailbox first. Josh was the oldest, so it was he who retrieved the prize and delivered it to her.

She thumbed through the pile of bills and junk mail, and it was obvious that the envelope with the money in it caught her eye right off. She held it up and looked at the handwriting on the envelope. She tore open the envelope and removed fifty twenty-dollar bills. Randy said she stood and dropped the rest of the mail on the porch. She looked inside the envelope for a note of explanation. There was none. Then she smiled at what was probably the only stroke of good fortune she'd ever had in her life. Josh grinned proudly, like he was the one responsible for their bonanza. Randy said it did his heart good to watch them and to know that this was only the first installment. When I heard that, any misgivings I'd had about stealing drug money from Legrand Warfield disappeared.

Mary Galphin's name and address on the envelope was in Randy's hand, but he didn't think she'd realized it. Perhaps one day when she puts it all together, it will come to her. I hope it does. It was the only clue he left that he was reaching out to help her from beyond the grave.

Mike Sanders was also watching when Carl Riley got his surprise package. He opened the box on his porch, looked inside, did a double take, and hurried inside his house. Like Mary Galphin, he examined the inside of the package for an explanation. Like her, he found nothing.

That afternoon, he was riding around town driving a new Dodge pickup. That evening over at Butch's Bar, he bought drinks for the house, bragging how he had won a ton of money in a high-stakes poker game in Elmwood. The next morning, Sonny Brooks found him at Lee's Pond trying out his new casting outfit and dropped the news that Legrand Warfield was looking for him. Legrand wanted the rest of the money Carl had stolen from his cache in the swamp.

"I been set up," Carl complained. "Somebody mailed me that money out of the blue."

"I thought you won it in a poker game," Sonny said.

Sonny claimed Carl took off down Highway 21, heading away from Brownville, and that was the last anybody ever saw of him in Elmwood County.

Helen Noble was wrong about Bubba Wilson. As it turned out, I heard more than a peep out of him. One day after school, I stopped by the police station to deliver nomination forms to Martha Furguson, the dispatcher, who was also president of the Biographical Club, the civic group that was our Palmetto Girls State sponsor.

The police station was in the same building as town hall, an unadorned two-story brick structure with a tacky concrete facade that shared what little there was of Main Street with the bank, the café, several retail shops, and always a couple of vagrants standing on the street corner doing nothing. Bubba Wilson must have heard me talking to Martha. He poked his head in the door from the jail side of the office and said without preamble, "It's about time you and me had a talk."

"Really?" I said.

I'd seen him around school twice in the past week, questioning Bennie Norris before he boarded the alternative school bus and Pete Grubbs in the breezeway between buildings about the break-ins that had been reported around town.

He was squat and muscular, in his early thirties, with a confident voice and a quick walk. The reason for the stereotype of Southern lawmen as potbellied, tobacco-spitting, politically corrupt, good-ole-boy butchers of the English language is that there have been so many of them over the years. In Bubba Wilson's case, he actually worked at cultivating the image, and he'd probably be there in another ten years. I kept waiting for him to call me "boy."

He nodded toward the door that led to the town hall side of the building. "Do you mind?"

I followed him into the conference room where the town council had its weekly meetings. Bubba shut the door behind us.

Freddy Seaton's portrait hung at the center of the room, behind the mayor's chair at the conference table. It rested below the same American flag that had draped his casket. It was set in a mahogany frame with the sheen of a fine coffin, a flat print in black and white. The lack of color struck me as a fitting symbol of death. He was a handsome young man with a military cut and neatly pressed Army dress greens. The chest was virgin, empty of the garden of battle ribbons he sported in death. The dearth of ribbons, along with the gold second lieutenant bars, led me to believe that the still boyishly innocent face that looked out from the portrait was ignorant of the hell that awaited him perhaps only weeks away in Vietnam. What went through my mind was a line from *Mr. Holland's Opus* delivered in a similar situation: "*What a waste.*"

It suddenly occurred to me that photographs are like ghosts—frozen in time, forever young while we continue to age, windows to our lost youth and that of the children we lose to adulthood and the elders we lose to death. They can be quite sad.

Bubba rested his foot impudently on the seat of the mayor's chair. "Some strange things have been going on around this town," he said.

"What sort of things?"

"First, there's been a string of unsolved burglaries. Then I get a call from Tim Boyle the other day claiming you're behind some kind of prank that involves a wedding with his dead daughter. Before I can move on it, Tim calls me back and says it was all a misunderstanding. Funny thing is, when I check it out, I find you rented the First Baptist Church for a wedding three Saturdays ago. The preacher who performed the ceremony has moved on, but I found the lady in Elmwood who played the organ. She says the bride looked a lot like the picture I showed her of Linda Sue Boyle. Says the bride wore a ring with a big diamond that sounds a lot like the one that was stole from Thompson's Jewelers. Now, I want you to tell me what's going on."

"I did rent the church for a wedding," I admitted. "It was a private ceremony. The bride may have resembled Linda Sue Boyle. I think that's where the misunderstanding came from, plus the fact that someone—I can assure you, it wasn't me—wrote the wedding up in the *Pineville Chronicle* as Linda Sue Boyle and George Baucom's wedding. And I believe the bride did have a right sizeable engagement ring."

He eyed me suspiciously. "Who was the bride?"

I eyed him back. "That's none of your business."

He turned to leave. Then he made a Columbo-like about face. "Where were you last Saturday night?"

"Helen Noble and I went to Columbia to see the new Will Smith movie."

"Can she vouch for you all night?"

"You mean did I spend the night with her? No. Do I need an alibi for some reason?"

"I don't know. Somebody stole Legrand Warfield's life savings."

That's why he was interrogating me. He was on the take from Legrand Warfield, and Warfield was putting the heat on the law to get his money back. He was leaving no stone unturned.

"The word around town is it was Carl Riley."

He nodded. "Maybe. But I got a witness who thinks he saw your car parked on the old logging road off Highway 21 a couple of miles from the Warfield place. That's where we found Legrand's wheelbarrow that was used to haul out the money."

It was hardly likely that anyone had seen my car where I had parked it. Either he was bluffing me, or they hadn't kept the affair secret from Gordon Wallace after all.

"Well, Helen and I did stop to make out on our way back to Brownville. I can't say which road it was on, though."

His face and voice took on a deeper menace. "I think you know more than you're telling me, Fellars. I'm going to be watching you."

20

Tim Boyle called me at school and informed me that Melissa's adoption papers were in. The first thing I did was run down to the school library and inform Helen.

She gave me a quick hug, oblivious to the gawking eighth graders who stared up from their assigned tables and poked each other in the ribs.

We huddled together in her back office.

"Now we'll see if my theory was correct," I said. "We've been spinning our wheels, and nobody's gone over yet. This could have all been for nothing."

"Whether they go over or not, it wasn't for nothing," she said.

I stayed in Brownville until dusk and drove over to the church where the Baucoms were married. George and Linda Sue found me sitting in the parking lot. They had Melissa with them.

"Melissa's ready to go," Linda Sue said, with a mother's love in her eyes. "She's not scared if we go with her."

"I'm happy for you," I said.

"What do we do?"

"I don't know." I pondered it a moment. "Is there something you've avoided doing?"

"Going into the cemetery."

"That's it, then. Go to the cemetery and wait. I have an idea sleep will come."

I picked Helen up at her apartment. Tim and Charlene Boyle were at the cemetery when we got there.

Helen and I said our goodbyes. Melissa gave Helen her Barbie, the tattered doll with the nurse's uniform. "George says you can't take it with you," she said. "He says the toys don't wear out on the other side. So I don't need her now."

She flashed her snaggle-toothed charm on us one last time.

"I'll take good care of her for you, honey."

George shook my hand. "The guys are making their rounds tonight, returning the things we borrowed for the wedding," he promised. He held up Linda Sue's hand. "Even the ring." I saw that it was gone.

"I hope that takes some heat off as far as the law is concerned," Linda Sue said.

"It ought to give Bubba Wilson something to scratch his head over," I said. I hugged Linda Sue. "We'll see you when our time comes."

"We'll be waiting on you."

They said their farewells to Linda Sue's parents. Then, with Scuttles bouncing at their heels, her stubby little tail fanning happily, they walked up the hill to their graves. They left holding hands, looking like a family.

The elder Boyles held onto each other for a long moment, then walked over to us.

Tim Boyle held out his hand. "I never did apologize for coming off at you the way I did in your office," he said, with genuine regret.

"You had every right," I said.

"We thank you from the bottom of our hearts," Charlene said, wiping away a tear. Her voice cracked. "Tonight we lost her for the second time, and it wasn't any easier than the first. But I wouldn't trade this experience for anything in the world. I wish we could have shared it with George's and Melissa's parents, but this isn't something you can just bring yourself to tell anybody about."

I nodded. "I know. I couldn't tell you that day in my office either."

They both embraced Helen and me.

"Take care of yourself, Bill," Tim said. "People are beginning to talk about you. They see you riding around town at all hours and talking to yourself. They're starting to think you're a little strange."

I smiled. "It's going to get worse. I've got fourteen more kids to send over."

"If there's anything I can do to help you, let me know."

"I hope you mean that. I may have to call on you."

21

Tim Boyle's comment about my being the subject of town gossip was unsettling. I decided I needed a place where I could meet the gang without having to ride around town with them in my car or wait for them to contact me at school.

"We need a club house," I told them one night at a group meeting in Jerry Sinclair's south pasture.

We kicked around several suggestions, from the boiler room at school to the basement of one of the churches to the attic of the vacant mill. The trouble with all of the places we discussed was that the town cops checked them on unpredictable rounds each night. Then Chadwick Corley mentioned the haunted house on Brewer Avenue that Doc and Mable Levitt let the town decorate every Halloween. Everybody started trashing the idea simply because Chad had presented it. Putting Chad down was a knee-jerk reaction.

I came to his defense. "Hold on, gang. It's not a bad idea. Think about it. It's right in the middle of town. It's not on the police rounds, because there's nothing in there anybody would want to steal. If anybody comes meddling, it would be a cakewalk for you to scare them away."

So the haunted house it was.

My next problem was how to visit them unnoticed. I didn't want my car parked out in front of the Levitts' Brewer Avenue house while I was inside. On the other hand, if I parked on Main Street and walked to Brewer Avenue, people would think it odd that I was walking the streets at all hours.

I decided to stay after school twice a week and develop a regular habit of walking. People could be seen with their iPods taking their daily strolls in early morning and late evening. My route would take me down Brewer Avenue, where I would manage to disappear into the Levitt house for the regular meetings. If I got called there at some ungodly hour, I would just have to park in the church parking lot on the next block over and walk the short distance through the woods.

The Levitt house looked like it had been built to be a haunted house, which of course, it hadn't. At least, not originally. It had been the home of Brownville's town doctor in the early part of the last century. It had gables and dormers and comprised two stories, an attic, and a basement. The Levitts had deliberately left it unpainted so that it would look dilapidated, but they coated it with wood preservative each year (taking care not to disturb the places where old paint was flaking). They had remodeled the house ten years ago, not only building in a secret passage but constructing floors and stairways so that the boards would creak loudly when you walked over them. The hinges on the doors had been doctored so that opening and closing them produced a creepy whine.

In the attic were stored props adapted from modern horror flicks—chainsaws, Jason masks, Freddy masks, gorilla outfits, prosthetic limbs, skeletons, and assorted costumes. This paraphernalia was unboxed each October and given life in a display that delighted the town's children. It was backed up by a sound system throughout the house that, when activated, produced hideous laughter, screams, and the sound of chains rattling. Proceeds from the five-dollar fee to tour the haunted house went to the Lion's Club.

I got a skeleton key that fit the back door, and the dead, wasted youth of Brownville moved in. We put blankets over the windows and under the cracks of the doors so light from inside the house wouldn't be detected at night. Electricity was available in the house, but I persuaded them not to use it because I didn't want the Levitts' next month's power bill to give us away. So they stocked up on candles, which I thought was very becoming of a haunted house. (The candlelight made your shadow dance on the wall when you creaked your way up the stairs.) If a gadget didn't run on batteries, they didn't use it. It was mid-April, and with a little luck, they would only need to occupy the house for a few more weeks. I hoped to have all of them on the other side by the time school was out on June 1. Luckily, the living children of Brownville had their minds on Easter eggs and not Halloween thrills this time of year.

The dead youth brought an eerie simulation of life to the house. Sally Brock set up a studio in one of the attic dormers and set about writing the novel she had always meant to produce someday. I offered to procure a laptop computer for her, but like the others, she was stuck in the technology of her time. She tried to make do with an old manual Royal, but she found it too difficult to work the keys all day. She finally ended up writing the way Twain and Steinbeck had written, with a pencil. Before she got too far into the novel, I realized the laptop would have been a terrible mistake, since we would have to pass the novel off as a work produced in her lifetime. I scrounged up some old mimeograph paper from my mother's attic so the final manuscript would look aged.

Barbara Fields eventually joined her in her makeshift studio to work on a poem to her parents. Sally helped Barbara when she got stuck for a word, and Barbara proofed Sally's daily output.

The others sat in the living room laying plans, sharing ideas, and talking over old times. I was surprised at how upbeat they were on my visits. The sounds of the dead past echoed forth and carried about the house—the crack of pool balls in the game room as Will Masters and

Charlie Green took up their old sport; Johnny Brown's high-pitched "EEEEEEEEEEKK!" as he engaged in horseplay with Freddy Seaton, who reverted to his high school pranks; the pounding of a basketball in the den as Steve Hall went one-on-one with Tony Cunningham; Sharon Summer's liquid giggles as she took to flirting with Randy Galphin and Mike Sanders; and laughter as someone made a joke at Chadwick Corley's or Laval Crenshaw's expense.

They took turns playing CDs they had borrowed from the town library, each one favoring the music of his era. Freddy Seaton was into fifties early rock. Tony Cunningham liked mid-nineties heavy metal. Steve Hall was into anything Motown. Laval Crenshaw favored classical, but he had to fight the others to get to play it. Will Masters favored Waylon Jennings and Merle Haggard, early eighties vintage. One tune none of them seemed to get tired of hearing was Alabama's "Give Me One More Shot." They adopted that one as their theme song. Other universal favorites were Rod Stewart's "Forever Young" and Travis Tritt's "It's a Great Day to Be Alive."

There was an old Steinway in the parlor with half a dozen fallen keys. Sammy Tribble lit up before it and spent hours pounding out jazz numbers from the late forties and early fifties. He could take Duke Ellington's "Retrospection" and "Reflections in D" and improvise with them until they were basically pure originals. His fingers were magic over the keyboard, and his whole body jerked with each pulse of music.

When I began to overhear students in the hall at school talking about hearing piano music coming from the Levitt mansion, I forbade Sammy to play again, but he ignored me. One night, in response to a neighbor's complaint, Bubba Wilson flashed his light at the windows of the Levitt mansion and returned fifteen minutes later with Doc Levitt to inspect the place, barely giving the gang enough time to take down the blankets over the windows and put away their toys. When I heard about that episode, I realized something had to be done.

Helen and I tried to remove the piano from the house, but it was too heavy for the two of us to handle, and I had second thoughts about stealing a piano out of a private residence. I ended up removing all the wires from the piano.

Sammy was crestfallen. He sat on the piano stool and stared blankly at the impotent keys.

"I'm sorry, Sammy, but I had no choice," I told him. "You were attracting too much attention."

His big, hulking frame folded over as he sat on the piano stool. "I know, Mr. Fellars, but I couldn't help myself. I couldn't quit my music."

I patted him on the shoulder. "I understand, Sammy."

"If I could have quit my music, I'd still be alive. I was taking piano lessons from a White woman, and they told me to quit, just like you done. I was scared, but I couldn't quit. That's why they hung me."

I felt like a dog when he said that.

Sammy would continue to sit at the piano and pound on the keys, producing hollow clinks. I think he could still hear the music in his head.

Randy Galphin and Mike Sanders were the next two to go over. Randy walked into my office the Monday before spring break and perched on my window ledge. He asked me to see them off at the cemetery that night.

I bade them farewell by the light of the moon. The others came to the edge of the cemetery, and Freddy Seaton and Mike Sanders exchanged salutes.

"I'm as ready as I'll ever be, but I'm still scared to go," Randy confessed. You could see the fear in his eyes.

Jesus don't accept apologies from dead people.

I wanted very badly to comfort him, but I kept coming back to the realization that had dawned on me the last time I'd tried. I still had no idea what awaited him on the other side.

"You led the others to me, Randy. That's got to count for some-thing," I said at length.

It was hard saying goodbye to all of them, but Randy Galphin was special. I was going to miss seeing him sitting on my window ledge.

22

∞

The living and the dead took turns demanding my professional attention that spring. Just when I thought I had my hands full trying to fulfill my promises to the dead youth in the Levitt mansion, a problem at Brownville High would pile itself onto my plate. One of my most memorable problems was Shelby Nichols.

I got a referral on Shelby from Tammy Wilson, the school nurse.

Tammy stuck her head in my office one morning and said, "I've got a live one for you."

Tammy was good about referring students from the nurse's station to the guidance office. She helped keep me in business, and whenever I got the chance, I would return the favor by including her in my IEP conferences whenever medication was involved.

"Yeah?"

"Shelby Nichols."

"What about her?"

"She's pregnant."

"Oh no."

Normally it was no big shock when you heard a student was pregnant. We got one or two a year at Brownville High. But in Shelby's case, "Oh no" was an understatement. Shelby was a straight-A student, at the top of her class. She was president of the junior class, with a string of accomplishments listed after her name in the school year-book. Her dad was a lawyer in Elmwood, and her mom was a teacher over at Brownville Elementary. Her parents had high hopes for her, but she did not need their push to fuel her ambitions. She made no secret of her plans to attend Dartmouth and Harvard Law School.

"Do her parents know?" I asked.

"They know."

"How did they take it?"

"How do you think?"

"I hope the father isn't who I think it is."

"Who else would it be?"

"You're right. Shelby's not a promiscuous girl."

"No, she's not."

The baby's father would have to be Larry Ringer. The kid who fancied himself ahead of his time. He of the useless generation.

"Maybe this will straighten Larry out. Give him some sense of responsibility."

"Don't count on it," Tammy said. Evidently she knew him better than I did.

"I'll call Shelby in and talk to her," I said.

"Good luck."

I called Shelby out of psychology class the next period and sat her across from my desk. She was a pretty girl, with a mature face and a confident voice that had talked its way to good grades in classroom discussions and membership in student government. She was going to make a great lawyer if her pregnancy didn't derail her plans.

"Nurse Wilson gave me the news," I said.

"I know. She said she was going to talk to you."

"I hope you don't mind."

"No. It's no secret."

She had a point there. There were no secrets in Brownville. News of her pregnancy would soon be all over school.

"How do you feel about it?"

"I don't know."

"You've got mixed feelings?"

She thought about it.

"You could say that. I don't know what to do."

"What do you think your options are?"

She shook her head. "Not many. I could get a job and forget Dartmouth, or I could go to a clinic and erase the mistake. My parents have made it clear they won't raise the child for me. I'm not going to get any help from Larry."

"Larry?"

"Larry Ringer. You may as well know, Larry is the baby's father."

I played like I didn't already know that. "What does Larry want you to do?"

"He wants me to keep the baby."

"But you don't think he'll help support the child?"

She nailed me with a look. "Do you?"

"I don't know. Maybe becoming a father will help Larry grow up."

She smiled at that. "Don't get me wrong, Mr. Fellars. I love Larry. But my parents can't stand him. They tried to break us up. Me getting pregnant just proved them right in their eyes. I hate to think they were right, but I can't bet my future on Larry turning responsible."

"What do your parents want you to do?"

"They want me to get an abortion. They're together on that. My dad will pay for it."

"Shelby, you do have another option. You could put the baby up for adoption."

Her face clouded over, and I knew what she thought of my suggestion even before she opened her mouth. "I've thought about that, but what bothers me there is that twenty years down the road, the child might look me up and disrupt my life and demand that I explain why I abandoned it. How would you feel if your parents gave you away to somebody else?"

"I believe I would feel a lot better than I would if they decided to abort me."

"No offense, Mr. Fellars, but if they decided to abort you, you wouldn't have any feelings."

I guess she had me on that score.

I decided to call Larry Ringer in and get his take on the situation. He sat in the chair Shelby had occupied earlier in the day.

"Larry, I believe you owe me a cigar," I said.

He jerked his head back. "Say what?"

"I hear you're going to be a daddy."

A proud grin sprouted on his face. "Yeah. Neat, ain't it?"

"I believe the last time I talked to you, you said you planned to be a beach bum. Does expecting a child change your plans at all?"

"Why should it?"

"Why should it? Don't you think if you bring a child into the world, you have a responsibility to take care of it?"

"That's what my parents are for."

I stared at him for a long moment. "Let me get this straight, Larry. Your parents have an obligation to take care of you as long as they are alive, and to take care of any children you might spawn, no matter how old you get, but you have no responsibility to take care of any children you might bring into the world?"

A sheepish expression crawled across his face. "Well, you don't have to put it that way."

"That's the way it seems to me. Is this the new rule of your so-called 'useless generation'? Your parents have an obligation to your generation, but you don't have any obligation to your own offspring?"

Larry wasn't about to take responsibility for the new rule I had voiced. "Well, you can blame our parents. That's how they raised us."

I shook my head. "Larry, I don't know what I'm going to do with you."

Counselors are supposed to be nonjudgmental, but sometimes it's really hard.

23

∽

I hadn't planned to discuss Shelby Nichols's predicament with my friends in the Levitt mansion, but when I visited them that evening, they were in hot debate mode over the subject. I've said it before; there are no secrets in Brownville, and gossip made its way to the dead as much as the living. What got their hackles up was the subject of abortion.

Most of them were against it. Tony Cunningham put it best. "Shelby's baby is in the same boat we are. We all got cut off before we got to make our mark on the world. If she aborts her baby, it won't even get the chance we had."

Tony got support from Sally Brock. "Tony's right," she said. "We would all give anything to have our lives back. It's a shame to deliberately throw a life away."

They were crowded around the fireplace in the den, some of them sitting on the brick hearth, others claiming the camelback sofa across the room, while others stood in the corner, leaning on the wrought-iron spinel stair railing. Will Masters and Charlie Green sat off to themselves in a couple of antique Victorian gothic throne chairs, with a checkerboard on the Chippendale stool between them.

Sharon Summer voiced the standard pro-choice argument. "A

woman has a right to do what she wants with her body. Shelby has a right to make her own decision."

"If you've got a person living inside you, that's not your body, sweetheart," Freddy Seaton cut in. "That's a hitchhiker you stopped and picked up. You don't want it along for the ride, you should have kept your pants zipped."

"Hear, hear," from Tony Cunningham.

Sharon Summer put her hands on her hips. "You guys don't get a say in this. You don't have a uterus," she said.

"No, but I used to live in one," Chadwick Corley said.

That brought a round of laughter and high fives from the other guys. It was an odd sight because there was no sound as palms slapped palms.

Sharon was incensed. She turned on Chadwick. "Laugh it up, moron. The fact that you want anybody to bring a child into this horrible world shows how insensitive you are."

"Who says I want anybody to bring a child into this world? My life hasn't been all that great, or haven't you noticed?"

"Mine hasn't either. I'm with you there, Chad." That came from Laval Crenshaw. I found it odd that Laval, who got upset when he heard that an animal had been mistreated, would come down on the side of abortion when it came to humans.

"What do you think, Barbara?" Sharon said, looking to Barbara for support. She didn't get it.

"I think life is sacred."

"What's sacred about it?" Chadwick asked.

"Look at the odds each one of us had to overcome just to be born. We had to race against millions of sperm to get to fertilize our mother's egg. If our parents had picked another time to mate, we wouldn't have been born. If they had picked other partners instead of each other to mate with, we wouldn't have been born. If their ancestors before them had mated with anybody else, all up the line, we wouldn't have been born."

"Somebody would have been born, it just wouldn't be you," Sharon said.

"That's my point. Each of us had to overcome incalculable odds just to get here. That makes life sacred."

"It might be sacred, but it sucks," Laval said.

"Then why are you sticking around?" Tony said.

"Same reason you are. I don't know what's on the other side."

"That's not why I'm sticking around."

"Then why are you?"

"So I can make my mark. So what little life I had won't be wasted."

Sharon brought them back to Shelby's dilemma. "You guys are changing the subject. You know what you missed out on. If Shelby aborts her baby, it will never know, and it will be spared all the heartache we had to face."

"Let's take a vote on it," Tony suggested. "Pro-life or pro-choice. What do you say, Steve?"

"Pro-life."

"Sammy?"

"Life."

"Johnny?"

"Life."

"Will?"

"We don't care one way or the other," Will Masters said, not looking up from the checkerboard and answering for himself and Charlie Green.

"What about you, Mr. Fellars?"

"I suggested she put the child up for adoption if she didn't want to keep it."

"There you go," Tony said. It was one of his favorite sayings, purloined from Dennis Weaver in *McCloud* reruns.

"Typical male point of view," Sharon said.

"It's Shelby's business," I said. "She will have to make her own choice. And she will have to live with it."

It wasn't hard to figure each person's stance on Shelby's dilemma. Sally and Barbara had been spoiled by their parents and had been sheltered from the pain and suffering Sharon, Chad, and Laval had endured in their short lives. Somehow that made their appreciation for life more intense. Sammy Tribble had suffered as much as any of them had, but his love for music had counterbalanced the horror he had experienced. Freddy Seaton had had a good life until the end. The others had enough anger at having been cheated out of years of living to be incensed at the prospect of anybody throwing away a human life.

One thing they taught me that evening was that the subject of abortion was just as divisive and unresolved in the land of the dead as it was in the realm of the living.

BROWNVILLE
MILL HILL GHOST TOWN

The photographs on this and the following pages, collected by the editor from the Brownville Courier morgue, from school yearbooks, and furnished through the generosity of former citizens of Brownville, feature the principals in Bill Fellars's bizarre account.

As Brownville High's guidance counselor, Bill Fellars found himself counseling the living by day and the dead by night.
"It's going to get worse. I've got fourteen more kids to send over."

Helen Noble, the school librarian with a heart of gold, was recruited to help Bill Fellars rescue the dead.
"Oh, this is just great."

Bubba Wilson, Brownville's good-ole-boy town cop, tried to settle a grudge against Bill Fellars.
"I'm going to be watching you."

Legrand Warfield was Brownville's answer to Al Capone.
"I'm not the kind of man you want to toy around with."

Designed as the community haunted house, the Levitt Mansion became the real thing. The sounds of the dead past echoed about the house.

Although he started out wanting to have Bill Fellars arrested, Tim Boyle ended up helping him get a dead child adopted.
"You've got some explaining to do."

"The Old Married Couple"
George Baucum and Linda Sue Boyle were high school sweethearts. They got back together after they died.

Will Masters and Charlie Green (left) were a couple of rednecks with no ambition. They only wanted one last party.
"We ain't even got to see Elvis yet."

Sharon Summer and her sister Julie share a selfie. Inset: The white cross that marks the spot on Lover's Lane where Julie Summer died on Prom Night.
"Our boat keeps sinking."

THE LOST YOUTH OF BROWNVILLE

You couldn't look at them and not feel that, the inevitable and mysterious dictates of Fate notwithstanding, they were all too young to die.
"You were all a sweet bunch of kids."

Todd Grant was the last one Bill Fellars sent into eternity.
"If I go to hell, at least I'll belong there."

It didn't take much to fall in love with little Melissa King, snaggle tooth, Scuttles, Barbie doll and all.
"George says the toys don't wear out on the other side."

"If I Should Die Tomorrow"
For her sixteenth birthday, Barbara Fields had asked for a car. Benjamin Fields rued the day he so readily agreed to buy her one.
"What are you going to do, Moses? Lead us over?"

Butt of a lifetime of jokes, Chadwick Corley set out to teach the town of Brownville the meaning of the word "retribution."
"Give me a dollar and I'll go away."

They still talked about Sally Brock in the teacher's lounge, about how much potential she had.
"She would have been somebody."

Gag photo of Freddy Seaton pretending to impersonate a general officer, taken seven weeks before he was killed at Pleiku, Vietnam, in 1967. They buried him with full military honors and proudly hung his burial flag in town hall, but Freddy found no peace.
"What are you going to do without me after I cross over?"

Sammy Tribble, flashing the smile that would have charmed audiences had he been allowed to pursue his dream of becoming a jazz pianist. Sammy Tribble was lynched for breaching the Old South caste system. The murder scene (inset above), Crybaby Bridge, derives its name from what local legend attributes to Sammy Tribble's nocturnal wailing.
"Every time I hear that whiny voice of yours, I turn over in my grave."

Tony Cunningham's pride and joy was his red Buick. What is left of it rests in an Elmwood junk yard, referred to by locals as "Jalopy Hell" (inset).
"Any way you cut it, being dead's a real drag

Life threw Steve Hall a curve ball he couldn't dodge, leaving him fifteen forever.
"He can't do nothing to me. I'm already dead."

Mike Sanders clowning around in a coffin the year before he fell asleep at the wheel on his way home from boot camp and never woke up.
"It's a lot harder to move things around after you're dead."

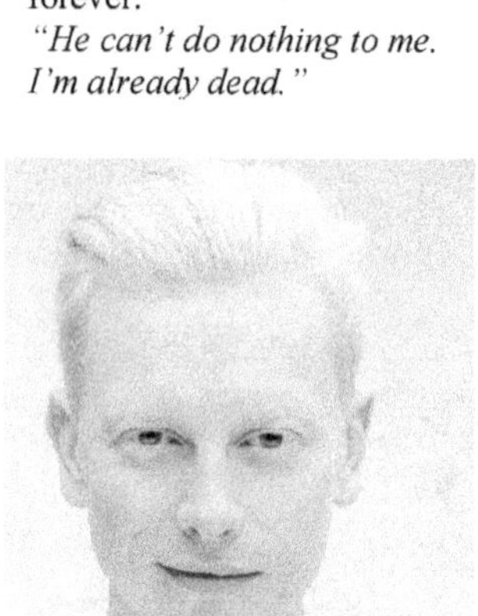

Laval Crenshaw loved animals because they didn't reject him the way people did.
"There's a lot of prejudice out there against dead people."

Gordon Wallace caught in a pensive mood by a yearbook staff member. Bill Fellars's brush with Gordon Wallace, his nemesis, nearly cost him his life.
"We're going to explore the bright side of death together."

Johnny Brown hated school and drove his teachers up the wall.
"She has to love him. She's his mother."

Randy Galphin chose death and then changed his mind. Inset: The .32 Smith & Wesson with which Randy Galphin killed himself.

"Stealing from a crook ain't regular stealing."

Brownville High and the L. B. Brown mill today. Announcements that the mill and school would be closed marked the beginning of Bill Fellars's visits from the dead.

The swamp where Legrand Warfield buried his drug money. Inset: The millstone that marked the treasure spot is now a landscape feature in an Elmwood residence.

Cemetery Drive, where Bill Fellars bade farewell to his dead students.

24

౧

Laval Crenshaw loved animals because they didn't reject him the way people did. In life, Laval had felt isolated from even his own family.

Laval had the misfortune of having his time on earth occur years before gender identity became a focus of the progressive wing of society. The town said Laval had always been a mama's boy, hanging onto her apron strings all the way through puberty. He was into things his mother and sisters were into—making cakes, building dollhouses for his sisters and helping them furnish them, sewing, making papier-mâché flowers, and his greatest love, computers. Laval also had the misfortune of having his time on earth cut short just as the computer age was coming into its own.

Laval's feminine demeanor attracted scorn on the playground, where children are ruthless at an age before tact is born and ruled by the law of the jungle bars. But as unkind as his peers were, they didn't hold a candle to Laval's father.

The town knew an entirely different Clyde Crenshaw from the one his son knew. Clyde Crenshaw, the one the town knew, was a deacon in the Brownville Baptist Church, and although he owned a used car lot over on the south side of town near the Guard armory, he had a reputation for giving you a straight deal. Clyde Crenshaw didn't drink or run around on his wife, but he didn't look down on you for doing it either. In fact, he was a good buddy to take along on a drinking spree, because he didn't need to be tanked up to have fun; he was the natural choice for designated driver, and he knew how to keep his mouth shut. The Clyde Crenshaw the town knew had all the charm and personality of a good salesman.

His popularity had manifested itself in high school, where he had lettered and won MVP honors in three sports, served as co-captain of the football team his senior year, and brought home a mantel-full of trophies he still displayed in his den. Two years after Laval died, Clyde was inducted into the Brownville High Athletic Hall of Fame. His spirit of competition had survived into adulthood, and a big part of his life was participating in the Bass Busters competition on Indian Lake every year. He was also a member of the Old Lodge Hunting Club.

After siring three daughters, Clyde Crenshaw had been overjoyed with the birth of a son, whom he'd hoped to mold in his own image and to whom he'd looked for companionship in his manly exploits. But the boy had proved to be a disappointment almost from the start.

Clyde Crenshaw had had the mistaken idea that he could shame his son into masculinity, and out of this endeavor emerged the Clyde Crenshaw that the town never saw. Whenever Laval came home from school with a black eye or bloody nose, Clyde would taunt him for not fighting back. Laval's mother would come to his rescue, and his parents would end up in a knock-down, drag-out argument over "what's best" for their son.

Somewhere along the way, Clyde seemed to give up on changing his son and settled for seeking out ways to punish him for being different. His most potent tool of torment became Laval's emerging love for animals. Father and son were opposite in this respect too. As a child, Clyde Crenshaw had been bitten by a stray cat and, as was the medical prescription of the day, had had to undergo a series of painful rabies shots in the stomach. He'd never forgiven the feline species for this horror.

Clyde set out to destroy every stray cat that appeared at his doorstep. To this end, he constructed a large rabbit box, which he would bait with cat food and set in his backyard. He would watch from his kitchen window as the stray cautiously investigated the contraption, followed its nose inside, and tripped the door shut. Then he would back up his Ranger to the cat box, leave the motor idling, attach the hose of his wife's vacuum cleaner to the exhaust pipe, and place the crevice tool up to the crack beside the door of the cat box. He would make Laval watch as the dying animal screamed and shook the cat box. Sometimes he would gun the motor, cackling as he sent gales of death into the contraption.

From such experiences, a powerful rift of hatred developed between father and son. The further Laval was pushed from his father, the closer he became to his mother. By the time Laval was an adolescent, his father could not speak to him without betraying his hatred. The day finally came when, after hearing rumors about town, Clyde confronted Laval about his alleged budding homosexuality. When Laval openly admitted it, Clyde disowned him on the spot and banished him forever from his home.

If Laval Crenshaw loved animals because they didn't reject him, his other great love, for the same reason, was technology. In 1977, when he was twelve, his mother and grandmother pooled their savings to buy him an Apple II computer for Christmas. They hid the $1,300 cost from Clyde.

Laval would later look back and see that he had gotten in on the dawn of the personal computer age. His heroes Steve Jobs and Steve Wozniak had formed Apple Computer Company on April Fool's Day of the previous year, and his other heroes Bill Gates and Paul Allen had founded Micro-Soft (the hyphen was later dropped) the April before that.

In 1980, Laval begged his mother for an Apple III, but she was unable to come up with the $5,000 it cost. It was the only time in his life Laval could remember that she had not given him what he asked for. Laval pitched a fit, then brooded and pouted for long periods and generally made his mother's life miserable for months. After she died, he figured it had nearly killed her not to be able to give in to his wishes, and he regretted his childish behavior. His last computer was an Apple IIe, which his mother and grandmother bought for him in 1984, a year after his father had exiled him and the year his mother died of ovarian cancer. Laval was also dying, but he didn't know it at the time. He wasn't diagnosed until 1985, the year Rock Hudson died and the year Ryan White was barred from school. Laval supposed he must have contracted the disease when he was sixteen and went on a trip to New Orleans with his high school forensics team.

Laval came back to Brownville in 1986 to die. He was nursed in his last days by his maternal grandmother, who was the only one he had left. His sisters made infrequent visits, but they kept their distance. He never saw his father again.

I was in my office filling out a college recommendation for Barbara Donner, who was on track to be this year's valedictorian, trying to think of something brilliant to write, when there was a knock on my door. I looked up to see Sally Brock, Barbara Fields, and Sharon Summer standing in the doorway to my outer office.

"Hello, girls. I didn't hear you come in."

I wouldn't, though, would I?

"We need to talk to you, Moses," Barbara said, taking the lead. The air blowing from the ceiling vent did not disturb her perfectly coiffed hair as she passed under it.

"If you're not busy," Sally said. She was taller than the others, older and more mature.

"It's about Laval," Sharon said. Her straight, dark hair contrasted sharply with her pale face.

"What about Laval? Sit down, girls."

Sharon and Barbara sat in the two chairs I kept in front of my desk. Sally took Randy Galphin's window ledge.

"He's stealing," Barbara said.

"He's talked the guys into helping him," Sharon said.

"He stole from my uncle. That makes it personal," Sally said.

I held up my hand. "Back up, girls. Don't all talk at one time. What did he steal from your uncle, Sally?"

"Salt blocks."

"Salt blocks?"

"My uncle Bill sets out salt blocks for his cows. Laval stole them and took them into the woods for the deer."

I knew that Laval's bout with AIDS had left him gaunt and feeble. I couldn't imagine him lifting a salt block.

"How did he manage that?" I asked.

"He talked the guys into helping him. They found an old wagon at the dump, and Will Masters repaired the wheel."

That's the way they were. The others often picked on Laval and Chad Corley, and Laval and Chad often picked on each other, but when serious business was at hand, they all helped each other out. I later learned that it was on one of their excursions on behalf of Laval's crusade for animals that they had stumbled on Legrand Warfield burying his drug treasure.

"Did you confront Laval about this?" I asked.

"Yes," Sally said.

"And?"

"He said my uncle would replace the salt blocks, so it was no big deal to him. He said since it wasn't deer season, it wasn't likely that hunters would stumble on the salt blocks and use them for bait."

"Has he stolen anything else?" I asked.

"He's been stealing bread out of the Sunbeam bread truck when it stops to make deliveries to the Community Cash," Sally said.

"He does the same thing at Fred's Market and the café downtown," Barbara said.

"Whenever the driver goes inside to settle his accounts with the store manager, Laval steals bread out of the back of the truck and takes it in the woods to feed the birds," Sharon said.

I turned from the girls and typed on my computer. I googled Tractor Supply and looked at salt blocks.

"He's not doing too much damage. Looks like a salt block costs about ten dollars. A loaf of bread can't be more than, what, three bucks?" I said.

"You're making excuses for him?" Barbara Fields said with fire in her eyes.

"A block of salt might not cost much, but it all adds up," Sally said. "Especially to a farmer, who can lose his whole crop in a bad year."

Their comments put me to shame. "No, I'm not excusing Laval's stealing. But I do want to point out his heart is in the right place."

"That hardly makes it right," Sally said.

"What are you going to do about it?" Barbara asked.

"I'll talk to him. I'll come around after school."

"I would appreciate that," Sally said. The girls exchanged looks, then turned and walked to the door.

"Maybe you shouldn't let on to him that I'm coming," I said. "I don't want to spook him."

Bad choice of words, I know. It didn't occur to me until it had slipped out of my mouth.

Laval turned on Sally Brock when I confronted him about stealing her uncle's salt blocks.

We were in the parlor of the Levitt house, and the scarce light coming through the slanted blinds on the bay window beyond the staircase cast a dim veil of gloom over the room.

"You didn't say anything when George stole the diamond from Thompson's Jewelers and gave it to Linda Sue," Laval said.

"That was different. They were borrowing it. They put it back. There's no way you can replace the food you've stolen."

"Why should I worry about replacing something nobody's going to miss?"

"What makes you think they won't miss it?" Barbara asked.

"Little Miss Sunbeam didn't seem to mind. She was still smiling on the side of the bread truck last time I looked."

"You think this is funny?" Barbara said.

"Do you see me laughing?"

"You'd better quit while you're behind, Laval. Her claws are coming out," Tony Cunningham said.

Barbara cut her eyes to Tony. "You stay out of this. You helped him."

"I wasn't the only one," Tony said.

"Thanks a lot, Judas. Rat us out, will you?" Chadwick Corley said.

"Yeah, Benedict Arnold," Will Masters said.

"Sellout," said Charlie Green.

"It's not like they didn't already know," Tony said. "We didn't keep it a secret."

Freddy Seaton had been sitting at the bottom of the staircase, taking in the conversation. He rose and walked over to join the group.

"Stand down, guys," he said. "The girls are upset."

"You're not my daddy," Laval said.

I placed a hand on Laval's arm. "Freddy's right. We need to do some healing here. Let's all just take a deep breath."

I let them cool down for a few minutes.

I looked at Laval. "Your intentions are good, Laval, but we need to figure another way for you to carry out your animal crusade. Stealing is wrong."

Laval cut me a look. "Was stealing wrong when you helped us steal Legrand Warfield's money?" he asked.

It was the perfect checkmate. I watched as the girls' faces fell. They knew Laval had presented me with a question for which I had no answer.

I tried just the same. "It was wrong, but sometimes a wrong choice is the moral one," I said.

Laval grinned at me.

"There you go," he said.

"Hey, you stole my saying," Tony Cunningham said, not acknowledging the fact that he had stolen it from Dennis Weaver.

25

Laval Crenshaw was not the least bit discouraged by my stricture against his stealing habit.

One Thursday morning, while Laval was staking out Fred's Market for the Sunbeam truck, Langston Marsh made the mistake of pulling up to the gas pump. Langston was on his way to the Elmwood stockyard, and he had a year-old Angus bull in a trailer behind his pickup. The bull was one of those animals no fence could hold, and every day, Langston got his exercise by chasing it out of the road and through the woods until he was able to get it up. Langston prized the bull enough to tolerate its wanderings, but his wife was unwilling to have her daylily beds trampled, so she had put her foot down. The bull had to go.

Langston's trailer had been built by Larry Wells during slack time at his body shop, and it was much too sturdy to permit escape. Just the same, the bull kept rattling it, poking around for weak spots, standing on his hind legs to seek a way over the top, dancing frantically around and around.

"Easy now, boy," Langston said over and over, with no effect, as he replaced the gas nozzle. As soon as he fished his wallet out of his oil-stained overalls and hurried into the store to pay for the gas, Laval made his move. He untied the rope securing the gate and slid it open.

"Move it, stud," he said, "or you're going to end up in the locker room at the Community Cash."

The bull started up the highway, but Laval spooked it toward the woods.

Not long after the bull episode came the great turkey escape. I learned about it one afternoon when I entered the Levitt mansion and heard a heated exchange between Laval on the one hand and Freddy Seaton, Chadwick Corley, and Tony Cunningham on the other.

"What's all the commotion about?" I asked as I entered the parlor.

Tony turned to face me. "You heard about the wreck on Highway 21?"

I nodded. "I heard the sirens go by. What happened?"

Chadwick Corley looked at Laval. "This moron totaled a semi."

Chadwick, the universal victim, was often Laval's chief tormentor. I'd tried to get them to take up for each other, since they both were often picked on by the others. But I guess Chadwick felt that if he could put Laval down, he wouldn't be the lowest man on the totem pole.

I started. "What?"

"I didn't mean to," Laval said sheepishly. "I was trying to stop it so I could let the turkeys out."

"You let them out, all right," Freddy said. "They're scattered all over the county."

"At least they won't be butchered," Laval countered.

"Half of them got creamed in the wreck," Tony said.

"No, they didn't. Most of them ran off into the woods."

"They were missing half their guts," Chadwick countered.

I held up my hand. "Hold it, folks. Let's start at the beginning. Laval, what happened?"

"I was walking along Little Goose Creek," Laval began. "I went to cross over the bridge on Highway 21, when I saw an eighteen-wheeler loaded with crates of turkeys bearing down on me. So I stood in the road and waved my hands. The driver leaned on his horn, and when I didn't budge, he applied his air brakes. The truck couldn't stop in time and plowed right through me. The driver lost control of the truck. It fishtailed down the road and finally stopped when the body jackknifed against the guard rail on the bridge. The turkey crates were jarred open in the wreck."

"Was the driver hurt?" I asked.

Laval shook his head. "He walked away."

"He limped away," Tony corrected him.

Laval laughed. "He must have thought he killed me. He drove right through me. You should have seen the look on his face."

I wanted to grab him and shake him. "That's not funny, Laval. You could have killed *him*. When he tells the highway patrol he ran down a pedestrian and they don't find a body, what then? What about the hundred-thousand-dollar rig you totaled?"

Laval's lip began to quiver, and he huffed, "I'm sure he has insurance."

"Maybe he does, but that's not going to solve all the problems this caused."

"What problems? The driver wasn't hurt."

"He wasn't killed but think of the trauma you put him through. He could get fined for reckless driving. His insurance will go up. He could lose his job. Do you not see how serious this is?"

Laval's gaunt face soured and his eyes narrowed. "So you're going to start on me, too, huh?"

I almost said something ugly to him, but Chadwick Corley took the words out of my mouth. "Laval, who lit the fuse on your tampon?"

Laval faced Chadwick and puffed up, his lips quivering again. I could see why they ridiculed Laval, but I couldn't afford to give in to the negative feelings he'd aroused in me at the moment. When Laval was in one of his moods, you had to baby him.

"No, Laval, I'm not starting on you. Your heart is in the right place. But you can't put humans in danger to save animals."

"And while we're on the subject," Freddy Seaton cut in, "what you did to Langston Marsh bothers me. The man's just trying to make a living raising his cows. Turning that bull loose is going to cause all sorts of problems. It could wander into the road and wreck a car. It'll trample all over people's gardens this spring. You're not doing domesticated animals any favor by turning them out into the wild."

"I'm not doing them any favor by letting them get butchered either."

"It's called the food chain, moron. Humans are on top. Deal with it."

"Chadwick, you're not helping the situation by name-calling."

Laval pouted with us for a week after that, but I think he got the message. From then on, he turned his attention to relocating homeless cats and dogs. He watched the streets in the evenings and noticed who had a habit of walking their dogs. Anyone riding around town with a dog hanging its head out the window of the vehicle caught his attention. He hung out at the Community Cash and made a mental list of people who bought pet food. If he didn't know the people, he would follow them home and find out where they lived. Soon he had a file on the names and addresses of the animal lovers in Brownville.

He then went looking for strays. He found wild dogs roaming in the woods, abandoned kittens at the garbage dump, stray dogs dodging cars in the streets, homeless cats eking out a meal in the dumpsters. They were the canine and feline proletariat, for the most part curs and mongrels, flea-bitten, half-starved, and mangy.

Each time he found an orphaned animal, he would lure it to one of the addresses on his list of animal lovers, where he would feed it, then find a way to make enough noise to attract attention from the homeowner. In most cases, the people he selected continued to feed and care for the animals, some doing so reluctantly until they became attached.

It's been over ten years since I last saw Laval, but I still think about him whenever I see a stray animal on the side of the road, or whenever someone abandons an animal at my doorstep. I'm sure my reaction is different from what it would be if I had never known him.

The time came when Laval found stray animals scarce in Brownville, and he realized that his work was done. He said his good-byes to us and to the animals of Brownville. But on the evening he had planned to go over, Sharon Summer caught him at the edge of the cemetery.

She begged him not to leave.

"I've finished my work," he told her.

"I still need your help."

"Doing what?"

"There's a coven of devil worshippers in Legrand Warfield's shack off Highway 21. They're into animal sacrifice. My sister's in with them."

Laval decided to stay and check it out.

26

In my line of work, I see all kinds of family situations. Some kids don't have a dog's chance from the word *go*. Like Seth Warfield, whose parents are into drugs, or Jamie McFarland, whose mother stays out drunk all hours and whose father has abandoned him. Sometimes parents do everything right and the kids still turn out rotten, like Jerry Hill, the preacher's son who was busted for breaking and entering Butch's Bar last fall. Sometimes kids seem to have everything going for them, when—bam—tragedy strikes, and suddenly they find themselves on the road to hell and can't get off.

Julie Summer, the little sister whose life Sharon Summer wanted to turn around, was in the latter category.

"We had it all," she once told me in a counseling session. "My sister and I were Little League cheerleaders. We went to church every Sunday. We sat down at the table together and ate as a family. We made the honor roll every term, had plans for college, had parents that made a good living. You name it; we had it. We were living the American dream."

The dream began to crumble when her mom died of cancer, and then shattered completely when her dad remarried and her stepmom didn't want her or her sister.

The sisters ended up living with their grandmother, who worked a swing shift in a nursing home and couldn't properly supervise them. They could be seen walking the streets at all hours, hanging on the corner of Main with the wrong crowd. Their skirts got shorter, their makeup got heavier, the backs of their teeth became stained with tobacco, and their breath was often a mixture of Certs and Budweiser.

They became chronic truants at school. Sharon dropped out on her seventeenth birthday. She was killed in a wreck shortly after that.

Fueled by festering anger at her father and stepmother and by grief over the loss of her mother and sister, Julie went from bad to worse. She went from cigarettes and beer to marijuana and crack, and her friends changed from delinquent teens to lowlife drifters in their twenties and thirties. Somehow, she managed to stay in school. She had a pattern of dropping out in the spring and returning the next fall, which was why she was only in the ninth grade at age seventeen.

By the time Sharon Summer made up her mind to try to turn her little sister's life around, she had her job cut out for her.

Sharon Summer began her campaign to rescue her little sister Julie from her aimless life by doing what kids often do to get their siblings in hot water: tattling on her.

One night, she saw Ben Cannon and a carload of drunk kids pull up into the parking lot of Li'l Cricket and pick Julie up. She called the Brownville police with the license number, then slipped unseen into the car.

Ben was trying to see how much noise he could make tearing down Main. He looked over at the blonde riding shotgun, who had a case of Miller between her feet. "Hey, sweetheart, you want to hand me one of them flushers?"

"No. You're driving."

He reached down. "Never mind, I'll get one myself."

She smacked his hand. "No, you don't."

The car jumped the curb.

"Watch it," a guy said from the back seat. "The road don't go over that far."

"Somebody moved the road," another girl said. She giggled gleefully.

Ben reached for a beer. This time he was successful. "I got it."

Before he could take a drink, a guy from the back seat reached up and knocked the drink out of his hand.

"Hey, now you got it all over my seat!"

"You're the designated driver. You gotta stay dry."

"It's my car." He snatched a beer out of the hand of the blonde beside him.

"It's my beer," she retorted and smacked it out of his hand. It spilled in his lap and rolled on the floor.

"Thanks a lot. Now I smell like a brewery."

"Wring your shirt out and suck on it."

"I ought to pull over and make you walk."

"You ought to pull over for that cop behind you," Julie said from the back seat.

Ben looked in the rearview mirror. "Oh, crap. I've got a bag of crack under the seat."

"Outrun him, Ben," the guy in the back seat said, his mind clouded with inebriation.

"Stay cool. He's not onto you yet," the blonde said.

Seconds later, the cop's blue light flashed.

"Now he is," Julie said.

The blonde smirked at Ben. "I can't wait to see how you're going to talk your way out of this."

The blonde was not able to hide the case of Miller at her feet. As soon as he saw it, the cop said, "Out of the car, all of you."

Five minutes later, he found the bag of crack.

The next time Sharon ratted, Julie was with Billy Martin. Her grandmother was working the night shift, so Julie asked Billy to come over and play house. Sharon called the nursing home without giving her name and left word for Grandma that there was some hanky-panky going on at home; she needed to get over there.

When Grandma walked in on them in a compromising position on the couch, Julie had enough presence of mind to yell "rape." Billy tried to hold his hand over her mouth, but then he ran out the back door, hitching up his pants as he ran. He looked just guilty enough to get Julie off the hook with Grandma.

She wasn't off the hook with her friends, though. Word soon got around that she was trouble. When Sharon kept ratting on her, her friends decided she was jinxed and began dropping her. The only way she could attend parties anymore was to crash them, because invitations were not forthcoming.

Sharon escalated her attacks. She began knocking drinks out of Julie's hand, just like the drunk carload of kids had done with Ben Cannon.

"Somebody knocked it out of my hand," an exasperated Julie would say to the party's host, who likely as not would be looking disapprovingly at the stain on their carpet.

"You're stoned. Nobody touched you."

On a night after one such incident, Julie went outside and looked at the stars. "God, are you trying to tell me something? I thought we were supposed to have free will."

I called her into my office for a guidance session not long after that.

"You look stressed out, Julie," I began. "I was wondering if anything was bothering you."

"No."

"Everything going okay with your schoolwork?"

"I guess so."

"How did you do on your last report card?"

"I failed English and history."

"Have you managed to pull your grades up?"

"Not really."

"Sometimes when things aren't going well outside of school, it's hard for us to keep our mind on our schoolwork. Are you sure nothing is bothering you?"

"Well, I've kind of had a case of the nerves lately."

"What's happened to give you a case of the nerves?"

"I know I've been into some things I shouldn't be doing, and I've gotten caught at it. But every time we get caught, my friends blame it on me. It's not fair, because it's not my fault. Now I've lost all my friends."

"Well, Julie, I can't tell you what to do, but you know what I'd do?"

"What?"

"I believe if the friends I hung around with were into things that caused me to get into trouble, I'd try to cultivate some new friends."

She took my advice and got some new friends, but it wasn't exactly what I'd had in mind. Jackson Smith, one of Legrand Warfield's drug smugglers, got out of prison and rented Legrand's old shack in the woods off Highway 21. Smith brought a motorcycle gang of devil worshippers to Brownville with him, and Julie Summer took up with them.

Modern satanism began in 1966, when Anton LaVey founded the Church of Satan and wrote its doxology in *The Satanic Bible*, published in 1969. LaVey preached a hedonistic philosophy based on individualism, nonconformity, and self-indulgence. He neither believed in a literal devil nor worshipped him. Nor did he practice any of the rituals of child sacrifice or animal sacrifice that have long been associated with satanism.

LaVey's heirs in the Church of Satan may not practice or condone animal sacrifice, but other satanists, usually misfit teens, have been arrested for sacrificing animals, vandalizing graveyards, and spraying satanic graffiti on church walls and railroad underpasses. Many of society's malcontents seem to be attracted to satanism for its shock value. It is my guess that such was the case with Jackson Smith. Satanism was his ticket to a reputation as a frondeur.

When Sharon Summer overheard Smith, who had crowned himself high priest of the Brownville Order of Satan, plotting to offer an animal sacrifice, she ran to Laval Crenshaw for help.

She found Laval and Will Masters at the edge of the cemetery. Laval was sitting on the grass, trying to muster up the courage to cross over, and Will was giving him assurance that he had made a difference with his animal projects.

"What's shakin', bacon?" Laval said when he saw Sharon.

"You're not leaving?" Sharon said.

"I've finished my work," Laval said.

"Please, don't go yet. I need your help."

She explained about the coven of devil worshippers in Legrand Warfield's shack.

She finished with, "They're going to kill a goat."

Laval stood. "Slow down, girl. Who's going to kill a goat?"

Sharon paused to catch her breath.

"Jackson Smith."

"What does he have against goats?"

"They're going to offer one as a sacrifice. Jackson wanted to sacrifice a lamb, but there aren't any sheep farmers around here. I heard him tell Pete to go steal one of Jerry Hall's goats."

Pete Scarborough was Jackson Smith's chief disciple.

"Jerry Hall lives on the other side of Elmwood. At least we've got some time."

They didn't have as much time as they thought. Pete Scarborough was too stoned to drive his Harley to the other side of Elmwood. He kidnapped Gwen Snider's poodle instead.

Sharon and Laval saw him swerving his Harley up Long Canyon Road toward Warfield's shack in the woods with the poodle wriggling under his arm.

"What are we going to do?" Sharon asked.

"We need a bugle," Laval said.

"What for?"

"Because I'm about to call out the cavalry."

The cavalry consisted of Laval's friends, some of the meanest dogs in Brownville. He went about freeing Dobermans from their pens and unleashing Rottweilers from their yard chains, as well as the homeless mongrels he had saved. He cast his spell on them, and they followed.

"That don't look like no goat to me," Jackson Smith said when Pete Scarborough dismounted his Harley and brought the yelping poodle through the door by the scruff of its neck. Smith was tall and stocky, with a shaved head, a stud in his left lobe, a gray-speckled goatee, and plenty of ink hiding under the sleeves of both arms.

"That's 'cause it ain't a goat," Pete said. He was tall and wiry, with a black goatee and a ponytail shooting out the back of his red paisley bandanna. He walked over and placed the poodle on an altar at the center of a pentagram drawn in chalk on the pine floor of the den of the house.

He snapped his fingers and said, "Front and center, angels."

Two women in faded, ragged jeans and tattered shirts walked over and began stroking the poodle.

Jackson walked over to the altar.

"I can see it ain't a goat. What did I tell you to get?"

"You said get a goat."

"Yeah, I did. How come you didn't get one?"

"There watn't none trip-trapping over the bridge."

"What bridge?"

"The one in the story. *The Three Billy Goats Gruff*."

Jackson gave him a long stare. "Man, you all messed up."

Pete grinned. He looked at the poodle. "You want I should take him back?"

"Naw. I expect if I cut your chin whiskers off and glue them on the mutt, it'll be close enough to a goat."

Pete instinctively reached his hand up to his goatee. For a fraction of a second there, he wasn't sure Jackson was kidding. When he realized he was, he said, "We'd better cut your horns off and glue them on his head too."

Jackson didn't smile.

Ten minutes later, Jackson Smith had the poodle on the altar, with the two women holding it down. The blinds were drawn, and a tray of daggers flickered in the candlelight. The room reeked of marijuana smoke and burning incense. A heavy metal beat from Danzig's guitars erupted from an old portable boombox on the end table. The circle of thugs, Julie in their midst, sat at the foot of the altar, smoking dope and drinking Wild Turkey. Jackson Smith stood by the altar in a black robe.

Smith began the Black Mass by offering a prayer to the dark one. The congregation of misfits responded in a chorus in the right places. They all seemed to know the words.

Smith had just picked up a silver dagger when they were distracted by a thudding noise from outside that could be heard over the hypnotic pounding of Danzig's "Mother."

"Pete, go see what all that racket is," Smith said.

Scarborough walked to the door and looked out.

"Jackson, I think you'd better come look at this," he said from the doorway.

Smith walked over and looked out the door to see Legrand Warfield's Jersey bull trashing their motorcycles.

"Hey, that thing cost me twenty grand! Get away from there!"

They all ran out to shoo away the bull, and that's when the dogs attacked. Jackson Smith managed to make his way back inside the house. He emerged moments later with a shotgun. When he took aim at one of the dogs, the shotgun was inexplicably shoved straight up in the air by some unseen force just before it fired.

I was watching from the curve of the road, and when I saw Julie run toward the highway, I cranked up my Mazda and pulled up beside her.

I opened the door of the passenger's side. "Julie, hop in."

We met Bubba Wilson's cruiser, lights flashing, on our way back into Brownville.

I don't know what I expected to hear about the incident the next day at school, but I didn't expect to hear what I actually ended up hearing.

"It's just terrible," Priscilla Crumpton was saying when I stepped into the office to check my mail. "She never had a chance."

"Who would do such a thing?" asked Sandra Burnsides.

"What happened?" I asked.

"Somebody turned loose everybody's dogs last night. Carl Harris's Doberman got loose and attacked Mrs. Halfacre. She's eighty years old. It took four grown men to beat the dog off her."

My heart stopped. "Did it kill her?"

"Might as well have. It chewed her to pieces. She's in Columbia at Richland Memorial. It'll be a miracle if she makes it."

It wasn't my regular walk day, so I parked at the church and took the back way to the Levitt house.

"Did you hear?" I asked as I stepped into the living room. They were all there.

"It wasn't any of us. We never got near Carl Harris's Doberman," Laval assured me.

"We stayed with every dog we turned out," Freddy Seaton said. "Carl Harris's Doberman wasn't one of ours."

"Are you sure?"

"It wasn't any of us," Laval repeated.

"All right," I said. "I want you to go out and find Gordon Wallace. Bring him here. I want to talk to him."

I could tell by the way they looked at each other that they didn't want to do it. I waited until they returned.

Freddy broke the news to me. "He wouldn't come. He says he doesn't have anything to say to you."

It would be a while yet before I had the pleasure of meeting Gordon Wallace.

I helped Julie Summers's grandmother get her into Charter Rivers Hospital. When she came out ten days later, she was on her way to recovery.

27

The first time I laid eyes on Chadwick Corley was when I was over at Brownville Elementary to see the custodian about having her son tested by the school psychologist. The fourth graders were lined up at the water cooler, and this chunky kid kept breaking out of line to tap other kids on the shoulder. The other kids kept swatting him away like a blowfly. Two fourth grade teachers were standing in a doorway talking and ignoring the commotion.

When the chunky kid bent down to untie somebody's shoelaces, one of the teachers looked over and said, "Chadwick Corley, pull your pants up. I can see your crack!"

Chadwick was just as obnoxious in high school. As Red Maynard, our band director, who knew him in elementary school, once put it, "He acts the same. He's just bigger."

Of course the kids all picked on him, and half a dozen teachers blessed me out every August when they saw his name on their class rosters. I would have predicted that the ridicule would have subsided as Chadwick grew older, because he grew into a hulking 250-pound teenager who was fully capable of defending himself. But the comments that continued to issue from his mouth were so asinine and his behavior so crude that most kids were willing to risk getting sat on, and the putdowns continued. Even from little eighth graders.

The running joke around school came from a remark Coach West said in the hall one day after watching Chadwick drive a group of normally timid girls into a snarling rage by just walking up to their group and grinning. "That kid could make a fortune," the coach observed. "All he has to do is walk up to you and say, 'Give me a dollar and I'll leave.' I know I'd give him a dollar."

Unfortunately, some students overheard Coach West's remark, and every time Chadwick walked down the hall, you could hear students say, "Here comes Corley. Get your dollar out."

Chadwick Corley's appearance seemed to go with his abrasive personality. His teeth were rows of green and brown kernels through which his nasal voice fanned bad breath when he spoke. His hair grew in long, unkempt spikes that shot out from his scalp and when clipped short showed the beginnings of a receding hairline. His ears, flat against his head, were always caked with wax. A mild condition of esotropia, also known as being cross-eyed, gave him a Jerry Lewis goofy appearance. Two or three times a year, a teacher would send him to me to talk about his body odor.

I liked Chadwick, but then, I didn't have to put up with him in class. It was difficult for most teachers to feel sorry for him because he seemed to always bring the ridicule on himself. Most teachers had to sit on him or he would have kept their classes disrupted all period. Whenever a teacher was short with him or a student made a derogatory remark or someone told him to go away, he would always grin and toss off some silly retort. Most people assumed from this standard response that you couldn't hurt his feelings.

But Chadwick Corley had managed to store up quite a bagful of hurt feelings, and when I asked him what he wanted to accomplish in the time we had left, his thoughts at once turned to revenge. At first I tried to discourage him, but I ended up bowing to his stubborn will. I knew I would have to let him find peace in his own way. I also knew I would have to try to hold him on a leash, or he would try to destroy Brownville the way Carrie White destroyed the small town of Chamberlain in Stephen King's first novel.

Fortunately, the people Chadwick Corley wanted most to punish, the ones who had accidentally drowned him at band camp in the summer of 2006, were out of his reach, because they had all moved out of Brownville. But there were plenty of former persecutors still around for him to toy with.

Chadwick set up headquarters in the basement of the Levitt mansion and made a list. At the top of the list was Elbert Snead, a school bully whose daily highlight was getting a laugh at Chadwick's expense during the 10:15 break. (Elbert was one of the few students who actually sought Chadwick out.) Elbert's bullying habits had continued into adulthood. By day he patched tires at Bill's Tire Shop across from Fields Service Station. In his off hours, he was an imperial Kleagle of the Elmwood County Knights of the Ku Klux Klan. With that, Chadwick found a willing ally in his plan to get even with Elbert Snead. Sammy Tribble had his own score to settle with the Klan.

Sammy Tribble had spent a good deal of his life barefooted, living in a wooden shack without screens. The dog came in and out at will; the hog lived under the house; the rooster woke him up in the morning; and in the summer, flies and mosquitoes were permanent guests. Sammy's father sharecropped a corner of what had once been a plantation and often hired on with a dairy farmer. He was paid in hand-me-down clothes and home-canned vegetables, but hardly ever in money. The Tribbles had ten children. They could not afford electricity to power the radio Sammy would have died for.

Sammy's mother was a cook at Brownville Elementary, "the White school," which is where she met Louise Harris, the music teacher. One summer day when the Tribbles were at the Harris home, helping them butcher a hog, Sammy was sent into the kitchen to fetch a butcher knife. When he didn't return forthwith, Louise Harris found him in the parlor listening to a Duke Ellington number on the radio. She was moved by the rapt expression on his face. She went to her piano and played the Ellington number they had just heard. She offered to let him try his hand at the keys, and discovered he had a remarkable ear for music.

Louise had never had a student who so thirsted for music. She persuaded first her father, then the Tribbles, to allow her to give Sammy piano lessons. This was 1951; she was twenty-two and Sammy was fourteen.

The lessons went on for more than two years. Although Sammy was handicapped by the fact that he couldn't practice at home, a piano being out of the reach of his family, Louise felt he made remarkable progress. He would compose songs in his head as he plowed his father's mule, then release them through his fingers at her piano every Wednesday during his lessons. Louise had a record player, and Sammy would sit on the back porch with her and listen to jazz albums she had bought just for him. His favorite artists, besides Duke Ellington, were Bud Powell, Red Garland, and Charlie Parker.

Louise had enough faith in Sammy's talent to believe it was his ticket off the cotton farm. She regretted that he hadn't started his lessons in childhood. She knew that if he was to make up for lost time, she would have to find a way to get him a piano. After several months, she picked one up at an estate auction in nearby Deep Valley. The keys had fallen, but it could be repaired.

In a way, the piano Louise bought him is what led to Sammy's demise. A member of the crew her father hired to deliver the piano to Sammy's shack was Brent Hackleworth. Fueled by curiosity over how a "colored" family had come to own an heirloom piano, Hackleworth learned it had been purchased for Sammy by one of the local White schoolteachers. Hackleworth reported the incident to his superiors in the Klan.

The Brownville Klan had nothing better to do in December of 1953 than hassle Sammy Tribble. Although Brown vs. the Board of Education was only months away, no one knew it at the time, and Blacks in Elmwood County were relatively complacent. They would stir with the rest of the nation in the 1960s, but in 1953, they presented absolutely no challenge for the Klan. Almost for sport, the Klan took an innocent situation involving a student who wanted more than anything to learn music and turned it into a racial tragedy.

Byron Keating, grand dragon at the time, began delivering threats to the Harrises. A colored boy taking music lessons from a White woman was not to be tolerated in Brownville. When the Harrises threatened legal action, the Klan backed off and began to intimidate the Tribbles. They trashed Sammy's father's barn and burned a cross in their yard. When that didn't work, they intercepted Sammy on his way to the Harrises' and accosted him under the Little Goose Creek bridge, where they threatened to drown him. Sammy skipped his piano lesson that day, but the next Wednesday he showed up at the Harrises' again. Music was his entire identity by then, and no amount of fear could force him to give it up.

When he left Louise Harris's house that evening, he never made it home. The next morning, they found his body hanging from an oak tree near the Little Goose Creek bridge. It was December 31, 1953, six days after Christmas. Later, the Little Goose Creek bridge would be referred to as Crybaby Bridge, after local legend had it that Sammy Tribble's nocturnal wailing could be heard by passersby.

When I found out what Chadwick Corley and Sammy Tribble had in mind for Elbert Snead, I asked them to let me be a fly on the wall and watch.

The week after Easter, Elbert Snead participated in a big Klan rally in Langston Marsh's south pasture. The festivities started with a picnic that looked as innocent as a Sunday school Fourth of July barbecue. Children frolicked to and fro among the cluster of pickups and jeeps while their mothers and aunts set out casseroles, sandwiches, and pies on folding tables. The men stood around in clusters, spitting tobacco juice and telling jokes. Two Bluetick hounds made the rounds, begging for table scraps.

The only hint that anything sinister was afoot was in the three crosses at the far edge of the pasture, which could have been mistaken for props at an Easter service, and the handful of teenage boys with T-shirts showing hooded Klansmen and the caption *The Original Boy in the Hood*. Three of the boys, Mike Pinson, Teddy Wheeler, and Torry Johnson, had worn the offensive T-shirts to school and been sent home by Mr. Jacobs to change.

Helen Noble and I had sneaked through the woods off the Pine Valley Highway and were watching through binoculars from the wood line.

After they were finished eating, the women cleared the tables, and the men donned their robes for the ceremony. By the time they were ready to rock and roll, it was getting toward dusk, and the torches the Klansmen held did not provide us with adequate illumination, so we edged our way around the pasture for a better look.

The first speaker was Rev. Jimmy Sheldon, who used the bed of Joe Campbell's pickup as a speaker's platform. Shouting into a megaphone, he asked God's blessings on the White race and prayed that God would help the Klan to "turn America around." He ended by offering God the hate organization's heartfelt thanks.

He was followed on the truck bed by a number of speakers. The last one was Elbert Snead, who launched into a vile attack on the government, the judicial system, the schools, the FHA, the ACLU, the National Organization of Women, the United Nations, the Catholic Church, the Israeli government, the Black Caucus, and, to make sure he didn't leave anybody out, the High School League. It was a rambling and pointless speech. His voice whined and cracked over the megaphone.

"He made thirty-seven grammatical errors," Helen whispered to me when he had finished.

"He used the N-word thirty-one times," I replied.

By now they had reached the climax of the evening, the cross burning. The crowd shifted to the foot of the three crosses in anticipation. Thad Mosby, who owned the truck stop just outside of town, was the torch man. He stepped up to do the honors. When the crosses ignited, the crowd cheered like the Brownville Bulldogs had just made a touchdown during the homecoming game.

The first thing that caught my attention was that the cheering suddenly died, only to be replaced by the frantic baying of the two hounds. They snarled and leaped so close to the flames that two hooded figures had to hold them back.

The crowd stared at the three burning crosses in awe. What mesmerized them was that there were three figures hanging on the crosses. The flames were so bright that you couldn't make out who they were, but I already knew. Chadwick Corley and Sammy Tribble had recruited Freddy Seaton to help them confront Elbert Snead.

Chadwick was hanging on the first cross. Unlike Jesus, he came down off the cross, floating until he landed in front of Elbert Snead.

Elbert finally managed to find his voice. "How in blazes did you do that?"

Chadwick grinned in his face. "It ain't nothing I could teach you."

Elbert stared at him. "Who are you?"

Chadwick grinned wider and said, "I'll give you a hint, Elbert. Give me a dollar and I'll go away."

The hounds whined and struggled to get away. Two more Klansmen had to help hold them.

"The dogs have more sense than the people," Helen whispered to me.

Elbert struggled to speak again. He shook his head. "This ain't happening."

Chadwick kept grinning. "Sure it is, Elbert. You're just in denial."

Sammy Tribble came down next. He stood on the bed of Joe Campbell's pickup. It was the first time in Elmwood County history that a Black man had crashed a Klan rally.

"I'm Sammy Tribble. I got hung by the Klan in 1953." He pointed to the rope burn on his neck. "That was before your time, Elbert, so you don't know me, but you know who I am. I was the last Black man hung in Elmwood County. You folks talk about Sammy Tribble every time you meet." Sammy paused for a moment to stare at Elbert Snead. "You might not know me, Elbert, but I know you. Every time I hear that whiny voice of yours, I turn over in my grave. I figured it was time for me to come topside and tell you personally that I don't appreciate having my sleep disturbed."

Before Snead could react, Freddy Seaton came down to have his say.

"I'm Freddy Seaton. I died in Vietnam in 1967. I came here to give you folks some advice. You boys need to leave your hoods and bedsheets at home. Otherwise, people are liable to mistake you for ghosts. And that would give us a bad name."

The crowd began to mumble, but no one moved.

Shorty Hascall only had an eighth-grade education, but he came up with what they all seemed to think was a brilliant suggestion. "Let's make like a fetus and head out of here."

They let the hounds go, and the hounds ran in one direction while the people ran in another. Truck doors opened and slammed. Ignitions coughed to life. Tires squealed. When Troy Baxter's Jimmy sideswiped Phil Addey's Bronco, neither stopped to check the damages. They left the crosses burning and the picnic tables standing.

Chadwick watched them snake their way out of Langston Marsh's south pasture.

"I'm coming after you, Elbert," he screamed. "I never did get my dollar!"

I never heard anybody talk about what happened in that pasture that night. As far as I can tell, Mike Pinson, Teddy Wheeler, and Torry Johnson never breathed a word of it at school. News must have gotten around, though. There was hardly any Klan activity in Elmwood County after that.

The incident brought closure for Sammy Tribble. He unexpectedly announced that he was ready to cross over.

"Are you sure?" I asked. "What about your music? We were going to do a jazz album."

"It don't matter now," was his reply. I couldn't get him to elaborate on it.

He looked tired. I was reminded of a term my mom used to use when she got old and talked of being ready for death. She would say she was "world-weary." That's how Sammy Tribble looked when he finally gave it up. He looked utterly worn out.

So he went, leaving us with his big, ivory-toothed smile and leaving Steve Hall as the only Black man among them. We saw him off into the tombstones, then went back to the Levitt mansion and put a Duke Ellington CD on the battery-powered player. I strung the wires back on the old Steinway, and we sat around staring at it the way Sammy had, like we expected to hear his music in our heads.

28

Barbara Fields had been the only child of Benjamin and Pat Fields, and as such, she had been their entire life. She was quick to admit that she had been spoiled rotten, but she never showed it at school. Her discipline record was spotless during her time at Brownville High.

When it came to her family life, Barbara had enjoyed something only a minority of Brownville High students ever had—a stable home with parents who had never been divorced and who still showed love to each other.

Her father owned a service station on the corner of Church Street and Main, and although he earned more than the mill workers who bought gas and tires from him, he was by no means a wealthy man. He and his wife used what income they had to provide for the material needs of their only daughter. They willingly sacrificed vacations, stylish clothing, and frills for themselves so that they could make sure their living room spilled over with gifts on Christmas morning and on their daughter's birthday.

Unlike many parents, who use material gifts to substitute for not spending time with their children, the Fields doted on their daughter. When she came to her father's service station, he would stop whatever he was doing, no matter how impatient the customer, and attend to her needs. When Barbara was small, her mother and father could be seen in the yard playing with her every day. You never saw the parents going to a movie or driving anywhere that their daughter did not accompany them. As Barbara became older, their life was a series of pajama parties, trips to the bowling alley or skating rink with Barbara's friends, trips up the street with her to sell Girl Scout cookies, trips to root for her as she participated in the Little Miss pageant each year, and parties they hosted at their daughter's request. When she fretted over a spat with a friend, they fretted with her. When she sweated a biology exam the next day, they sweated with her.

For her sixteenth birthday, Barbara had asked for a car. Benjamin Fields rued the day he so readily agreed to buy her one.

Barbara Fields's sole wish was to find a way to tell her parents she loved them. We decided to let her write her feelings in a poem. I would deliver the poem to her father with the pretense that she had written it before her death and that it had been recently found at the high school.

She began by studying books on poetry. I went to the library and checked out *The Poet's Handbook* by Judson Jerome and *The Art and Craft of Poetry* by Michael J. Bugeja for her. I visited the back issues stacks at the University of South Carolina and ran off several years of Bugeja's columns in *Writer's Digest*. I brought her books by Emily Dickinson, Edna St. Vincent Millay, James Dickey, and Bennie Lee Sinclair.

She worked for several weeks on her composition. Although she proofed Sally Brock's novel daily, she would not let Sally or anyone else read the poem before it was finished.

It was with a great deal of reluctance that she finally showed it to me.

"I'm finished with it, Moses," she said, "but if you laugh at it, I'll stay right here and haunt you till Doomsday."

"I'm not going to laugh at it, Barbara. Even if it's bad."

"In that case, how will I know if it's any good?"

"Are you satisfied with it?"

"Yes."

"Then let's have it."

Despite weeks of study and practice, and for all her efforts at emulating the masters, she produced a simple schoolgirl poem entitled "If I Should Die Tomorrow."

It went like this:

If I should die tomorrow
Let me share my thanks today.
You've been the perfect parents—
A gift I can't repay.

If I should die tomorrow
You'll mourn me for a while.
But when you've dried your tears,
Recall me with a smile.

If I should die tomorrow
You'll have your lives to live.
Indulging yourselves for me
Is the best gift you can give.

If I should die tomorrow
Please keep this truth with you.
You wouldn't wish that I stay sad
Had I survived instead of you.

If I should die tomorrow
Our love will always be.

Take my love where'er you go.
I'll take yours to heaven with me.

If I should die tomorrow
I'll wait until your day.
And when it's time to leave this life,
I'll guide you along the way.

If I should die tomorrow.

It was the kind of poem that you see in the obituary columns on the anniversary of deaths. It's also the kind of poem that looks corny unless it's your daughter writing it to you. Or unless it's you writing it to your parents.

"I'm touched," Helen said when I showed her the poem.

"You should be. She condensed ten pages of notes into six stanzas. It says everything she wanted to say."

"When are you going to give it to him?"

"Right after school, I guess."

"I've got something else you can give him." She led me to her back office and pulled out a box of old yearbook photos. "I found some school pictures of Barbara in the extras. They weren't used in the yearbook. I'll bet her parents would like to have them."

I stopped by Fields Service Station on my afternoon walk. There were several customers in the station, so I called Ben Fields aside and gave him the poem.

"We found some pictures of Barbara and a poem she wrote in the library. Ms. Noble and I thought you'd like to have them."

He thumbed through the photographs and read the poem. It brought a sad smile to his face. He looked up and said, "Did you read this?"

"Yes."

"It sounds almost like she knew she was going to die. I wonder when she wrote it."

"That I can't tell you."

"Well, I really appreciate this, Mr. Fellars. I'm sure Pat will too."

I was somewhat disappointed by the lack of emotion he showed. But Barbara was watching us, and she said he was hiding his feelings because his customers were nearby. She said he didn't hide his feelings when he showed the poem to his wife.

To his credit, Gordon Wallace had enough decency not to spoil Barbara's gift to her parents.

Barbara went over soon after that. Her cold farewell kiss reminded me just how much they all had needed human warmth. She left me a parting gift. It was a glass paperweight—I still have it at home. I didn't ask where she got it, but I seem to remember there was one just like it on Mr. Jacobs's desk, right next to where he used to put his feet.

Five nights later, Laval Crenshaw followed. The dogs howled soulfully all across town the night he went over.

29

〜

Will Masters and Charlie Green were a total frustration to me when I first met them. My goal in those days was to make sure every student made something of himself, and I ran into a brick wall with Will and Charlie. Their only aim in life was to make it to the 2:35 dismissal bell so they could ride up and down what little there was of Main Street, light up on a corner somewhere, and watch the world go by. They were pioneers of the useless generation almost a decade before Larry Ringer proclaimed it as his future.

Will's old man didn't work—he claimed a back injury, but he'd never managed to document it sufficiently to qualify for disability. His mom's paycheck from the local textile mill was their only means of support. It was always tight, because Gary Masters managed to drink away a good chunk of the family budget at Butch's Bar. To make matters worse, he would squander their money in other ways. If Irene gave him ten dollars to go to Li'l Cricket for milk and bread for the kids' breakfast the next day, he'd often as not drop by Willards Pharmacy and waste it on a box of Whitman's chocolates with which to surprise the children.

"He didn't have a bit of responsibility," Irene confided to me. "Whatever the kids wanted to do, he'd let them. If I told them no, all they had to do was go ask their daddy. Of course, they loved him to death, but it sure made it hard on me. I was always the heavy. Everybody else could say, 'Wait till your daddy gets home' when they wanted the kids to mind, but that didn't float at our house.

"Most kids eventually come to appreciate their parents being strict when they grow up and have kids of their own. That's what causes me the biggest heartache about Will dying so young. I'm afraid he went to his grave thinking I was mean."

Out of this dysfunctional situation, Will developed a don't-give-a-crap attitude about life. While kids all around him fretted over a history test or frantically searched for somebody's homework to copy so Old Lady Larimore wouldn't chew them out in American Lit, Will took it all in stride.

Will's attitude was often interpreted as insolence by teachers like Jane Larimore, who was from the old school and who was convinced I'd put him in her class just to make her earn her money the hard way. Will would greet her with a big, sappy grin and a friendly "Hello, Sugarlips, you're looking mighty fine today." The greeting drove her bananas, but the more she protested, the worse it got. "Hello, Sugarlips. I think you're the prettiest teacher on the faculty. Don't tell your husband, though. I hear he's a good shot with a deer rifle." She brought him down to my office and demanded that I refer him to the school psychologist. I had a talk with Will about respecting his elders, but it went in one ear and out the other. The next morning, I heard his voice carry all the way down from the end of the east wing. "Hello, Sugarlips. Mighty pretty shade of nylons you got on."

I couldn't help but laugh. Ned Spruce, the assistant principal, was standing by me outside the office. Ned shook his head and said, "That's one kid Mrs. Larimore won't dare fail."

"Maybe that's why he does it," I said.

Unlike most kids his age, Will took no pride in his personal grooming and would come to school in hand-me-downs, with his hair disheveled and fingernails dark with half-moons of dirt. All the same, he had no problem finding female companionship, thanks to Charlie Green's popularity. Charlie was a lady's man and had more girlfriends than he could shake a stick at, so Will got his share of tagalong leftovers.

It was always good to have a guy like Charlie Green along when you were cruising the parking lot at McDonald's or the strand at Myrtle Beach, because he could pull up to a carload of girls and shoot them a line smooth as silk, sidestep their putdowns, and have them eating out of his hand within five minutes.

Charlie was a latchkey kid from a single-parent home and had basically had to raise himself. All things considered, he hadn't done such a bad job of it. His basic flaw was that, like Gary and Will Masters, Charlie had no sense of responsibility. When he got Melissa Lanford pregnant and refused to marry her, her parents threatened litigation. In the end, Charlie's reputation saved him. Melissa's parents took a long look at him, saw how shiftless he was, read the writing on the wall, and took Melissa to Atlanta for an abortion.

I tried to steer Charlie toward a career in sales, but he and Will ended up working in the same mill where Will's mom worked, Charlie pushing a broom and Will running the card machine. They lived for ten months after graduation, putting in their time at work, hanging out on the street in the afternoon, going to a party at somebody's house in the evening, and rounding out the night by drinking beer and shooting pool in the back of Butch's Bar on Highway 21 until 2:00 a.m. Although the legal drinking age in South Carolina had been twenty-one since 1984, they had no trouble getting Patsy Hascall, the girl at the cash register, to look the other way when one of the local yokels would hand them a couple of Buds.

It turned out to be a dull life. Will and Charlie tried to put some spark in it by drag racing home from Butch's Bar one night—their last on Earth. They tried to pass on a curve and collided head-on with an eighteen-wheeler on its last leg home from a seven-state jaunt, leaving their spot on the highway with the unimaginative name Dead Man's Curve. The driver of the other car in the race was never identified.

Ira Cavandish's parties were legendary. For years I'd heard about them from the students who frequented my guidance office. Not that any of the students had ever been. They'd overheard their parents talk about them. Nor did any of the students' parents ever admit to attending a Cavandish party; it was always a friend who had witnessed the decadence. Amazingly, these parents who had never attended the bashes had absorbed an incredible amount of detail about what went on at them. They were wild affairs during which booze and drugs floated about the Cavandish farm from sunset to sunup, and more than one marriage had broken up because of acts of indiscretion that had taken place there.

Will Masters and Charlie Green were basically a couple of rednecks with no ambition. It didn't take much to make them happy. They only wanted one last party with the friends they used to hang out with—the ones who still lived in Brownville—Bud Griffin, Pete Mosley, Ted Graham, Pee Wee Wiggins, and Stumpy McElrath. They were all regulars at the Cavandish bashes, and since I could think of no pretext by which to get them together otherwise, I decided that Will and Charlie would simply have to crash Ira Cavandish's next party. Although they had observed the celebrated event unseen for years, they would get to go as participants this time.

Rumor had it that Ira Cavandish was throwing a bash the last Saturday night in April. I waited until almost midnight to take Will and Charlie to the Cavandish farm, because I wanted to give everybody time to get stoned. I figured if anybody recognized them, the sight of two dead boys would be easier to deal with if you were stoned.

We made our way up a maze of dirt roads on the west side of Brownville, bouncing over ruts where April showers had eroded the topsoil, our headlights weaving through the shadows of pine trees, until we came to an open aluminum gate. Two guys stood a few yards from the gate, their cigarettes winking in the dark. One of them turned on a flashlight and walked over to me. When he reached my car, I saw that he wore camouflaged hunting fatigues and carried a Winchester. I recognized him as Toby Crouch, a former student. When you've been a counselor at one school as long as I've been at Brownville High, you recognize a lot of people as former students, and if you knew Toby Crouch, you'd realize how melodramatic the fatigues and Winchester were.

I blinked as he caught my face in his flashlight beam. He moved it over to Charlie and Will. We were all sitting in the front seat.

He was shocked to see me. "Mr. Fellars, where do you think you're going?"

"Trying to crash a party."

"I don't believe this one's your style."

"You let me be the judge of that."

He looked extremely uncomfortable. "I don't know . . ."

"Look, the school's closing down. The town's closing down. I'm getting transferred to Elmwood High next year. I want to have one evening to remember before I leave Brownville. These are my nephews. They've heard about Ira's parties and wanted to come."

"We're not supposed to let teenagers in."

"They're not teenagers. They're older than they look."

"Well, I don't know—"

"You can search us if you want. We're not wired or anything. We're not narcs, or anything. Think about it. If I narced on anybody, I couldn't do my job, because nobody would trust me. Word gets out."

"If word gets out that you came here, you could lose your job."

"That just goes to show that I've got more to lose than you. Give me a break."

He paused a moment in indecision. "I'd better check with Ira."

I pulled out my wallet. "Don't check with Ira. I already checked with Ben Franklin. He says it's okay."

I took a hundred out of my wallet and handed it to him.

While he was gawking at it, I said, "Thanks," and drove on.

Despite what I had said to Toby Crouch, I had no intention of going to Ira Cavandish's party myself. I pulled up in the pines behind a cluster of jacked up pickups and Blazers with Confederate flag stickers on the windows and cut off the ignition.

"Okay, guys, you're on your own. Have fun."

I crawled in the back seat and went to sleep.

They floated around until they came across Bud Griffin and Pee Wee Wiggins making time with Ed Hazel's and Bob Blackmon's wives under the shed of the barn.

It took Pee Wee about fifteen minutes to make the connection. "You guys look like Will Masters and Charlie Green."

"We are."

They were too drunk to be shocked.

"Well, I'll be," Pee Wee said, sucking on a reefer. "Have you run into Janis Joplin and Jimmy Hendrix lately?"

"We ain't even got to see Elvis yet," Will complained.

Pee Wee turned to Bud and said, "We must be hallucinating, Bud."

"We must be."

"How come we got the same hallucination?"

"You stole mine. You was always copying my homework in school."

That brought gales of laughter from all of them. Pee Wee looked around and noticed that the two women had drifted off. He seemed to experience a flash of sobriety. "I don't think I'm going to like this tomorrow morning," he said.

They went off to find Pete Mosley, Ted Graham, and Stumpy McElrath.

Toby Crouch knocked on my window at 4:00 a.m. He had Will propped up against the tire of Johnny Pugh's four-by-four and Charlie's arm draped around his neck. They were belting out the refrain from Elton John's "Crocodile Rock," trying for a duet, but missing each other's beat by a mile.

Toby helped me dump them into the back seat of my car, where they promptly passed out, stone drunk off of old memories.

We said goodbye to Will Masters and Charlie Green the next evening, on Sunday. There was a funeral that day, Todd Broxton's grandmother, and we had to wait until they had finished their business. When it was time for their final stroll up the hill, Will and Charlie left this world as happy-go-lucky as I'd ever seen them.

30

The Brownville rumor mill was in fine working order, humming overtime. Monday morning, Mr. Jacobs summoned me to his office.

"Bill, I'm worried about you," he said with paternal concern. "Are you feeling okay?"

I slumped down in the cushioned chair in front of his desk. "I'm fine."

"I know we've been under a lot of strain this spring, with the school closing and everything, but you haven't seemed yourself lately. You seem distracted. The faculty has noticed it too."

Helen had warned me that he had asked her about my welfare.

I took my cue from his remark about the school closing. "It's the transition blues, Mr. Jacobs. Having to box up all my records to move them to Elmwood next year."

"I know what you mean. I see you walking in the afternoons. Does that help?"

"Yeah. When you have a desk job like ours, you need to stir around a little in your off hours."

"That's true. I get my exercise on the golf course." He folded his hands and bowed his head. His tone shifted. "Bill, I've been hearing some rumors about you that I need to ask you about."

I eased out of my slouched position. "What rumors?"

"I heard you were at Ira Cavandish's party this weekend. I hope that's not true."

"It's not exactly true. I did drive up to the Cavandish farm Saturday night, but I was just giving a couple of guys a ride. I didn't attend his party. In fact, I don't think I even got out of the car."

He expelled a visible sigh of relief. "I figured that's all there was to it. It's amazing how people in this town twist the facts around."

"Yeah, it is. Were there any other rumors you wanted to ask me about?"

"No. You can't pay any attention to rumors anyway." If he'd heard anything else, he must have figured there was an explanation to it just as innocent as my Cavandish story was, and he decided not to pursue it.

He was still worried about me. "Bill, if you need a day off, just let me know."

Bubba Wilson started following me around town after that. He would park along the curb and watch me as I took my walk. When I reached the end of a street, he would pull up to the curb of the next street and watch me the length of the street. He followed this pattern of park and watch, park and watch, the entire length of my four-mile walk. I missed my Tuesday meeting at the Levitt house on Brewer Avenue.

By Thursday I'd had enough. I worked at school until dark and drove out to Highway 21. I picked up Bubba's headlights in my rearview mirror after I passed Li'l Cricket. I stopped at the county dumpsters just outside the town limit.

Bubba pulled up behind me. He got out and strutted up to my window.

"You're out of your territory, Bubba," I said to him. "We're outside town limits. Are you going to follow me to Elmwood?"

He assumed a bully cop stance and looked down at me.

"I told you I was going to keep watching you, Fellars. Things I can't explain keep happening around this town. All those items that were burglarized turned back up where they belonged. Somebody got in Martha Driggers's bedroom twice without waking her or her cocker spaniel. They got in and out of Coleman's Treasures twice without tripping the alarm. And there was the business with the dogs the night Legrand Warfield's bull got out and Carl Harris's Doberman chewed up Mrs. Halfacre. You were seen speeding away from the Warfield place."

"Did Warfield's money turn up?" I couldn't resist asking that. He glared at me like he knew I was toying with him.

"No, it didn't. I still want to know what's going on, Fellars. I still got a feeling about you. I'm thinking about having the sheriff take you in for questioning. I hear you took a couple of teenagers to Ira Cavandish's booze and pot orgy Saturday night."

I threw up my hands. "All right, Bubba, you win. You want to know what's going on? Follow me. I'll take you to my leader."

I led him over to the churchyard and got out of my car.

"This way," I beckoned, deliberately leading him through the tombstones of Confederacy-era graves that had not been moved when the town cemetery opened up on Cemetery Drive many decades ago.

The back approach to the Levitt haunted house was even more sinister than the front, because there was less light and more shadows. You had to go through an iron gate that I had learned to muffle by lifting up and pressing against the hinges. This time I let it creak.

I rattled my skeleton key in the lock.

"Breaking and entering is against the law," Bubba told me. His voice was unsteady.

"I've got an officer of the law with me," I said.

The door creaked open. Candlelight danced about the room.

I stepped inside and Bubba followed me.

I turned and looked at him. "Remember, you asked for this."

"Just get on with it, Fellars."

The floor creaked as I walked to the center of the room. I cupped my hands around my mouth and called upstairs. "Front and center, gang. We got company."

Sally Brock and Sharon Summer descended the stairs. They were the only two females left. Tony Cunningham and Steve Hall came into the foyer from the kitchen entrance. Freddy Seaton and Johnny Brown entered from the parlor. Chadwick Corley, whom nobody could stand to be around, came up from the basement. As they navigated their way up and down steps and across boards designed to creak, they moved in total silence. Somehow the silence was more ghastly than all the hideous laughter and chain-clinking and creaking the house was capable of manufacturing.

There were only seven of them left now, and I wished I'd had the others to show off to him. But seven was enough. At first Bubba looked like he feared I had recruited a coven of drug-crazed skinheads to Brownville and hidden them out in the Levitt house. He soon found it was much worse. I did not try to be gentle in initiating him as I had with Helen Noble.

"If you see anybody here you don't know, Bubba, I'll introduce you. But since you've lived in Brownville all your life, I believe you knew most of them before they died."

He gaped at them like a wide-eyed idiot, his eyes darting from one to the other and back again.

He took a step back and said, "Oh Jesus!" It was a prayer, said in awe, rather than profanity.

"Here's the story, Bubba," I said. "They've got some unfinished business to take care of before they pass into eternity. I've been helping them. Perhaps you'd like to help too." I summoned menace into my eyes and voice. "Either that or get off my back."

He looked like a camper who had just blundered his way into a den of rattlesnakes. He began backing away from us. "Okay, Mr. Fellars. You folks go on about your business. I'll leave now, 'cause, ah, I got work to do."

The flickering candles provided plenty of light, and the furniture was arranged so that there was plenty of space to move about the room. Even so, Bubba managed to knock over an end table in his clumsy and hasty exit.

Three minutes later, I heard his tires squeal from the next block over.

31

With an enrollment of just under three hundred students, Brownville High was one of the smallest high schools in South Carolina. In a vain attempt to stem its declining enrollment, the administration had added seventh and eighth grades to the high school several years before. Most of my problems came from seventh and eighth graders.

So I was hardly surprised when Patsy Freeland, the eighth grade English teacher, marched Dawn Vernoy, Kathy Bain, Sandy Keeler, and Amanda Montgomery into my office and said they needed conflict resolution. They had been involved in a pushing and screeching match in the hall at break.

They were still mouthing back and forth after Patsy left. Out of the maze of lies, accusations, and countercharges, I pieced together the following facts. Amanda had told Kathy that Dawn slept around because Amanda was jealous of Dawn's boyfriend Keith. Kathy told the girls in her first-period pre-algebra class what Amanda had told her, and the rumor had gotten back to Dawn. In retaliation, Dawn told Sandy that she had heard that Amanda's mom used to be a hooker and had slept with every man in Brownville, "except for my dad." That rumor made its way back to Amanda. Both girls had confronted each other at break, backed up by their witnesses. Both girls also claimed they had no idea what the other girl was talking about.

If you find that hard to follow, so did I. Now you see what guidance counselors have to put up with. While I was sorting through it, Amanda threw in for good measure that she had heard that Dawn used drugs.

That brought an instant denial from Dawn. "I would never use drugs. Not after last night."

That was my jumping-off point. "What happened last night?"

"I had a creepy dream."

"Would you care to share it with us, Dawn?"

"It was about Tony Cunningham."

I started at the name and hoped they didn't notice it. "What about Tony Cunningham?"

"He came to pick me up in his red '95 Buick. We went and picked up Tommy Gable and Toby Pracht. Kathy, you were in it too. We picked you up standing by the benches on Main Street."

"Tell me you didn't," Kathy said.

"She's making it up," Amanda said.

"We drove out to Miller's Pond and got stoned on pot. Then we polished off a bottle of Johnny Walker Red. After that, we got back in the car and tore up the road down Lover's Lane and got on Highway 21. When we got to the two-mile straightaway in front of John McCutcheon's house, Tony said he could open her up. He got up to a hundred and ten, then the car left the road and hit a tree. God, it was awful. We all got killed except for Tony. I started floating away, and I could see my body crushed against the dash. Tony didn't have a scratch on him. He grinned and said, 'This time I lived and y'all didn't. I just thought you'd like to know what it's like being dead.' It was so creepy."

"Oh! My! God!" That came from Kathy, whose eyes were like quarters. She said it just like that, with exclamation points in her voice.

"It was just a dream, Kathy," Dawn assured her.

"I had the same dream last night," Kathy said.

"No, you didn't."

"No, I did so. I was sitting on the bench across from McKinley's Hardware, and y'all drove up and parked in a handicapped spot. You rolled down the window and the radio nearly blasted me out of my socks. 'Stuck Like Glue' was the song, I think. The whole dream was clear as a bell. I could smell spilled beer when I got in the back seat between Tommy and Toby. Tommy kept tickling me, trying to make me pee in my pants, and Toby kept making fun of my nails."

"This is so wild," Dawn said. "Tony did park in a handicapped spot. He said, 'Do you think the local fuzz—'"

"'—would consider being dead a handicap?'" Kathy finished the sentence with her, then said again, "Oh my God!"

"You guys are making this up," Amanda said.

"And when we got to Miller's Pond," Kathy continued, "Tony got stuck cutting through the pasture. When the car started sliding, Toby told him whatever he did to keep going."

"And I said I wasn't going to mess up my shoes pushing the car out of the mud."

"Oh my God, this is so unreal."

"It's so creepy."

"You guys are absolutely making all this up."

"I don't think they're making it up, Amanda," Sandy said. "I had the same dream last week. Only it was Sharon Goggans, Crystal Ling, and Billy Grant I was in the car with. Tony Cunningham picked us up."

"Now you're in on it with them."

"I most certainly am not. I didn't even know about their dream. Besides, I had mine first."

"I hate to sound dense," Amanda said, "but who's Tony Cunningham?"

"I didn't know either till I asked my mom," Sandy replied. "He got killed in a car wreck back before I started school."

Dawn nodded. "My uncle was in school with him."

"Ted Simmons was in the wreck with him," Kathy added. "That's why he still limps."

"I went down to the library and looked in the old yearbooks," Sandy said. "It was the same guy in the dream. Long hair and all."

Amanda flipped her hair. "Well, I really feel left out. I'm the only one that didn't get to go for a joyride with him."

"You don't want to go for a joyride with him."

Dawn looked at me. "Mr. Fellars, how could we all have the same dream?"

I shrugged. "Maybe he's trying to tell you something."

Helen was hardly surprised when I relayed the account of my morning session to her.

"Half a dozen kids have come into the media center and asked for the '99 yearbook. Tony Cunningham's name is going around school like wildfire."

"Good."

She cocked her head. "Why good?"

"The prom's coming up. By the way, do you want to go with me?"

"What's the prom got to do with Tony Cunningham?"

"You remember what his wish was?"

"I believe he wanted to warn kids not to follow in his footsteps."

"Smart girl. I guess spooky dreams are more effective than a film on car crashes during assembly."

She batted her eyes at me. "Smart guy. Were you serious about the prom?"

"Dead serious."

Her smile was playful. "Don't you think that's a poor choice of words, considering the people we're trying to help?"

"Quit torturing me. Yes or no?"

"You already know I'll go with you, don't you?"

"Well, I didn't want to take you for granted."

"You'd better not," she said.

"Why do I feel like you're training me?" I asked.

She let out a cute little giggle.

Kids continued to report visits from Tony in their dreams. I tried to downplay the phenomenon whenever I heard the faculty puzzling over it in the teacher's lounge.

My line of razzle-dazzle went like this: "I wouldn't make too much out of it. It's probably some sort of psychological suggestion. A couple of kids start off the story as a prank. The others hear about it and either fabricate a similar experience because they don't want to be left out, or their subconscious mind takes over and turns it into a dream."

32

〜

"She would have been somebody," is what everybody says when they talk about Sally Brock, the town lawyer's daughter. When somebody as talented as Sally dies prematurely, it gets you to thinking, and you wonder how many potential John Grishams died in Vietnam with Freddy Seaton, or how many kids with Tom Hanks's talent never make it out of St. Jude's Children's Hospital.

Sally Brock, an intelligent and studious girl, was always on the shy side, until her last two years in high school. Her junior year, she began writing a column called "Sally's Corner" for the school newspaper, and suddenly everyone became aware of a secret previously known only to her few closest friends. Sally Brock had an outrageous sense of humor. The acclaim her column stirred boosted her self-esteem and caused her to blossom among her peers.

In her senior year, she surprised everybody, including herself, by trying out for the female lead in the school play. She got the part and stole the show, amazing everyone except those who know that introverted people often have a wild streak hidden on the dark side of their personalities.

On the plain side and slightly overweight, Sally never had a steady boyfriend, but that seemed to be all right with her. She was into horses and more than once lamented that she had been born a hundred years too late. She would have preferred to live in the horse-and-buggy era. Her father, grateful that she was horse crazy instead of boy crazy, kept a palomino for her in the stables on Langston Marsh's farm a couple of miles out of town, and Sally kept the family on the road (when she could pry her father away from his law practice) with rodeos and trail rides.

When she wasn't riding out to the stables on her bicycle, or later in her Grand Am, Sally would likely be at the town library, picking over the shelves for something she hadn't already read. She was a voracious reader, selecting an author, devouring their works, and moving on. One summer she was into Zane Grey; the next winter she was working her way through Mary Higgins Clark; and by the next summer she had moved on to Erle Stanley Gardner.

She began writing in the eighth grade but was somewhat secretive about it, because she was by nature a private person. When everyone began raving about how good "Sally's Corner" was, Sally began showing her stories around during her senior year. She had been writing for four years and by now had become quite polished. Her teachers were astonished, and they encouraged her to submit her work to magazines. To my knowledge, she was never published but eventually worked her way up from form rejection slips to a few encouraging letters from magazine editors.

Sally affected a grungy dress code, refusing to wear makeup. She wore her thick, long hair tied into a ponytail, until she decided to have it cropped short so that it would be easily managed. Her lack of polish worried her mother, but when her literary ambitions became known, people began to assure her mother that it was perfectly okay for Sally to be a little eccentric, because that was just her artistic streak showing.

By the time she graduated, Sally's potential was evident to her teachers and her classmates, who voted her "Most Likely to Succeed" in the senior superlatives. What wasn't evident was the disease that had already started growing in her body, which would not manifest itself for two years and which would suddenly close the curtain of her life long before the play should have been over.

Sally Brock turned out between one and two thousand words a day on her novel. She worked in the mornings, with the birds singing outside her window and soft '60s rock playing gently inside the dormer room. In the afternoons, she would read Anne Rivers Siddons and Joyce Carol Oates. I monitored her work in progress regularly, and I was confident she would achieve her goal of turning out a good novel, even if she only got one crack at it. After all, she wasn't exactly a novice. The years of steady writing during high school had allowed her to get out of the way the million words of junk the late John D. MacDonald said aspiring writers had to turn out before they began to get any good.

I had another goal for her. I wanted to see her finished work published. Because my mother had been an aspiring writer in her younger days, I was well aware of the overwhelming odds that face even the most talented unknown writers in their quest for publication.

Without telling my mother what I had in mind, I decided to pick her brain. We had just finished supper one evening, and she had settled in the living room to read the latest large-print mystery she had checked out from the library.

"Mom, why did you stop writing novels?" I asked her.

She looked up, and the light from the ceiling shone on her glasses. "Oh, I haven't thought about that in a long time. I had a lot of ambition back when I was younger. I could turn out a novel in a month if I pushed it. I started writing the same year Stephen King published *Carrie.* I must have written seven or eight novels. I thought the last couple were pretty good. But I never was able to break through."

"So why did you stop?" I asked again.

"I got interested in other things. My flowers and raising a family. The farm took a lot of time. And I was always having to bring work home from school. I figured I'd done the best I could with my writing, but it wasn't good enough to get published. After so many rejection slips, you just give up."

"Do you still have any of the novels?"

She considered. "I think the last one is in the attic somewhere."

"Would you mind if I read it?" I asked tenuously.

"I guess not, if I can find it." She chuckled. "I haven't read it in twenty years. It ought to give us both a good laugh."

Her manuscript was pretty good for a trunk novel. It was a mystery, and it turned out to be a fast read. What impressed me as much as the novel was the last rejection letter she got. It was a personal letter of encouragement from Hiram Thompson, an acquisitions editor with Pathway Press in New York. The letter suggested to me that Mom was closer to being published than she thought. A writer who begins to collect personal letters rather than standard form rejections is making progress. It was a shame she hadn't kept at it.

A little more digging told me why she might have gotten discouraged. She had evidently revised the novel and resubmitted it about a year later. Her query letter to Hiram Thompson was returned with the notation that Mr. Thompson was deceased and that Pathway Press was not taking on any new authors.

I examined the first letter carefully. It was dated March 3, 1988. It consisted of a full typed page and three lines and a closing signature on the second page. The seed of a marketing plan for Sally Brock's novel began to take shape in my head. I folded the letter and put it in my pocket.

I showed a photocopy of the letter to Freddy Seaton in the parlor of the Levitt haunted house.

"There's a five-by-eight Kelsey hand press in the basement at school. The journalism class used to use it before the school had computers. I noticed on your transcript that you took journalism under Mrs. Hinson. Do you remember the printing press?"

He nodded. "Sure do."

"Do you know how to use it?"

He frowned. "Yeah, but I always hated it. It's a messy job. You have to put down newspapers and clean up the press. What do you need?"

"I need a Pathway Press letterhead on blank stationary." I pointed to Mom's rejection letter. "It has to look just like this. Can you handle it?"

"If I absolutely have to."

I patted him on the shoulder. "I appreciate it. It's to help Sally."

Sally finished her novel in just a few weeks. She left it in a hat box on the dresser where she had worked with a note for me that said, "Mr. Fellars, I've reached the end. It's time for you to tear it apart. Leave it here when you're finished. Sorry I'm gone, but I can't bear to watch you read it. Sally."

I made a copy of the novel at FedEx Office in Columbia so I wouldn't have to spoil her original with red marks. Then I took it home to read.

The title of Sally's novel was *No Fear of Death*. Like my mom, she had turned out a murder mystery. At least, on the surface it was a murder mystery. The multiple murder takes place between 11:30 p.m. and 12:30 a.m. in a lake cabin. The victim is an emotionally disturbed mother and her three children. The mother is both killer and victim. Her motive is revenge, and she strives to implicate her estranged husband, who is also a failed writer, as the murderer. She does this by provoking a fight the day before the murder so both will sustain bruises and by luring him to the lake cabin so he will discover the crime scene. The hapless husband discovers his wife and children murdered. What really grabs his attention is that the crime scene has been lifted, detail for detail, out of one of his unpublished novels, in which a husband snaps and does a *Fatal Vision* on his family. The wife, after ice-picking her kids, has managed to electrocute herself in the bathtub with a hair dryer while making her suicide look like murder. All right out of the husband's unpublished novel. In trying to hide the incriminating manuscript from the authorities, the unfortunate husband makes himself look guilty.

On the surface, a murder mystery, but underneath, an insightful psychological probe into the human heart.

Helen and I took three days "tearing apart" Sally's novel, as she put it. We made surprisingly few changes, and only one suggestion for a major structural alteration. To tell you the truth, I think we were afraid to tinker with it too much.

Though we had made few changes, getting Sally to accept them was a bloodbath. She fought me for every added comma and minor word change.

Her novel started out like this:

I have no fear of death.

You may suppose that to be an asenine pronouncement, that any prudent man should fear death, because death is an unknown kingdom of darkness from which no living being has returned to speak of the evil that awaits us there. But that isn't true. We were all dead before we were born into this miserable life, and we slept away the eons undisturbed. I slept dreamless through prior eternity, and I brought no memory from the void.

In the second sentence, asinine is misspelled, and she accepted that change. But when I broke the sentence in two by placing a period after death and capitalizing *because,* she bristled.

"It's one thought. You've totally disrupted the flow."

"The sentence is too long, Sally. It reads quicker if it's broken up."

"It doesn't read any quicker. Time yourself."

"It seems to read quicker."

"I'm not writing for people who move their lips when they read," she said.

I gave in. "All right, Sally, it's your book. If it means that much to you, we'll put the comma back in."

That's the way it went with most of the minor changes I made, and believe me, they were minor. At first she took the changes in good humor.

"Ouch. That hurts," she'd say.

Or, "That manuscript is my baby. You're cutting off part of his foot."

In some cases, I merely reversed the order of words to conform with the expected flow of modern English usage. Where Sally had written, "He went often to see the marigolds in the park," I amended to "He often went to see the marigolds in the park."

She became more defensive.

"No, no, no," she erupted. "You've done it again. You've taken something that sounds lyrical and made it trite. Leave it the way I wrote it."

I gave in to her again and again.

One thing I fought her on was the major structural change I'd suggested. In her novel, one of the patrolmen sent to secure the crime scene happens to be an old family friend of the framed husband. He discovers a scrap of paper in the fireplace that missed getting burned. The paper is a description of the crime scene that the wife lifted from her husband's novel to make sure she had duplicated it at the lake cabin. Thinking that the paper scrap incriminates the husband, the cop hides it. Later, at the end of the novel, he gets drunk in a bar and discloses the existence of the paper scrap, the "smoking gun," to a private detective who is working on the case. The way the missing evidence is disclosed was too contrived. I suggested to Sally that it be disclosed through a different scene.

"I think that scene works just fine," she said stiffly. By now she was working up to full-fledged hostility.

I tried to be patient with her. "Sally, you're too close to your work to see it clearly. Most writers set their first draft aside for a couple of months and let it cook in their heads. They go back and revise it, and they see it in a new light. We don't have time for that process. If it has flaws, we've got to fix them now. Have you ever read *Under the Lake* by Stuart Woods?"

"No."

"All his other novels are great, but this one reads like magic for an hour and a half, then falls apart in the last fifty pages. Not even the cover blurb from Stephen King can save it. I'm not saying your novel does that, but it could be strengthened in this one scene."

She finally became totally put out with me. "You write your novel the way you want to write it, but leave mine alone," she finally said.

"I'm trying to help you, Sally. Remember, you asked me to 'tear it apart.'"

We left the novel the way she wanted. When Sally's novel was finally published, two reviewers criticized the very scene I had wanted to change. But it was her call. And who is to say that the two critics and I were right?

On the whole, Sally had produced a stunning first and only novel. When I told her that, she smiled, and I realized that was something I hadn't seen her do lately.

"Are you okay, Sally? You seem kind of down."

She took a long moment to answer. "I miss Barbara. She was a big help to me. I don't think I could have gotten through this book if she hadn't been there for me when I got stuck. I was afraid I wouldn't be able to keep on when she left."

"I miss her, too, Sally. She kind of grew on you. 'If you laugh at my poem, Moses, I'll stay here and haunt you till Doomsday,'" I said, imitating Barbara's voice.

Sally laughed. Then she reached out and hugged me to let me know we were still friends. "Thank you, Mr. Fellars. You gave us all another chance. I hope you don't get in trouble for doing any of this."

She was the only one of them who ever actually thanked me, though I knew the others felt what Sally had expressed. I didn't hold it against Sally for being so abrasive about her novel. It was her only legacy, and I admired her fighting for it. But it did let me know what editors have to put up with.

I hugged her back. "Don't get sappy on me, Sally."

She laughed again.

I wrote Sally a bogus letter of rejection on the Pathway Press letterhead Freddy furnished. The letter was as close to Hiram Thompson's letter to my mom as I could get it. I even borrowed an IBM Selectric from the museum in the back of Hickson's Antiques so the type would look similar. This detail was important, because I paired my bogus first page with the original second page, which contained Thompson's signature. It was important that the signature be authentic. The three lines on the last page formed a logical ending to the bogus letter I'd composed. The stationary I had provided Freddy Seaton came from my mother's attic. It was thirty years old, expensive fifty-pound Bond paper my mother had used for her query letters and was a close enough match to the texture of the original letter.

I secured the services of a remailing service in New York City. Using Pathway Press's return address, I sent the manuscript to Sally Brock at her parents' address. The remailing service would forward it using a New York City postmark.

Sally's rejection letter informed her that Hiram Thompson had just discovered a manuscript Sally had sent him twenty-two years ago. He was terribly sorry the manuscript had been misplaced, and since Pathway Press no longer published fiction, he couldn't fit it on his list. However, the quality of the manuscript was such that he didn't have the heart to destroy it, so he was returning it with encouragement for her to try to place it elsewhere, "as it seems timeless."

Word of Sally's lost novel soon spread around town. The town librarian proofed it, as did two English teachers at Brownville High. The local newspaper did a nice spread on Sally's story, which was picked up by the Associated Press.

When a publisher did not snap up *No Fear of Death* immediately, the Brocks decided to subsidize publication themselves. Sally's mother hired a publicist to get her on the talk show circuit to push the novel. As the novel gained recognition, an *Atlanta Journal* book reviewer became suspicious at the implausible scenario of a publisher returning a novel manuscript after twenty-two years. A quick investigation revealed that Hiram Thompson had been dead for twenty years and Pathway Press went bankrupt in 1992, the year before Sally Brock died. The book reviewer cried hoax. Ironically, one reporter went so far as to accuse Sally's parents of having the novel ghosted in her name.

The Brocks saw enough of Sally in the writing to know it was her work. Stung by the criticism, Aaron Brock enlisted a noted handwriting analyst to examine Hiram Thompson's signature on the rejection letter and the draft of the novel in his daughter's hand. Without knowing whose handwriting he was authenticating, the expert rendered the mind-boggling verdict that the signature on the letter and handwriting of the manuscript were both authentic. Two tabloid talk shows hired handwriting experts, who reached the same conclusion.

I suppose had the FBI been called in, they could have established that the first and second pages of Hiram Thompson's rejection letter were produced on different typewriters. But everybody's attention was focused on the handwriting, which in both cases was authentic.

So that was my marketing hook. A dead publisher returned the manuscript of a dead girl twenty-two years after she sent it in, almost two decades after both had died. I hoped it would make people want to go out and read the book. Unfortunately, the quality of Sally's writing was dwarfed by the circus of notoriety in which I had cloaked her book. I counted on Sally's parents to keep the book alive long enough for readers to take a second look and see just how good her story was.

It took three years for this drama to play itself out. Sally did not wait around to see it through. She crossed over the day after her parents got the manuscript. She went with the satisfaction of knowing she had managed to achieve some measure of immortality on this side.

33

꙼

Prom night is an annual high school ritual that adds a touch of Cinderella magic to the often equal parts mundane and troubling adolescent experience. Along with homecoming, the senior trip, and Friday night football, it sprinkles a little sunshine on what many students consider to be the equivalent of a twelve-year prison sentence.

At Brownville High, prom night was drawn out like the twelve days of Christmas, because kids started begging to get out of school early to decorate the National Guard armory a full two weeks before the event. There were always plenty of volunteers to hang balloons and streamers from the armory rafters—but very few volunteers to return to the armory for cleanup the Sunday after the prom, when most kids were suffering from hangovers and lack of sleep.

Brownville High always held its prom on a Saturday night, usually in early May. The Friday before the prom, the absentee sheet was always three times longer than normal, because most kids took two days to prepare for the prom, getting perms, renting tuxedos and evening gowns, or just sitting at home contemplating the big event. I noticed in the days leading up to the prom that the Brownville High student body seemed to come alive again. For months, their depression over the closing of the school had been building, until most of them had come to look as dead as the gang I had living in the Levitt mansion. This year's prom would be special. It would be their last one at Brownville High.

This year, I shared in their enthusiasm as prom night approached, because Helen would be coming with me as my date. In past years, I had worn a sport coat and tie and thought nothing of it, but this time I went all out and rented a tux.

I picked Helen up at her apartment. I had to wait for her to put the finishing touches on her attire, but the wait was worth it. She was decked out in a dark brown evening dress that matched the shade of her eyes, with a split up one side almost to her hip, and her hair had been freshly permed. Maybelline highlighted her facial features to best advantage. Her perfume was so pleasant I took my sweet time about pinning on her corsage. She could have passed for one of the students, perhaps a homecoming queen. I felt like a cradle robber.

Couples stared approvingly at us as we approached the armory, but Matt Strong and Grady Fletcher stole our thunder. They pulled up with their dates in a rented limousine, complete with a uniformed driver.

This year's prom theme was early rock 'n' roll, and the armory was decorated with pictures of early Elvis, the Everly brothers, Bill Haley and the Comets, Buddy Holly and the Crickets, Fats Domino, Little Richard, Jerry Lee Lewis, Carl Perkins, James Dean, and young Marlon Brando, despite the fact that the latter two were not rock singers. I couldn't help but reflect that the Levitt mansion was not the only place in Brownville where there were ghosts tonight.

The band was in full swing when we arrived, but no one was dancing. Helen and I made our greetings to the other faculty members and lit at a corner table.

Mr. Jacobs paced back and forth from the refreshment table to the exit, looking uptight, like he expected trouble. Every year he had to run off somebody's drunken date who was talking too loudly or who fell on the floor when she tried to get up to use the bathroom, and he always had to argue with students who wanted to go out to their cars to take a nip of Wild Turkey. This year everybody behaved, thanks to Tony Cunningham's dreams. I supposed when they talked in the future about Brownville High's last prom, the verdict would be that it was a rather dull affair.

It was anything but dull to Helen and me. We laughed and talked all evening and did all the slow dances. When the other faculty members looked at us, I detected some envy. They were here out of duty, and the magic did not seem to rub off on them the way it did on us.

The students seemed to realize that we were caught up in the spirit of the prom. They ushered Helen and me over for a portrait. When I went to get Helen some punch, Terry Graham pulled me aside and said, "I hope you get lucky tonight, Mr. Fellars."

"I'm already lucky, Terry," I told him.

At one point, I ran into Julie Summer. She was with Marty Wilcox, a good sign. Marty was in the Beta Club and was a far cry from Julie's usual pick in guys.

"You're looking good tonight, Julie," I told her.

She gave me a million-dollar smile and squeezed my arm. "Thank you, Mr. Fellars. And thanks a million for helping me."

It was the last time I would see her alive.

Helen and I sat at our table a while longer and watched the students mingle. They were all beautiful, even the ugly ducklings who were nobodies in a corner desk at school. I still wonder what sacrifice some of their parents had to make to allow them to show up in the attire they wore.

At one point during an oldie, I think it was a Tams song called "I Been Hurt," I looked over in the corner where the candlelight didn't reach and thought I saw Tony Cunningham slow-dancing with

Sharon Summer in the shadows. When I poked at Helen and pointed, they were gone.

At another point, when I went to use the men's room, I spotted Bubba Wilson standing by Mr. Jacobs, helping him look for trouble. Bubba stared right through me, as if I were a ghost.

I saw Jane Larimore, now shriveled like fruit at the end of the season, a wallflower by the punch bowl. I was glad Will Masters had taken his leave when he did. I don't think he could have resisted waltzing over to her, tapping her on the shoulder, flashing his crooked smile, and drawling in her ear, "Hello, Sugarlips. You're looking mighty spiffy tonight in your Sunday best."

When the music paused long enough for me to be heard, I leaned over to Helen and said, "Let's go outside and get some fresh air."

The highway in front of the armory was up a hill, and we sat on the retaining wall below the road.

I took Helen's hand. "Thanks for coming with me tonight. It's the first time in a lot of years I've had a date for the prom. It makes it a lot more fun."

She smiled, showing her dimples. "Thanks for asking me, Bill. I just hate it we didn't attend the last two proms together."

"If I'd only known then what I know now, I'd have asked you."

She lowered her head. "Just what did you think of me before we started seeing each other?"

"First impression?"

"First impression. Be honest."

"I wasn't very impressed. I thought you were a little too gung ho. You seemed a little too eager to please the administration. When you explained the new computer system, I thought you were talking down to the faculty. It's a good thing first impressions aren't always lasting. I came to see you're a good person. If I hadn't believed that, I wouldn't have asked you to help me get the Baucoms a marriage license. I never considered asking you to the prom."

"Why not?"

"For one thing, I'm eleven years older than you."

She giggled. "You obviously don't read romance novels."

I shook my head. "Can't say as I do."

"It's not unusual for the hero to be ten years older than the heroine. That goes along with what psychology texts say."

"Those I do read. And you're right. The most stable relationships occur when one of the partners is a decade or so older than the other. That's because you have a father figure or a mother figure."

"So you see, Dad? You don't have an excuse for not asking me earlier," she said with a twinkle in her eye.

"Okay. I plead guilty. Now, what did you think of me before we started seeing each other?"

"First impression?"

"Yeah. Be honest."

"I wasn't any more impressed with you than you were with me. I couldn't get over how messy your office was the first time I saw it. It's worse than your room. But I thought you were a good counselor. You're good with kids."

"Yeah, I'm good with kids and animals. It's women that give me fits."

"Maybe you haven't picked the right women to be friends with."

"I didn't pick the right one to be married to." I immediately regretted bringing up my ex. "It's a shame that one woman can give you a bad opinion of the whole female sex."

She leaned her head on my shoulder. "If that's true, then the right woman could give you a favorable opinion of the whole female sex."

"You've already done that. Thanks."

"I'm flattered."

"I mean it. My mom worries about me because I haven't wanted any female companionship since I got divorced. She likes you."

"Does she pressure you to see women?"

"No. Does your mom? To see men, I mean?"

She laughed. "Every time she calls. She thinks it's terrible that I'm twenty-nine and haven't gotten married. She's afraid I'll be an old-maid librarian."

We were quiet for a long moment. It was a clear night and the stars were particularly bright.

"I love you, Helen," I said.

She squeezed my hand. "I love you, too, Bill. That's a start, isn't it?"

"Yeah. I can't wait to see where it leads."

I held her for a long kiss. We broke up when the sirens started. A couple of minutes later, Toby Pritchard came running out of the armory in his tux, minus his date, and hopped in his car. He peeled out of the parking lot. He was on the rescue squad.

It was a good half hour before he returned. He was walking with his head down.

"What happened?" I asked when he reached us.

"A car wreck on Lover's Lane."

"Who was it?"

"Marty Wilcox and Julie Summer."

"Oh my God!" Helen said.

"How bad was it?"

"It's bad. They took Marty to the hospital. But I think Julie is dead."

"Oh my God!" Helen said again.

"How did it happen?"

"Marty hit a deer and lost control. The car skidded into a tree on Julie's side."

He turned and went into the armory.

"Poor Sharon," Helen said. "She's going to be fit to be tied."

"I know," I said. "I dread seeing her."

34

∾

For the next few days, I counseled the living by day and the dead by night.

The district always got its money's worth out of me when someone in the community got killed. Brownville was a close-knit town, and any death affected the whole student body. Even the sixty-five-year-old drunk who got hit by a train last fall while staggering home from Sam's Party Shop was somebody's grandfather. When the victim was a member of the student body, the emotional carnage was almost more than I could handle.

Julie Summer's death virtually shut the school down the Monday after prom. By 8:30, my office was overflowing with wailing students, and teachers were sending for me to come down to their classrooms. I called Elmwood High and asked if they could spare a couple of counselors. The reinforcements came at 9:15.

After the 10:15 break, I was left with a dozen hard-core grievers. They were mostly Julie's friends, or students who'd sat next to her in class. A couple of them, Jake Cavanaugh and Tyrone Phillips, had hardly known Julie and wouldn't have given her the time of day—they used any pretext to get out of class. I predicted they would grow up to be ambulance-chasing lawyers if they could stay in class long enough to pass.

I let them all grieve for the first hour. After they had vented their frustration about how unfair life could be, I tried to help them focus on fond memories they had of Julie. The whole experience was particularly painful for me, because I had my own grief to deal with.

It wasn't any better at night at the Levitt mansion.

When I made my first visit in the wee hours of the morning after prom night, Helen and I could hear Sharon Summer's wails from the street. She was the only female left, and the guys were at a total loss in dealing with her.

She was in denial. "She can't be dead. She can't be dead," she kept saying. Helen's warm embrace seemed to comfort her.

I pulled Freddy Seaton aside. "Has Julie shown yet?"

He shook his head. "She may have crossed over if she was at peace with herself. If she didn't cross over, she won't show until the undertaker fixes her up."

"Let me know if she does."

He nodded. "She's going to be confused and upset. The first night's always the worst."

Aside from Sharon, Tony Cunningham took it the hardest. I decided to start with him and work my way up to Sharon and Julie.

He sat in a rocker in the second-floor bedroom, creaking back and forth, saying nothing, staring at the black cats on the wallpaper. His eyes were unfocused.

I sat on the floor beside him and crossed my legs. "It's tough, isn't it, Tony?"

"Yeah, it's tough. I went all out to keep anybody from ending up like me."

"She didn't end up like you, Tony. It was a deer. It couldn't be helped."

"It don't make me feel no better."

"You've got to focus on what you've accomplished, Tony. You set out to give kids an important message, and you succeeded. This was the first dry prom I've ever seen."

He was silent for a moment. The creaking of his rocker was a lonely sound.

"I was looking forward to the prom, Mr. Fellars. That's how I was going to rate myself. I know they didn't get wasted because of alcohol or drugs. But it still spoils it for me."

I nodded. "It spoils it for me, too, Tony. It was a night Miss Noble and I were going to remember. But considering what Sharon is going through, I figure it's kind of selfish of me to dwell on my ruined evening. Does that make sense?"

He cut his eyes away from the wall to meet mine. They were no longer unfocused. "I get your drift."

"Who knows?" I continued. "If you hadn't reached all those kids, there might have been a carload of them killed. Maybe you feel like what you did won't last. But these kids experienced something nobody can explain. I've got a feeling they'll be talking about it for years."

His lips curled into a faint sad smile. "I did have them going, didn't I?"

"You sure did. How did you group them in the dreams?"

"I picked girls that hung together and guys that hung together, mostly. I paired the girls up with guys they went out with, or talked about going out with. I did a lot of eavesdropping. In some cases, I put people together that hated each other's guts, like Millie Hinson and Perry Logan, just for the sake of variety."

"You're a real dog, Tony."

His smile became more distinct. "I know."

"Your job's not over yet. I'm going to need all the help I can get with Julie."

"I know that too. I been there."

I waited until Sharon's hysteria died down, and then I went to work on her. We sat on the couch in the den. Somehow she had managed to manufacture tears that streaked her mascara. I dabbed her cheeks with a Kleenex. Her tears were cold.

"It was all for nothing, Mr. Fellars," she said. "We worked so hard to set her straight. Just when we get her turned around, this happens. It's just not fair."

"No, it isn't fair," I agreed.

"She would have made it, too. If she was just going to go out and waste her life, it would have been different. But she would have made her grandmother proud. It was too late for me, but she had a chance. How am I supposed to handle that?"

"I don't know. I'm not sure how to handle it myself."

"It was all for nothing," she said.

"It wasn't all for nothing. You turned her away from her old life."

"This pretty much cancels that fact out, doesn't it?" she said bitterly.

"No, it doesn't."

She gave me a puzzled look. "How do you figure?"

"Most people would rather face eternity with clean lives. Think about it. When people find out they're terminal, what do they do? They try to clean the slate. You were trying to help her make a decent life for herself, but you also helped her prepare to face death."

She stared down at her hands. She was slowly wringing them. "Sorry, that doesn't help."

"I'm not finished. You don't know that she hasn't already crossed over. You're all stuck here because you're not ready to go on. Maybe you got her ready."

She didn't say anything for a long moment. The tick-tock of the grandfather clock in the next room filled the void.

"I almost went over last weekend," she said. "Now I wish I had. I wish I'd never seen this."

"I wish I'd never seen it either, Sharon. But I'm glad you didn't go over. It's like I told Tony. Your job's not finished yet. If she is stuck on this side, she's going to need you now as much as she ever did. You're going to have to help me send her over."

"I can't even send myself over now."

"That's what I'm trying to tell you. You and Julie are going to have to find your way over together."

35

∽

Julie Summer showed up Monday evening in her prom dress. Her appearance was a credit to the mortician's skills. Death had not robbed her of her beauty, a fact that somehow added to the tragedy of her untimely demise.

She was an emotional wreck. I had not had to deal with the others in the immediate after-throes of death. It was a horrifying experience I hope I never have to endure again. It took a full two hours to get her to the point that I could reason with her.

I sat her on the same couch in the Levitt house where I had talked to Sharon the day before. The others clustered around and watched. Sharon sat on the other side of her, holding her hand.

She went through predictable phases of grief. First, as with her sister, there was denial.

"I can't believe it. I can't be dead. I'm too young to die. I'm only seventeen."

Her words reminded me of the old news clipping that made the rounds during Red Ribbon week, in which a dead teenage victim of an alcohol-related car wreck lay in his casket and watched the grieving file by. As he observed his broken friends and family members and as he reflected on the things he would never get a chance to do, the dead youth concluded by saying, "I'm too young to die. I'm only sixteen."

The others understood her feelings.

Tony Cunningham said, "Honey, I've been dead for eleven years, and I still can't believe I'm dead."

Freddy Seaton added, "I got killed forty-three years ago, and I haven't been able to put it behind me yet."

Their words did not mollify her. "I didn't do anything to deserve this. I was living right, for a change. Why did this have to happen to me, Mr. Fellars?"

"I can't answer that, Julie. I don't know why children get leukemia, or why some kids are born crippled, or why young people have to die. What I do know is that when you're faced with something you can't change, you've got to find a way to deal with it and move on. The longer you wait, the harder it's going to be."

She wasn't ready to hear that just yet.

She remained in denial. "I had my whole life ahead of me. I can't believe it. I can't be dead."

Her grief finally gave way to anger. She was determined to cheat death at any cost.

"I'm not going," she vowed.

"If you don't go, I don't go," Sharon said. "You were my project."

"That's your problem."

"No, it's our problem. We're in the same boat now, in case you haven't noticed."

"Oh yeah, I've noticed. We were in the same boat when Mom died. We were in the same boat when Dad married Brenda and Brenda kicked us out of the house. We were in the same boat when Grandma tried to make us go to school and not hang out with creeps and we wouldn't listen. And now that we're dead, we're in the same boat. Our boat keeps sinking, in case you haven't noticed."

Sharon's voice took on an edge of exasperation. "Julie, we can't stay on this side."

"Watch me," Julie said defiantly. "If anybody over there wants me, they'll have to come and get me and drag me over."

Julie Summer's funeral was on Tuesday afternoon, and practically the whole school was there.

Most of the students turned out in their Sunday best, and it was the only time except for prom night and, for the ones who went, Sunday school that they dressed up. The ones who came in blue jeans and sneakers and baseball caps did not do so out of disrespect. They did not consider their attire to be an index of their grief.

The service was held in the First Baptist Church, where George and Linda Sue Baucom had been married six weeks before. Unlike that night, when the furnace malfunction had brought a chill to the room, we sat in a sweltering late spring heat, and paper fans undulated across the pews. The crowd spilled over into the churchyard.

In twos and threes, the grieving made a quiet pilgrimage to Julie's open casket beneath the pulpit, where it rested in a garden of many-colored flowers. They looked down on her sleeping body, the one she'd left behind, and their quiet sobs could be heard over the peaceful death hum of the church organ. Helen and I didn't go up. We knew we would say our goodbyes later.

The ushers led the family in. The grandmother had to be supported by both arms. Her face was covered with a black veil. Brenda Summer tried to comfort her husband, but he seemed to distance himself from her with his body language. She had made him choose between wife and daughters. He had chosen the wife and lost both daughters. Regret was written all over his pinched face. The strain between the couple showed.

There were two sermons, one inside the church and one at the graveside in the cemetery that would eventually claim Julie and her sister. The poor minister searched for words where none would suffice. Two of Julie's classmates delivered tearful eulogies that made their voices crack. It was a touching service.

I knew the Summer sisters were watching.

36

～

True to his word, Bennie Norris returned to Brownville High from the alternative school in the middle of fourth quarter and strutted down the hall with his pants sagging and his cap on backward, belting out the lyrics of Kanya West's "Runaway" at the top of his lungs, always late to class. The alternative school was forced to release him for lack of space due to an influx of more violent referrals. Whenever a teacher or Mr. Spruce, the assistant principal, called him out in the hall, he always had plenty of lip to give back. He kept pushing the envelope until he was finally expelled for the remainder of the year after the drug dog sniffed out a half-eaten hamburger in his locker and turned up a stolen Glock under his algebra book.

Shelby Nichols returned from spring break and claimed she'd lost her baby. The Brownville gossip machine claimed her father had sent her to Atlanta for an abortion. The school nurse made an attempt to refer her to me, but she decided she didn't want to discuss her situation with a male. I get that sometime with girls and their female problems.

Larry Ringer was another matter. He came to me fuming because he had been left out of the decision on whether to keep the baby, and in the process confirmed the abortion rumors. I listened and sympathized, but when I tried to point out that fatherhood was a lifelong commitment and that he had not given Shelby confidence that he would make the commitment, he tuned me out and went his way.

The school drop files were housed in a fireproof vault up a flight of stairs from my office, in a small room that had once served as the projector room for the auditorium just down from my office. Permanent records of Brownville High grads had been computerized some years back, but the files of dropouts were not computerized. They were housed in two filing cabinets in the corner of the room, discarded like the students they represented. I had an occasion to visit the drop files the day I added Julie Summer's permanent record to the collection of students who would never graduate.

I rifled through the files, as I always do, reacquainting myself with the faces of students who never made it past the ninth grade and wondering what happened to them.

I knew what happened to some of them. You could see them hanging out on street corners, watching traffic go by. Ben Farber, the town drunk thumbing a ride to Sam's Party Shop. The usual gang of loafers who gathered at Wertz's Café for breakfast every morning. Fifty-year-old Tony Garrison still living with his elderly mom and helping her spend her social security check. Mazie Cannon bumming cigarettes off people coming out of the Pantry. These were the ones that never left Brownville. The wasted youth of Brownville decades out of high school. Opportunity was just as dead for them as it was for Randy Galphin and Tony Cunningham.

The sad thing is, I could look at the current student body and predict who would end up in the drop files. Bennie Norris would probably never finish school. Nor Larry Ringer. Wendy Echols, who had a reputation as everybody's girl, would probably end up pregnant and use the baby as an excuse to drop out.

To me, the school drop files represented a failure of the education system. I was part of the system, promoting the message to stay in school. Kids dropping out was a slap in my face. I took it personally.

Maybe Larry Ringer was right. Maybe they were the vanguard of the useless generation. Maybe they were ahead of their time.

It was a depressing thought.

It's funny how looking at the drop files had never bothered me so much before the dead teenagers began to unload on me. They changed my whole outlook on life.

37

Andy Bundrick wasn't exactly at the top of Chadwick Corley's hit list, but when the opportunity for revenge presented itself, Chadwick wasn't able to resist.

Andy had tormented Chadwick only once, but in this case, once was enough. It had been on the eighth grade class trip to Sea World. They were staying at the Holiday Inn in Orlando. Andy had lured Chadwick's roommate out of the room their first night, then poured lighter fluid across the threshold and lit it. He had pounded on the door and run.

When Chadwick had opened the door and faced the wall of flames, he had panicked and screamed his head off. Students had popped out of their rooms to see what the racket was. Chadwick still remembered them standing there laughing at him on the other side of the flames. Mrs. Peabody had come and thrown a blanket over the fire. Nobody would tell her who the culprit was, but scuttlebutt had it that it had been Andy. When Chadwick had tried to return the favor, Mrs. Peabody had become more vigilant, and Chadwick was caught. He had been restricted to his room the next day while his classmates explored Sea World.

Chadwick remembered the incident when he saw Andy's blue 2008 Chevy pickup pull up to Fred's Market the Saturday afternoon of the prom with a fishing boat behind it and Pete Grogan and Joe Hall in the cab with him. When he saw Andy come out of the store with two cases of Bud, he knew he might get a chance to repay an old debt. He knew where they were going. They often camped at Ira Cavandish's pond and fished into the night.

They had killed off half a case by the time they reached the pond. They unloaded the boat and fished until dark, then made a campfire and cooked up a mess of their catch. They told dirty jokes and traded gossip they had heard from their wives. When they finished the two cases of Bud, they cracked a bottle of Johnny Walker Red and sang bawdy songs. They had a tent, but they passed out in folding lounge chairs before they got around to erecting it.

Chadwick waited until Joe got up in the early morning hours to go relieve some of the pressure on his bladder from the considerable amount of alcohol he had taken. Using the anchor rope from the boat, he tied Andy's arms and legs to the lounge chair. He took the gasoline can from the boat and poured a circle of gasoline around Andy's lounge chair. He ignited the gasoline and screamed, "Fire!"

Pete leaped to his feet and Joe ran out of the bushes.

Andy fought his way out of a drunken stupor and blinked at the fire.

Joe and Pete stood staring at him. Then they began to laugh.

"Wake up, Andy. You're in hell," Joe said, and they laughed harder.

Andy struggled violently to free himself from the chair.

"Help. Help!"

"I would put it out for you, Andy, but I just emptied my water tank." Laughter.

Andy gaped at the circle of fire around him. "Untie me. This isn't funny."

"It looks pretty funny from this side of the fire," Pete said.

Andy continued to wriggle in bondage. "Get me out of here, hang it. I'm going to be burned."

"Aw, Andy, you got a good foot and a half before the flames get you. I'd curl my toes up, though, just to be safe."

"If you don't get me out of here, RIGHT NOW, I'm going to kill you both."

They continued to laugh, and their laughter inspired a string of obscenities. The obscenities were met with more laughter.

In his struggle to free himself, Andy managed to tip the chair over. Joe and Pete slapped their knees and bent double in laughter.

With no help from his friends, Andy finally managed to free himself from the rope. He stalked over to the pickup, making no effort to extinguish the fire.

Joe and Pete continued to laugh until they saw Andy walk over, cradling the Winchester. The blood in his eye doused their laughter.

Joe held up his hand. "Now, wait a minute, Andy. We were just having some fun. Put the gun down."

"I told you I was going to kill you if you didn't get me loose."

"If you'da been in any real danger, we'd have helped you, Andy," Pete said, his voice now serious.

A maniacal grin consumed Andy's face. "Yeah? Well, guess what? Right now you guys are in real danger. You need somebody to help you."

"Come on, now, Andy. Put the gun down."

"First I want to hear you beg."

"Please put the gun up, Andy," Joe said.

"We're real sorry, Andy. We won't do it again."

Andy nodded. "That's good. Now I want to see you dance."

"Aw, come on, Andy."

He fired the Winchester, kicking up dirt a foot from Joe's feet.

"Hang it, Andy, this ain't funny."

"From this side of the gun, it looks pretty funny."

He fired again. On the third shot, the rifle was violently deflected by some unseen force. The bullet hit the front of Andy's pickup. There was the sound of spilling water.

Joe walked over to the truck. "Nice shot, Andy. I think you've killed the radiator."

"Your aim was about ninety degrees off," Pete said.

"I didn't do it! The gun moved itself!"

Joe walked back over to Andy. "Why couldn't you have just shot the tire? At least we could have changed it."

"What do you care? It's my truck."

"Maybe I don't feel like walking four miles back home."

Andy's temper had not cooled all the way down. "Mind your tone with me, Joe. I still got this gun in my hand."

"He's right, Joe," Pete said. "That was a pretty dumb trick for you to play on him."

Joe wheeled around. "Me? You did it while I was taking a whiz."

"Oh, no, I didn't. I woke up when you yelled, 'Fire.'"

"I never yelled, 'Fire.'"

"Well if you didn't do it, who did?"

Andy lowered the Winchester. "Well, I sure as blazes didn't do it."

38

Johnny Brown had always been a hyperactive child, and he was one of the hundreds of thousands of students who go to the school office every day at lunch time for their dose of Ritalin. Before the doctors made their diagnosis, Della Brown was convinced she had spawned a child of the devil. She always marveled at the Hyde-to-Jekyll transformation that took place half an hour after he swallowed the pill. She once vowed to skip the country if they ever ran out of the magic stuff.

Johnny Brown hated school and was what one of my college professors once called a "seven-hour idiot." That is, from 8:00 a.m. until 2:35 p.m., when faced with the academic challenges of the classroom, he was dumb as dirt. But get him away from a school setting and put some tools in his hand, and he suddenly became a genius.

Every time I poked my head in Johnny's classroom on business, Johnny would always beg me to get him out of class. Whenever there was a call for a volunteer to run an errand, his hand would be the first one up. If all else failed, he would sit in class and pick at a scab to make it bleed so he would have an excuse to go to the office for a Band-Aid. He always took the long way there and back.

If Johnny's teachers made him miserable, the feeling was mutual. He had a habit of running down the hall and skidding to a stop at the door, providing vocal effects along the way, "EEEEEEEEEEEKKK!" that made his homeroom teacher cringe.

"Look at it this way," Sandra Burnsides had said after hearing her complain. "At least you don't have to take him home with you at the end of the day."

"But Della Brown excuses everything he does."

"She has to love him. She's his mother."

Della Brown got fed up with Johnny's teachers sending notes home every other day complaining about his atrocious behavior. She finally threw up her hands and told the eighth grade team leader, "If you want to see a bad child, I'll show you a bad child. I'll take him off his medicine, and you'll see how good you've had it." She made good on her promise, and two weeks later, the teacher called back to say "uncle" and beg her to restore his medication. That incident broke Johnny's teachers of complaining about his behavior.

Lester Brown, Johnny's dad, had been a farm hand at Carl Frazier's dairy. He had recruited Johnny to help him, and one summer he witnessed what no parent should have to witness, the death of his child. Lester Brown was an Army reservist who had survived Desert Storm, but barely a year after Johnny was killed, he died in a helicopter crash during maneuvers at Fort Benning. He left behind a small son named Otis and a wife who struggled to make ends meet as a beautician.

During the week of Julie Summer's funeral, when I was helping her and her sister over their grief, I was also helping Johnny Brown put the finishing touches on his project to help his mother. Like Mike Sanders, Johnny Brown figured he owed his mother big-time. She'd always stuck by him despite all the grief he'd given her. Like Sandra Burnsides said, she was his mother; she had to love him. The one thing he figured she needed was a decent man in her life to help her raise up her remaining son.

Johnny had seen enough men around Brownville like Carl Riley, the deadbeat stepdad Mike Sanders had run off, to know that Flannery O'Conner was right: a good man is hard to find. Like Helen Noble, Johnny was very picky.

Johnny spent his days watching men at the post office, at the café, at the Community Cash, at the library, and on the corner of Main Street. He soon started following a rural mail carrier named Martin Northridge. Martin was a lifelong bachelor who lived with his parents on Holliday Road. He spent a lot of time at the library in the magazine and biography sections. He had a green thumb and seemed to dote on his nephew and niece. He was probably the best Brownville had to offer, but Johnny knew instinctively that there would probably be no magic between Martin and his mom. Martin was just too different from the kind of man his dad had been. He became very discouraged.

"I've got an idea," I said to him one evening as we reviewed his progress. "There's no flame like an old flame. Who was your mom's high school sweetheart?"

"I have no idea."

"I'll get Miss Noble to check the old yearbooks and see if we can find any clues."

He gave me a dejected look. "That's no good. She didn't go to Brownville High."

"No? Where did she go?"

"Deep Valley. She moved to Brownville because that's where Dad was from."

"All right. You go snooping around in your mom's house and see if you can find anything that will help us. A yearbook, old photos, letters. Even the names of old friends will help.

The next time I visited the Levitt house, he had the goods for me. A 1993 yearbook and two old school newspapers he'd found in his mother's attic.

"It looks like Mom and a guy named Danny Vaughn were a hot item," he announced. He opened one of the newspapers. "They're mentioned in a school gossip column. It says, 'Ask Danny Vaughn and Della Peale who caught them necking in the book room third period.'" He turned the newspaper to the masthead and looked at the date. "This is during my mom's freshman year. Two years later, Danny Vaughn graduated. Here's the class will."

He opened the other newspaper and read, "'I, Danny Vaughn, being of sound mind, hereby will my curly locks to Mr. Norton, my ability to talk my way out of traffic tickets to Coach Jones, and all my love to Della Peale.' So they were together for at least a couple of years."

"What does he look like?"

He leafed through the yearbook until he found the picture again. "Here."

He was a nice-looking young man, who indeed did have curly locks, along with a firm jaw and eyes that probably would make a young girl's heart flutter.

"What do you think?" I asked.

"He's worth checking out."

"Okay. I'll take a drive over to Deep Valley and see what I can find out."

Johnny closed the yearbook. "He's probably married."

"Maybe so," I said. "But even if he did marry, statistically speaking, you've got about a fifty percent chance he's divorced by now."

I drove over to Deep Valley the next Saturday and stopped at the first barbershop I came to. I've learned that if you want male gossip, that's the best place to go.

I leafed through a couple of issues of *Guns and Ammo* and *True Detective* magazines while I waited. Along the wall opposite the barber chairs, above the mirrors, was a stuffed trout, a painting of a mountain lake, and a sign that said, "If Guns Are Outlawed, Only Outlaws Will Have Guns."

When it was my turn to sit in the chair, the barber said, "I don't believe I've seen you around these parts before."

He had a bad haircut—not particularly good advertising, but I didn't figure he'd cut his own hair.

"No, I'm just passing through. Do you happen to know a guy named Danny Vaughn?"

Several customers sitting in the chairs waiting their turn looked up.

The barber chuckled. "Ain't many folks around here that don't know Danny Vaughn."

"I've got a friend that went to high school with him. What's he up to now?"

I got a quick report on Danny Vaughn. He owned a local hardware store and construction business. He was indeed no longer married, but not because of divorce. His wife had died of breast cancer two years ago. He had two teenage daughters. Some of the other customers chipped in comments that added to his resume, and they all lauded him highly.

Johnny was pleased at what I had learned. We both agreed that Danny needed to be evaluated further. I went to Spartanburg and hired a private investigator. I was tempted to borrow from Randy Galphin's Warfield funds to pay him but concluded that would set a dangerous precedent. I ended up drawing $750 out of my savings for the retainer fee. Johnny gave me four questions for the detective to answer.

I received the report in less than a week. I dropped by the Levitt house and sat down with Johnny.

"First question. 'How does he get along with children?' He has two daughters who have exemplary school records. He coaches Little League. He chaired two Special Olympics. He lets the neighborhood kids swim in his pool. How's that?"

"It gets a passing grade."

"Second question. 'How does he treat his mother?' He visits her regularly. He takes her out to eat twice a week. He pulls the chair out for her to sit down and opens the car door for her. He still says, 'Yes, ma'am.' Nobody's heard him say a cross word to her, except for when he was a teenager, and that doesn't count, because teenagers aren't human."

Johnny let that crack pass. "Go on."

"Third question. 'What kind of marriage did he have?' Basically, he treated his wife the same way he treats his mother, except for saying, 'Yes, ma'am.' And he doesn't French kiss his mother."

"I hope not. So far he's batting a thousand. Let's hear the final one."

"'What are his faults?' No skeletons in his closet. He's a workaholic. He smokes three cigars a day. He has a reputation for being forgetful. His daughters complain at school because he leaves the toilet seat up. That's all the guy could find."

I gave Johnny a recent photo of Danny Vaughn the detective had furnished. Johnny stared at it for a long moment.

"I wonder why they broke up."

"Who knows? I've seen a lot of high school romances, and very few of them end up in marriage."

He gave me back the photo. "Let's go for it. How do we get them together?"

We brainstormed half a dozen schemes to bring them together and settled on the strong arm of the law. We would deliver phony subpoenas to Danny Vaughn and Della Brown to appear at 8:00 a.m. one morning at the Deep Valley courthouse. The subpoenas would be served close to 5:00 p.m. the previous day so neither could call the courthouse for an explanation. They would show up at the courthouse and be told that the subpoenas must be a mistake. They would each find out that the other was available, and if there was any magic left, they would have an opportunity to pursue it.

After we made final plans, Johnny seemed to have second thoughts. "What if he turns out to be a wife beater?"

"There's no guarantee they'll be happy, Johnny," I told him. "You've got to realize that. Any relationship is a risk. But we've screened him the best we could. Do you want to back out?"

"No."

Johnny was very distraught when Julie Summer's death delayed the rendezvous between his mom and Danny Vaughn. Once the decision had been made to proceed, he was eager to get on with it. I had wanted to wait until Friday to deliver the subpoenas, but at his urging, we decided to do it on Thursday, two days after Julie's funeral.

I would deliver Danny's subpoena, and Freddy Seaton would deliver Della's. We would both need disguises. I dug my dad's Air Force blues out of my mom's attic, and Freddy borrowed a Sam Browne and two badges from the police station. With my dad's Air Force uniform and one of the badges and the Sam Browne, he looked like a cop.

I got out my blonde hair dye and went in a coat and tie. I wasn't about to drive into Deep Valley in a fake cop's uniform. I did take one of Freddy's badges but prayed I wouldn't have to use it. If Danny didn't buy my story, I hoped I could outrun him.

"I'm looking for Mr. Vaughn," I said to the lady at the counter of Vaughn's Hardware.

"I'm sorry. He took the afternoon off."

I looked at my watch. It was 4:55. It was too late to call off Freddy's delivery. If Della got her subpoena and Danny didn't get his, they wouldn't connect, and she would probably be more suspicious of our next ploy.

I smiled at the woman behind the counter. "I'm an old friend of his, and I was just passing through. Do you have any idea where he is?"

"He's probably at home."

I got his address and drove over. It was a two-story colonial in the right neighborhood, with two late-model Fords in the drive.

One of his daughters came to the door. I judged she was about fourteen. She had a sandwich in her hand.

"Hello. I'm looking for Mr. Vaughn."

"He's in the pool."

I flashed my badge just long enough, then quickly put it in my pocket before she realized it had Brownville instead of Deep Valley on it. "I'm from the courthouse. I've got to see him today."

She disappeared inside the house. He came out a couple of minutes later with a towel on his shoulders, dripping on the stoop. His curls had receded a little, and his gut spilled slightly over the top of his trunks. Otherwise, he looked pretty much like he had in high school.

"Can I help you?"

"Are you Daniel Vaughn?"

"Yes."

"Mr. Vaughn, I'm from the courthouse. I'm sorry to bother you at home, but I had to see you today. I have a subpoena for you to appear at the courthouse first thing tomorrow morning."

I slapped the subpoena in his hand.

He looked at it. "What's this all about?"

"Sir, I don't know. I just deliver them."

I turned to leave.

"This is kind of short notice, isn't it?"

"Yes, sir, but I just deliver them when I get them."

I backed out of his drive instead of going around the circle. I didn't want him to get a look at my tag number.

I can't tell you exactly what happened at the courthouse the next day, because Johnny wasn't there to hear it. From what he overheard later at his mom's beauty parlor, Danny Vaughn showed up with his lawyer. The court clerk and probate judge were puzzled over the subpoenas, then decided it was a hoax. They promised a full investigation. Danny was angry at first but soon dismissed his attorney and spent the next half hour talking to Della.

The call came that afternoon. Danny Vaughn phoned Della just before she closed her shop and asked her out.

I wish I could tell you that they married and lived happily ever after, but I can't. I did keep up with them for about a year, and the last I heard, they were engaged. But I also heard they were having some problems. Della was catching grief from the two daughters with exemplary school records, who probably felt jealous because Della was stealing time from their dad. Danny's mother, for whom he pulls the chair out to sit down and for whom he opens the car door, also disapproved of Della, perhaps for the same reason. I stopped keeping tabs on Johnny's mom because, as time went by, I was afraid of how the relationship might turn out. If the divorce statistics gave her an even chance that Danny Vaughn would be available, the statistics on second marriages were even more dismal. Besides, I didn't want to be over in Deep Valley checking on things and accidentally have Danny Vaughn hear my voice and wonder why it sounded familiar.

There were no dark clouds on the horizon that late spring, however, when Johnny brought magic back to his mother's life. I found it touching that, like Randy Galphin, he left his mother a clue that he had been her Cupid. The signature on her subpoena had been a poor imitation of Deep Valley Probate Judge David Clarkson's. But the signature on Danny Vaughn's subpoena had been his own. He hadn't put his own name on his mother's subpoena because it would have put her on guard that the document was bogus. Her reaction to seeing Danny's subpoena was that someone had played a cruel hoax by forging her son's signature.

But perhaps someday, if the romance blossoms to full maturity, she will contemplate the strange incident that reunited her with her high school heartthrob. And in doing so, perhaps she will dig out the old subpoena and compare the signature with her son's and see that they are identical. And perhaps she will recall that the cop who delivered it looked a lot like a dead soldier named Freddy Seaton.

I found something else Johnny Brown did touching. When I stopped at Walmart to buy my mother a gift the next day, it dawned on me why Johnny had been so desperate to pull off the reunion of old flames before the weekend. Sunday was Mother's Day, and Danny Vaughn was his Mother's Day present. I was sorry I couldn't let his teachers know what a big heart the little pain in the neck had.

39

M om had her stroke two days after Mother's Day. The United Parcel Service delivery man heard her call from her bedroom after he rang the doorbell. He summoned Silas Stanton, our nearest neighbor at the next farm over. Silas called me at school.

"Bill, you need to get back home. She's all right, but your mom's on the floor and she can't get up."

"Have you called an ambulance?"

"She wouldn't let me. She wants you here."

"I'm on my way."

I found her lying on the floor between her bed and the wall, and she couldn't move her right side. She had tried to get up to use the bathroom not long after I left for school and had rolled off the bed. She had soiled herself and wanted to be cleaned up before anyone carried her away. I sent Silas to call the ambulance while I cleaned her up.

She was remarkably upbeat about the situation. When the emergency technicians arrived, she smiled and said, "I suppose you wonder why I've called you here."

I followed the ambulance to the hospital. About halfway there, my heart cut a flip when the ambulance suddenly flashed its lights and accelerated from fifty-five to seventy-five. I sped after it.

By the time I parked my car, they had her inside. I spent two hours sitting in the emergency waiting room. When I was able to see her, she gave me a list of chores to do. That was her way. She was very methodical and in control. I went home and packed her suitcase.

I was able to talk to the doctor by early afternoon.

"How is she?"

"She's had a stroke. Her mind is clear and there's no problem with her speech. Her right side is paralyzed. She may eventually regain some control there, but at her age, it's doubtful. The first twenty-four hours are critical. She could have another stroke."

I went about my business and hoped for the best.

Her second day in the hospital, she called in the family attorney and turned over power of attorney to me. She updated her will.

She quickly lost the good humor she had shown when she was first stricken. She badgered the doctor until he finally released her after only a week under threat of a hunger strike. They wanted to send her to Roger C. Peace Hospital in Greenville for physical therapy, but she wouldn't hear of it. She wanted to go home.

I hired a sitter for her during the day, and I took the night shift. She had no control over her bodily functions, so I had to diaper her like a baby until she learned to ask for the bedpan when she had to go. The sitter bathed her each day, but I had to set my clock every two hours at night so I could get up and turn her to prevent bed sores. A physical therapist visited twice a week while I was at school.

Mom found her dependence on me degrading, and she begged me to put her in a nursing home. I wouldn't hear of it. She became depressed and expressed regret that she hadn't died.

"I don't want to be a burden on you," she said repeatedly.

"You did the honors when I was a baby. Turnabout's fair play," I told her.

I meant that, but I could never get it across to her.

My mother's illness kept me from my work with the residents of the Levitt house. Once I settled her into a routine at home, I asked Helen to stay with her in the evenings while I finished up with them.

40

Because I was able to work with Julie Summer immediately after her death, and because she had the support of a sister who was close to crossing over, she was able to find peace with herself much faster than any of the others did. She was spared the years of disembodied torment they had faced. When I asked her if there was anything she felt like she needed to accomplish before she crossed over, she took her time reflecting on the matter. She looked back over her life, and at what she had left behind, and concluded that she would abide by Fate's decision. Sharon was burning to cross over, and it was clear that Sharon would not cross over until Julie did. She decided it would be selfish to hold Sharon back any longer.

So a week and four nights after Julie's funeral, the sisters, who were always in the same boat that kept sinking, as Julie put it, held hands and walked into eternity together. Tony Cunningham followed them up the hill.

We went back to the Levitt house and listened to Alabama's "Give Me One More Shot." We did that every time we sent somebody over.

Johnny Brown went next. His mother was seeing Danny Vaughn regularly now. He, too, began to feel an overwhelming urge to go somewhere he should have gone a long time ago and decided not to wait to see if an engagement would materialize in the weeks ahead.

"If they don't make it, at least I gave her a summer romance she'll always remember," he said wistfully.

That left Freddy Seaton, Chadwick Corley, and Steve Hall. I knew what I was going to do with Freddy, and Chad was still working on his project, but Steve was a puzzle to me.

Steve Hall was one of those kids to whom life throws a curve ball, causing them to have to grow up in a hurry and forfeit part of their childhood. Steve had been a quiet kid, whose grandmother had been the only mom and dad he ever knew. His mother had been but a child herself when he was born and was wise enough to know she was not suited for motherhood. She hadn't had the heart to have an abortion, so she'd abandoned the child to her mother and gone to Philadelphia to make a better life for herself. She had managed to convince herself that the child would be better off, and perhaps she was right. Steve had seen her maybe once every two years during his lifetime, and although she always brought him nice gifts, perhaps to appease her guilt, he had never formed an emotional attachment to her.

Esther Minton, Steve's grandmother, was as poor as the proverbial church mouse, and I still remember how depressed I was the day I made a home visit to her shack, over in what the locals call "Brownville Watts," with its peeling plaster and water-stained ceiling and a cardboard patch over a broken window. The house was clean, however, and was sprinkled with icons that reflected Esther's religious faith and her pride in her African heritage—a portrait of Martin Luther King, Jr., a plaque of appreciation given by the AME Church, a velvet painting of a Black mother holding her baby.

Esther's pride was made evident one day when Steve was in the sixth grade and his teacher sent home a note saying that Steve would be excused from paying the three-hundred-dollar cost of a class trip to Sea World in Florida. Esther came to school the next day with the money and said indignantly, "We always pay our way." Like the

Galphins, Steve and his grandmother refused to let poverty become an excuse to leech on society.

Steve's ambition was to be a sports hero, like the ones whose posters hung from his bedroom walls, and here is where life threw him a curve ball. He had been too small to make the junior varsity football team in the eighth grade, and by the time he got his growth spurt at the end of the ninth grade, he'd had to choose between playing high school sports and getting a part-time job to take financial pressure off his grandmother, the only mother and father he had ever known. His sense of maturity led him to choose the latter course, and he started spending his after-school hours working for a neighbor installing sheet rock. Since he was only fifteen, he could not work without violating child labor laws, so he was part of the underground economy, which meant subminimum wages. But the money made him feel important.

When a March storm blew the television antenna off their chimney, Steve bought his grandmother a fifteen-foot standup model and enlisted his employer's help installing it. That day, life threw him another curve ball, one he wasn't able to dodge. The metal rod made contact with a frayed wire while Steve was holding onto it, sending ten thousand volts through his body and ending his dreams of being a superstar.

S teve Hall's grandmother had died some years ago, so he didn't have the same kind of ties on this side that most of the others did. He had never outgrown his desire to be a hero. I tried without success to convince him that he was already one.

"Steve, you worked to put food on the table when your grandmother and you were alive. That should be enough to make you feel like you accomplished something."

He shook his head. "It ain't enough. I just don't feel ready yet, Mr. Fellars."

"I can't get you in the Super Bowl, Steve."

He gave me a fond grin. We had had this talk several times before, because he was the only one who hadn't started on a project. Whenever I pressed him, he always said he was holding out for a spot in the Super Bowl.

"Well, what kind of agent are you?" he asked, still grinning.

We all had tried without success to help Steve come up with a project. I once tried to enlist his help in getting Larry Ringer to see the light. An old Chinese proverb says that if you save a person's life, you are responsible for that person. So in my mind, it stands to reason that if you save a person from going down the wrong road, you could take comfort in any success the person achieves in life. This is, after all, one of the strongest motivators behind the teaching profession.

"I've got several good candidates for you, Steve," I told him. "Larry has a good mind. If you can help me get him to use it, you can share in a lifetime of accomplishments."

Leave it to Chadwick Corley to throw ice on my efforts. "If what you say is true, Mr. Fellars, then Henry Tandey should be considered one of history's greatest villains."

"Okay, Chad, I'll bite. Who was Henry Tandey?"

"He was a British soldier who had Adolf Hitler in his crosshairs during World War I and didn't pull the trigger."

I later did research on Henry Tandey and discovered that Chadwick was correct on this footnote to history. Hitler claimed to have been spared by a British soldier who, out of compassion, did not take a shot when he had Hitler in his sights, and later concluded that the soldier was Henry Tandey. Although historians believe this story is an urban legend, it was the kind of affair that would appeal to Chadwick Corley.

Chadwick pressed his argument. "So if Tandey saved Hitler's life, by your standards, he is responsible for all the evil that Hitler caused. It cuts both ways."

Sally Brock, bless her, had come to my rescue. (This conversation happened before she crossed over.)

"I don't think that's true, Chad. It was an act of kindness to spare Hitler. There was no way to know what he would do later in life."

"Then why should you take credit for the good somebody does when you save them? There's no way you can know what they will do."

"The act of kindness is its own reward. The good the person does with their life is a bonus," I said.

"And the evil a person does after you save them doesn't count against you?"

"Not when you have no way of knowing they would do evil," I said.

"So there's an ignorance exclusion clause," Chadwick said, dismissing my argument and succeeding in derailing my efforts to steer Steve Hall toward a purpose by which he could come to terms with his aborted life.

I put my hand on Steve's shoulder. "Kidding aside, Steve, it's getting late in May. School's almost out, and I'll be moving on. When Freddy and Chad go, you're going to be stuck here with Gordon Wallace and Todd Grant. That scares me."

His grin faded. "It scares me too."

An odd thought occurred to me. "I wonder why we haven't heard from Gordon lately."

Steve shrugged. "He ain't forgot about us, that's for sure."

"I wonder if it's because we scared Bubba Wilson off. Gordon was siccing Bubba on us like a dog."

Steve nodded. "Could be. Gordon's good at getting somebody else to do his dirty work. Or he coulda been doing stuff to us all along and we didn't know it. He coulda spooked that deer out in front of

Marty Wilcox's car. Or he could be laying low, hoping we'll let our guard down."

"You know him pretty well," I observed.

"Better'n I want to." He looked me in the eye, and his tone grew serious. "You know what scares me, Mr. Fellars?"

"What's that, Steve?"

"If me and Chad and Freddy go before school's out, you're going to be the one stuck here with Gordon Wallace and Todd Grant. Gordon will come at you when you don't expect him. He's good at sniffing out a man's weakness and turning it on him."

"You let me worry about that."

"Then you let me worry about being stuck here with Gordon."

"Are you telling me you're not going over until I leave Brownville?"

"No. I'm just saying I ain't ready to go over yet."

"Steve, we can't be dancing around Gordon Wallace. I'm committed to helping every one of you go over, even Gordon and Todd, if they'll let me. I'm not going to leave Brownville until you go."

"Take my word for it, Mr. Fellars. It's better for me to be stuck here with Gordon than you."

"Why?"

"He can't do nothing to me. I'm already dead."

The Brownville Fun Day Festival had been instituted by the town fathers twenty years ago as an economic gimmick to tide local businesses over until the Christmas season six months away. Many small towns in South Carolina have similar festivals—the Salley Chitlin' Strut, the McCormick Gold Rush Days, the Whitmire Party in the Pines, the Newberry Egg and Dairy Festival. This year, Brownville's Fun Day Festival fell on the last Saturday in May.

The Fun Day Festival provided an opportunity for Brownville's entrepreneurs and civic organizations to entice or shame their fellow citizens into parting with moderate doses of their hard-earned cash. The mayor and town council used the festival as a rallying point for promoting civic pride, peppering it with the usual self-serving speeches and dignitaries posing for the cameras. Chadwick Corley planned to use the festival as an instrument with which to teach the town of Brownville the meaning of the word "retribution." Chadwick planned to take his revenge against the town for years of torment by wrecking this year's Fun Day Festival.

The traditional protocol for a Fun Day weekend consisted of a parade on Saturday morning followed by a carnival and crafts fair, in which street vendors peddled T-shirts, overpriced fatty junk foods, and overpriced cheap trinkets, and culminated in a street dance on

Saturday evening, during which some unknown country band would provide the entertainment.

The Fun Day committee had decided to forego the parade this year because of the one planned for Memorial Day two days later. In its place, they concocted a kickoff program of speeches that centered around the unveiling of a statue commissioned eighteen months earlier by the town council and done by a world-renowned artist nobody in Brownville had ever heard of. The statue was modeled on a photo of L. B. Brown, the founder of the now-defunct textile mill, as a young boy. It showed the young Brown in overalls with a fishing pole slung over his shoulder, turning to wave goodbye to whoever snapped the original photo.

Of course, when the original project was commissioned, the L. B. Brown textile mill was thought to be in good health, and when it closed its doors in January, a majority of council members had favored scrapping the project. Some argued that the fact that the statue showed the mill's founder waving goodbye was too ironic a symbol to be in good taste, considering the fate of the mill. But Milam Ledbetter, Brownville's mayor, who could be counted on to oppose the town council on every issue, had managed to keep the project on schedule by pointing out that the statue had already been paid for and that displaying the work of a renowned artist (even if nobody in Brownville had ever heard of him) would be a feather in Brownville's cap.

The kickoff program took place on the football field. The bleachers were packed with men in hunting caps chewing tobacco and nipping from brown bags while Bubba Wilson and the other local law looked the other way. Sprinkled among them were women who smelled of Estee Lauder and who sported fresh perms from the day before. Vendors worked the aisles, shouting, "Hot dogs! Popcorn! Icees!" and setting off a chorus of begging by children (the ones who weren't playing tag under the bleachers). On the platform, the same one they used for graduation, sat the dignitaries in metal folding chairs, trying their best to look important. At the center of the stage was the statue, hidden under a sheet. From their corner of the bleachers, the high school band struck up "Happy Days Are Here Again."

It looked like it was going to be just another kickoff program (if you've seen one, you've seen them all) throughout Rev. Lester Howell's prayer and the opening speech by Mayor Ledbetter, until they unveiled the statue. If Ledbetter had worried that the town would complain about the symbolism of the statue, he needn't have, because there was a distraction under the sheet. It was a huge posterboard sign tied onto the statue.

The sign read:

Give me a dollar and I won't wreck your party.
—Chadwick Corley

On top of the Brown statue's head was an offering plate pilfered from the First Baptist Church, placed upside down like a cap.

A wave of snickers made its way throughout the audience as the sign registered. In the far corners of the bleachers, people rubbernecked and asked, "What does it say?" and the word was passed to them, followed by another wave of snickers. After all these years, the name Chadwick Corley still had laughing power as the butt of a joke.

Mayor Ledbetter, a short, bald man in his early fifties who talked with a nasal twang, took one look at the sign and flushed. He tore the sign off the statue, whisked off the offering-plate cap, and dropped them onto the platform. Assuming the sign was a prank inflicted by some disgruntled teen but not realizing just how disgruntled this particular teen was, he took to the podium and launched into his "Sorry 2 Percent" speech. They'd heard it all before, how 98 percent of the teenagers of Brownville were decent kids, but the sorry 2 percent of teen thugs tried to ruin it for everybody, and how he wasn't going to let them. People rolled their eyes and joked among themselves while the mayor rambled on for twenty minutes, until band director Red

Maynard had the presence of mind to strike up "Dixieland Rag" when Ledbetter paused for breath.

It was a rocky start to a disastrous day.

The town used the term "mouthwatering" to describe George Goldman's hot dogs, and everybody agreed that what made Goldman dogs a cut above the rest was the chili. The blueprint for the chili was that ubiquitous Southern trademark, the "secret family recipe." Although the recipe was as closely guarded as the Manhattan Project, I can say I've tasted diced onions, potatoes, corn, and what might be a trace of tomato sauce among the ingredients. George sold his hot dogs at his store on Highway 21 just across the Little Goose Creek bridge. Every year, he would cook up about ten thousand for the Fun Day Festival, where they sold like Harry Potter books to a public that was tired of the usual skimpy carny dogs that vendors generally hawked at such events. This year, Chadwick Corley made sure the chili vats contained an ingredient George Goldman didn't know about. A liberal dose of castor oil.

While George Goldman had never personally done Chadwick Corley any harm, his son Roger had often laughed at the pranks perpetrated by the likes of Elbert Snead and Andy Bundrick. And while the pranks had rankled Chadwick, it was the laughter of all the Roger Goldmans through the years that still rang in his ears, and it was their laughter that had given legitimacy to the pranks. Therefore, he found it fitting that George Goldman should be his instrument of punishment. "It's a case of the sins of the son being visited on the father," he said, gleefully distorting scripture.

"Don't eat the hot dogs," I warned Helen as we passed the popular Goldman stand at the end of Main Street across from Kiley Abercrombie's kissing booth. Silas Stanton's wife was looking after my sick mom so I could attend the festival.

"Why not?"

"Trust me. You don't want to know."

On Fun Day, the entire length of Main Street was closed to traffic, and Bailey Amusements laid out their array of Ferris wheel, merry-go-round, bumper cars, whirly chairs, and other rides along the length of Main Street, joined by miles of electric cords that snaked along the asphalt. The stores along Main stocked up on extra inventory and propped their doors open and were joined by street vendors that gave the town the appearance of a third-world marketplace. The crowds that poured into the street took on the illusion of a stirred-up fire ant nest. On the tennis court at the near end of Main, the town had placed eighteen rented blue Porta-Johns for the convenience of the crowd. The quantity would prove woefully inadequate.

By 6:00 p.m., people were lining up at the Porta-Johns in unhealthy numbers, but it didn't seem to dawn on anyone that anything was amiss until the Ferris wheel got stuck. The operator, a grungy-looking man with a baseball cap on backward and a cigarette hanging out of the corner of his mouth, jerked the wheel to a halt, when suddenly the handle broke off in his hand. Two other Bailey Amusement employees walked over with tools. They fumbled around the bearing joints with a wrench and screwdriver for five minutes, then shook their heads. One of them walked over to a truck and began talking on a cellular phone.

Billy Wiggins, a fourth grader whose reputation for mischief had already reached us at the high school level, stood up in his seat at the twelve o'clock position and began to shout, "Mama, I got to go! I can't hold it!"

That's when everyone seemed to become suddenly aware that they, too, had to go, because there was a noticeable shift of movement toward the tennis court end of Main. The lines in front of the

Porta-Johns became longer, and people could be seen cradling their stomachs.

From the top of the wheel, Billy Wiggins continued to complain. "I can't hold it, Mama!"

Betty Wiggins, sitting next to him, echoed her son's complaint. "Hey, you down there! Get this thing moving. My boy's got to go, and I got to go too!"

I nudged Helen toward the Porta-Johns.

Like the others, she began to sense that something bizarre was transpiring. "Bill, what's going on?"

"Corley's revenge," I whispered.

"What?"

"You remember I told you not to eat the hot dogs?"

"Yes."

"Chadwick spiked the chili with castor oil."

"Oh my God. Why?"

"He's repaying an old debt."

"Who to?"

"The whole town."

"Oh, great. Thanks for warning me."

By the time we made it to the near end of Main, the Porta-John lines had snaked across the street and were still growing. I could still hear Betty Wiggins's voice from the other end of Main. "Well, you'd better hold it if you know what's good for you. Hey down there! Can you pleeeease get this thing moving?"

Some people began abandoning the Porta-Johns and heading into the shops along Main to beg use of the bathrooms, and soon lines backed out into the street like stopped-up toilets. Others trekked off to the grove of woods beyond the railroad tracks.

"Can you believe this?" a man next to me said. "Must be something in the water."

Somebody else laughed and said, "Or maybe Chadwick Corley's mad because we didn't chip in our dollars this morning."

"I went to high school with that creep," the other man said.

Helen and I avoided looking at each other when we heard that exchange. She squeezed my hand.

There was a pounding noise as someone began beating on a Porta-John door. "Hey in there! Don't take all day. Use it or get off!"

A muffled reply. "I got the runs. This is going to take a while."

The Wagner brothers, three representatives of the most uncouth element of Brownville's lower crust, perched themselves on a rail by the post office and enjoyed the show. They either hadn't partaken of Goldman's hot dogs or had cast-iron bowels, because they seemed unafflicted by the malady that had struck the rest of the town. They began heckling the less fortunate.

When Marty Farmer, who had once stolen Chadwick's gym shoes and filled them with syrup, got in line for the second time, they gave him a hard time.

"Hey, Farmer, you don't get your second dump till everybody's been served."

And when Mary Peabody, the retired eighth grade teacher who had banished Chadwick to his room at Sea World during the Andy Bundrick incident, emerged from a Porta-John trying to maintain her prim and proper demeanor, they cheered her. She glared at them indignantly, with eyes that had once withered preadolescents, but that only served to stir up the Wagner brothers, and they began cheering everybody who exited from a toilet.

Paula Riddle, a former cheerleader and prom queen who had more than once been grossed out upon receiving a forged love letter from Chadwick, became so flustered that she walked out of her Porta-John with a tail of toilet paper four feet long wagging from the top of her skirt. The Wagner brothers fell off the rail laughing, until Bubba Wilson sauntered over and shooed them on.

If Chadwick was keeping score, I knew he was busy chalking up his winnings.

Looking back, I suppose Chadwick came down so hard on Mayor Ledbetter because, more than any other single individual, he symbolized the town. On the other hand, you could make a good case for the opinion that the good mayor was asking for it.

Mayor Ledbetter was a walking paradox, because although everybody complained about how pompous he was, he always managed to keep getting reelected. When I met him years ago, he was all smiles, until he found out I lived in Elmwood and thus couldn't vote in Brownville. Since then, he'd never wasted a minute's time with me.

He glad-handed his way to the front of one of the Porta-John lines, working the crowd. When Kit Percival stepped out from the nearest toilet, the mayor said, "Excuse me, folks. This is an emergency. I've got a spastic colon," and cut in front of everybody else. The crowd muttered angrily as he darted inside and shut the door.

"I guess he'd rather lose votes than soil his pants," Helen quipped.

A few minutes later, the door cracked open and the mayor poked his head out, trying without success to hide his enormous body. He was holding his trousers up with one hand and working the door with the other.

He grinned sheepishly. "Sorry, folks. I seem to be out of toilet paper. Could somebody send some this way?"

He closed the door. The crowd groaned.

Billy Pendar, who was on the town council, ran over from Willard's Pharmacy with a six-pack of Scott tissue, trying to muster as much dignity as he could under the circumstances. He knocked on the door, but it didn't open.

There was a rattle from the other side, and then the mayor said, "It seems to be stuck."

"Unlock it," said Billy, his cheeks reddening by the minute.

"It locks from the outside, moron. You unlock it."

"I don't have a key."

"Well, run over to town hall and get one."

The crowd grumbled the whole time Billy was gone.

He came back wheezing and panting and managed to unlock the door. As the mayor reached to snatch the pack of Scott from him, his trousers fell down to his ankles. He cursed and slammed the door.

Billy Pendar slinked off without looking at anyone.

After several moments, the mayor's Porta-John began rocking.

"Cut that out!" he yelled from inside.

"Who's doing that?" somebody asked.

"I can't see. Must be somebody on the other side."

"It serves him right."

Suddenly the mayor's Porta-John tipped full over, causing the line to jump backward. People bumped into each other and trampled on each other's feet getting out of the way. There was a hybrid wave of laughter and angry shouts. With the Porta-John now lying horizontal, you could see that there hadn't been anyone on the other side.

At that point, everything seemed to happen at once. It's difficult to describe because I'm not sure I took it all in.

One by one, the other Porta-Johns began rocking and tilting over. Laughter was replaced by a murmur of amazement from the onlookers, which, when fed by the screams from inside the potties, soon gave way to hysteria.

The street took on an embarrassing stench. People started running for their vehicles, some with their clothes obviously soiled. Pounding and shouting arose from behind the doors of the fallen Porta-Johns, and then people began crawling out from under them, their pride in shambles.

They managed to turn the mayor's Porta-John over so that the door was on top. He pounded furiously on the other side. "Let me out of here! I'm drowning!"

"It's stuck again, your honor. Billy's gone for the key."

They got the door of the mayor's john unlocked and raised it like a coffin lid. The mayor came out cursing, drenched in excrement. People quickly backed away from him.

Suddenly the crowd thinned to almost nothing. Helen and I walked back down Main Street. By the time we reached the other end, the Ferris wheel attendant had succeeded in replacing the handle and was moving the big wheel.

"There's no hurry now, Mister," Betty Wiggins was saying. "Take your sweet time. Billy couldn't hold it. And neither could I."

By late evening Mayor Ledbetter was back, his stomach settled, word had it, by a dose of Kaopectate and his nerves by a shot of brandy. The band, a local outfit called the Whistling Drifters, was set up where the infamous Porta-Johns had been. People who'd missed the excitement of the early evening began trickling in (I didn't see many returning faces). The crowd wasn't one-tenth of the usual.

The mayor and other movers and shakers were determined to put the best face on the situation. But unfortunately, Chadwick wasn't quite finished yet.

During the street dance, Rev. Howell's wife suddenly turned around and slapped Mayor Ledbetter in the face.

"I beg your pardon!" she shrieked.

The mayor started. "Martha!"

The reverend was flabbergasted. "What on earth is wrong, dear?"

She glowered at Ledbetter. "He pinched me on the buttock."

"I did no such thing."

"There was no one else behind me."

"Mayor, how dare you!"

And from there, it got ugly. Half an hour later, the party was dead and the band was packing up.

Immediately after he succeeded in humbling the town of Brownville in the most base manner possible, Chadwick Corley began to experience an overwhelming sense of loneliness, a homesickness for the other side. I took that to be a sign that he was finally coming to accept his death.

When I saw him off at the edge of the cemetery, I realized my misgivings about his retaliation against his tormentors had been misplaced. It was the only way he had been able to regain his dignity. In the end, I was almost proud of him.

42

Like all Vietnam veterans, Freddy Seaton wanted a show of appreciation for his sacrifice. He had never had to face the hostility that greeted returning veterans, but he had seen it on television as he floated lost and hopeless and unseen about his house, and he had overheard enough conversations as he wandered aimlessly and endlessly through the streets to take the pulse of the town on the subject. He had been very disturbed by what he had seen and heard. Three and a half decades after the fall of Saigon, the nation had moved on, but Freddy hadn't.

I decided to arrange for the town to say thanks to Freddy on Memorial Day. I went to Tim Boyle and cashed in on his promise to help me. We cooked up a town parade and memorial in the town square in Freddy's honor. We cautiously approached Freddy's widowed mother for her approval. She was grateful to us and agreed to help us dedicate the memorial. We then approached the mayor and town council to have this year's Memorial Day declared Freddy Seaton Appreciation Day. The town council was out of money to fund the memorial, so we hit the churches up for donations. Freddy Seaton was still very highly regarded in Brownville, and it was an easy sell.

My mother's illness came after we had laid the groundwork for Freddy's honors, but during the last couple of weeks before Memorial

Day, most of the tasks fell on Tim Boyle. I spent the Sunday before the holiday in Brownville helping him attend to last-minute details.

I stopped at the Li'l Cricket for a Coke on my way home. When I walked out of the store, a big pickup with a roll bar and searchlights on the cab pulled up and stopped short of running me down. A burly man with hair draping his shoulders and a dark goatee hopped out quickly and got in my face. His face was tracked with scars that ran out from under the rims of his aviator sunglasses. Tattoos crawled up his hairy forearms.

"Mr. Fellars?"

"Yes."

"I'm Legrand Warfield." The name added menace to his deep voice. "I need to talk to you."

"What can I do for you, Mr. Warfield?"

"You know who I am?"

"If I'm not mistaken, you're Seth's dad."

I could tell that wasn't what he wanted me to say.

"You might have heard some bad things said about me around town."

"I try not to listen to gossip."

"Well, maybe you should, because in my case, it's usually true. I'm not the kind of man you want to toy around with."

I nodded. "I can believe that."

His brow furrowed over the sunglasses. "I got reason to think you might know something about some property of mine that was stole out of the swamps."

"What makes you think that?"

"Bubba Wilson thinks it. Or at least he did. He was hot on the case, then all of a sudden, he started dragging his feet. I figure you bought him off. With my money."

I rolled my eyes. "Mr. Warfield, I didn't buy anybody off."

He stuck his finger in my face. "I think you're lying. I think you stole my money. Now, you've got about five minutes to convince me you didn't, or we're going for a ride."

"Mr. Warfield, have you ever considered putting your money in the bank?"

That was the wrong thing to say. His face flushed red. He grabbed me by the shirt. "Your five minutes are up. Let's go."

He was so close I could smell cigar smoke on his breath.

Suddenly somebody grabbed him by the shoulder and wheeled him around. It was Freddy Seaton.

"Warfield, if you want your money, you need to take it up with me."

Warfield gaped at him. "Who in blazes are you?"

"You know very well who I am. I've got a bone to pick with you, Warfield. My kid brother claims your old man spit in his ear back in the third grade. That's grounds for a family feud."

Warfield looked at the name tag on Freddy's shirt. No doubt, he had seen Freddy's portrait in town hall on the many occasions, when he was being bailed out of jail.

Warfield reached out and touched him. He looked like he didn't like what he felt.

"How come you ain't in your grave?"

"I like to go for a stroll every now and then. If you want your money, Legrand, come around to the cemetery tonight around midnight and we'll talk about it. But I advise you to drop it. That money ain't worth getting on my bad side. And if you ever hassle Mr. Fellars again, you'll never have a peaceful night's sleep for the rest of your life."

Warfield hopped in the truck and fired it up.

"Hey, Legrand," Freddy called to him as he backed up. "I expect to see you at my parade tomorrow."

We watched him squeal out onto the highway.

Freddy turned to me and said, "Mr. Fellars, what are you going to do without me after I cross over?"

"I don't know, Freddy. You make a good attack dog."

Almost the whole town turned out for Freddy's memorial parade on Memorial Day, putting the fiasco of the Fun Day Festival of two days earlier behind them. Even Legrand Warfield was there, spitting tobacco into a gutter beside Al's Barbershop while he affected a detached look that belied the unease he must have felt in the wake of Freddy's menacing invitation outside the Li'l Cricket convenience store.

The parade was held after school, because Memorial Day wasn't a holiday for us and we wanted the students to attend. The high school band marched at the head of the parade and played patriotic songs. I heard "Stars and Stripes Forever" and "America the Beautiful" on my section of the street.

People who knew Freddy paid tribute to him at the dedication of the monument. First his high school classmates, then Mrs. Williamson, his senior English teacher, followed by his commanding officer in Vietnam, retired owner of a furniture store in Raleigh. I regretted that I couldn't put in a good word for him, but I wasn't supposed to have known him.

Freddy crossed over that night, at last able to heed the lonely bugle call of "Taps" that was played at his funeral those many years before. I got Silas Stanton's wife to stay with my mom again so Helen and I both could see him off. Steve Hall was there too.

"I'll stay longer if you want me to," Freddy said to me, no doubt mindful of my run-in with Legrand Warfield.

"No. You're way overdue."

He looked at Steve Hall. "Steve, you want me to wait on you?"

"No, man. I know you're burning to go over. I'll be along directly."

So we said our goodbyes.

"You were all a sweet bunch of kids," Helen told him.

He grinned and said with a twinkle in his eye, "We weren't saints when we were alive. Most people turn into saints after they're dead. I guess that's what funeral eulogies do for you."

43

My mom's death shouldn't have come as a surprise to me, but it did. She had been as healthy as a horse all her life, and just as hardworking. She couldn't adjust to a wheelchair and hospital bed, and she detested depending on others to care for her. I think she just gave up on life and willed herself to die.

She was sitting in her wheelchair in the kitchen and had just finished picking over her evening meal. She wasn't eating like she should.

I offered to wheel her over to the television set. The physical therapist wanted her to sit up as much as possible, but she said she was tired and wanted to return to bed.

I wheeled her into the bedroom and helped her into bed. I removed her bedroom slippers and cranked the bed back down into reclining position. I was adjusting her pillow when she began to pant heavily and roll her eyes.

"Are you okay, Mom?"

"I'll be okay once I catch my breath."

"I'm going to call an ambulance."

"Please don't. I'll be fine."

I called anyway. When I returned to the bedroom, she was sweating profusely.

"Just relax, Mom. The ambulance is on its way."

"Call them and tell them not to come. I'm not going back to the hospital."

When she heard the siren come minutes later, she suddenly developed the urge to go. I placed the bedpan under her.

I let the emergency personnel in and led them to her bedroom. Before they could place an oxygen mask on her, she began to vomit.

She vomited again as they were placing her into the ambulance. I placed my hand on her forehead. It felt clammy. She looked at me, then closed her eyes.

I followed the ambulance up the road as I had before. Again, as before, the ambulance suddenly increased its speed about halfway to the hospital. Again, I sped after it.

They had already unloaded her by the time I reached the emergency room. A nurse led me into a small room down the hall from the main waiting room. I went back out to the lobby and called Helen.

By the time she arrived, I still had heard nothing. We continued to wait.

Eventually the doctor on call poked his head in the door. "Mr. Fellars, has one of the nurses talked to you about your mother?"

"No."

"I'm sorry. She didn't make it."

Helen held my hand.

The doctor sent in a nurse, who gathered written information from me. Then I went home to grieve.

I attended the family visitation at the funeral home two nights later. Helen and I arrived early and viewed the body privately. As I saw her in repose, I recalled with a tinge of guilt the bad joke I had made about fearing that someday I would walk in and find her several days dead.

Mom had prearranged everything, so there was nothing for me to do but go through the motions. I greeted a long line of family members and old friends I hadn't seen in years. The district superintendent paid his condolences, along with Mr. Jacobs and most of the teachers at school. Tim Boyle showed up, along with many students and residents of Brownville.

At about 8:00 p.m., my ex-wife and daughter showed up. Karen had kept her age well. She was dressed in a sharp business suit, which was her usual attire since she sold real estate. Helen was standing at my side, and she and Karen instinctively checked each other out. Karen went over to look at my mother, and Pamela walked over to me.

She had grown several inches since I last saw her and was turning into a beautiful young woman. She was sure to break some young man's heart if she hadn't already.

She hugged me. "Daddy, I'm sorry. I wish I'd have visited her more."

"I've got lots of regrets, too, honey," I said.

Neither of us could think of anything else to say, but we had said volumes in that short exchange. I embraced her again. "I love you."

"I love you, too, Daddy."

One of the morticians had been watching us, and when we were finished, he walked over to me.

"I'm sorry to bother you, Mr. Fellars, but you have a phone call. The party says it's very important."

I took the call in his office.

"Hello, Mr. Fellars. This is Gordon Wallace. I hate to trouble you in your time of grief, but I need you."

A cold chill ran up my spine.

"Can't it wait a couple of days, Gordon?"

"No. If you're going to help me, it has to be tonight. Right now."

I quickly considered the situation. Gordon was bad news and could very easily be up to no good. But he had not opened a door to me before, and if I was going to help him, I didn't have much time.

"All right, Gordon. Where do I meet you?"

"In your office at school."

"I'll be right up."

"You have to come alone. If you bring anybody else with you, I won't show."

I knew Helen wouldn't let me meet him alone, so I slipped out of the funeral home without telling her.

44

He was sitting at my desk when I walked into my office. The light was on. I had seen it from the street as I drove by.

Just as Bubba Wilson had worked hard to cultivate the look of a good-ole-boy small-town lawman, Gordon had strived to look like a street punk. His hair was long and greasy, slicked back away from his forehead. He wore a leather jacket, despite the fact that it was almost June. His right ear sported an earring, common today but *avant-garde* in Gordon's day. He had the usual scars and tattoos. There was a line under his chin where his throat had been slit by the drug lord he had tried to skim. The mirror-tinted sunshades hid his eyes.

He leaned back in my chair. "Hello, Mr. Fellars. Thanks for coming."

I sat down in a plastic chair across the desk from him. "What can I do for you, Gordon?"

He placed his feet on my desk. The bottoms of his boots had horseshoe taps on both heels and a wad of smashed bubble gum under the left toe.

"Actually, nothing. I figured I could do something for you."

"Really?"

He gave me the grin that had seemed to charm the female student body population of Brownville High a decade ago. "I figure you're feeling pretty down about now. You need a friend."

"I'm touched, Gordon. Especially since you've been sabotaging me all spring. You sent Linda Sue's writeup to the *Pineville Chronicle*. You sicced Bubba Wilson and Legrand Warfield on me. You turned Carl Harris's Doberman on Mrs. Halfacre. And you think I need a friend?"

"It was just a game. Which you won, fair and square. You're in luck, Mr. Fellars. I'm not a sore loser."

"I'm not finished yet. I've got Steve Hall left. And I haven't given up on you and Todd Grant either."

He grinned again. No matter what drugs and alcohol had done to his lungs and liver, he had taken care of his teeth.

"I'm not going to give up on you, either, Mr. Fellars. I know a lot about you."

"Oh? What do you know about me, Gordon?"

"I know you're feeling pretty bad about yourself. You had wonderful parents, just like Barbara Fields. They did everything right. Gave you a happy childhood. Not like Mike Sanders, who had a stepdad that trashed his mom every night and battered his little brother every other day. Or Laval Crenshaw, whose old man belittled him every day of his life. Or Seth Warfield, whose old man is the biggest crook in Elmwood County. Or me. I could tell you stories about my old man that would make you chuck your cookies. Did you know my old man served twelve years in the pen for armed robbery?"

I nodded. "I've heard that."

"It doesn't seem fair, does it?"

"No, it doesn't, Gordon."

"Then you look at your daughter. You weren't able to give her the same happy, stable childhood you had. You brought her into the world and turned around and crapped on her. You gave her a broken home. She hardly even speaks to you. That's got to make you feel pretty bad, huh? How am I doing so far?"

I tried not to swallow. "Pretty well on target, Gordon."

"But now you think you've got a bright spot in your life. Helen Noble. Do you love her?"

I nodded. "Yes."

"You know what love is, Mr. Fellars? It's a sickness that warps your thinking. It blinds you to the other person's faults. You get married. Then your eyes are opened and you see the faults, but it's too late. You end up with a kid or two. Another marriage goes sour. Now you've got two or three kids whose lives you've crapped on instead of just one. Am I right?"

"I've seen the pattern."

"You've managed to fool yourself into thinking you did the others a favor, but you didn't. Think about it. Mike Sanders got rid of his stepdad, but his mother will just go out and find another abusive husband. That kind of woman always does. And there are plenty of them in Brownville. Will and Charlie frittered away their second chance on a drunken orgy. What good did you really do them? Chadwick Corley? Even his dead friends thought he was a joke. The critics are going to burn Sally's novel. Her parents are talking about paying to get it published. What did you do with Barbara Fields's family except open up old wounds? I could go on, but you get the picture."

"What about Randy Galphin's family?"

He thought for a moment, then said, rather begrudgingly, "All right, I'll give you that one. If you'd have given them the money all in one wad, they'd have blown it. So you were smart to dole it out to them. But if anything happens to you, they're back to square one, aren't they?"

"I plan to take care of myself," I said.

He let that alone and moved on. "I know something else about you, Mr. Fellars. A deep, dark secret."

"Oh?"

"Whenever you get depressed, you always bring yourself out of it by thinking of Ray Taylor."

His remark shocked me, and I'm sure it registered on my face. Somehow Gordon had managed to invade my deepest thoughts. I suddenly became very much afraid.

Ray Taylor had been a principal at Brownville Elementary when I first came to Brownville. At that time, mine was not a full-time position at Brownville High, and I was assigned to Brownville Elementary one day per week. I became quite close to Ray Taylor.

The pressures of his job eroded Ray's health over the years. First he suffered a heart attack and almost died. He was a sentimental old cuss and was overjoyed when I visited him in the hospital. I still remember feeling the stubble when he took my hand and held it to his cheek. Later, Ray ended up killing himself.

"You get to feeling rotten," Gordon continued, "but you tell yourself, at least I'm alive. Poor old Ray can't see the sunset anymore or enjoy the taste of a Big Mac.

"But if you look at it another way, Ray's got it made. He doesn't get cold or hungry anymore. He doesn't have any parents chewing on him. No financial worries. He doesn't have to fight the rat race. You're out of line pitying Ray Taylor. He doesn't have a worry in the world."

"If that's the case, why are you still around? Why do you fear death?"

He threw his head back so I could see the death scar on his throat.

"You see this? It means I'll never have to fear death. I haven't gone all the way over yet, but I'm still dead. I'm not like the others. I'm hanging around for kicks. When I run out of fun, I'll move on."

He removed his feet from my desk and opened his jacket. He extracted a paperback book and placed it on my desk. "I got you a present. I took it out of the library."

I looked at the cover. "Robert E. Howard. One of my favorite writers."

"Do you know how he died?"

One of the strangest feelings I have ever experienced settled in my stomach. "He lived with his mother. When she died, he went out and shot himself."

He grinned his trademark grin again. "Kind of hits close to home, don't it?"

By now he had me agreeing with everything he said. "A little too close."

He opened my desk drawer. "I brought you another present." He pulled a pistol out of the drawer and placed it on the desk.

I stared at it. "What's that for?"

"We're going to explore the bright side of death together."

"You're going to kill me?" I asked.

"No. I believe everybody should control their own destiny." He looked at the pistol. "It's the one Randy Galphin used to kill himself with."

I couldn't take my eyes off it.

He shoved the pistol across the desk to me. "You're going to think this is crazy, Mr. Fellars, but stroking a pistol can be a great relaxer when you're down. Pick it up and hold it."

I did as he said. I was completely under his dark spell by then.

"How does it feel?"

"Soothing. Very soothing."

"Do you feel your frustrations being soaked into the barrel?"

"Yes."

He leaned forward across the desk. "Open the chamber and take out the bullets. Feel them."

I stroked the bullets. "They feel good."

"I'll tell you something Ray Taylor knew about bullets. I spent a lot of time in his office in the sixth grade. He hated his job. He was good at it, but he hated it. He said parents and teachers were like wild Indians, always out to scalp him. And Ray gave me an old Indian fighting secret. Never let them take you alive, or they'll torture you. When your troops are wiped out and the Indians are closing in, always save that last bullet for yourself."

Suddenly I was consumed by a wave of hopelessness and despair. "I'll try to remember that."

"Put the bullets back in the chamber and we'll try an experiment."

I did what he said.

"Now cock the pistol and tell me what you feel."

The pistol clicked.

"Power," I said.

Gordon was pleased. "That's right. That's the most powerful anti-depressant drug there is. It gets rid of the Indians trying to scalp you. It makes you stop feeling like a dog because you crapped on your daughter's life. It fixes it where you don't have to worry about living in a nursing home or having your child wipe your butt in your old age. Now, are you ready for the big finish?"

I nodded. "I'm ready."

"Put it in your mouth and pull the trigger."

I brought the pistol up to the roof of my mouth. Gordon took off his sunglasses, and we stared each other in the eye. His eyes were gray, not just dead but evil. He never blinked. He drew me into the black hole of his gaze, and I remember swirling into a pit of darkness so black and beautiful I could almost see the bright side of death.

At the last second, he turned his eyes away, and that's when I snapped to. I heard him scream, "No!"

I became aware of pounding on my office door.

"Bill! Bill, are you in there?" Helen said.

I took the gun out of my mouth and uncocked it. Gordon ran to my closet and opened the door.

"Another minute and you'd have been free," he said to me. He stepped inside and closed the door.

I walked over and opened the door after him. He was gone.

I placed the pistol on the desk and opened the door for Helen.

She stepped into the room and looked around. "Are you all right?"

"Yes."

"Where's Gordon?"

"Gone."

She stared at the pistol on my desk. "What did he do?"

"He killed off all my troops and then turned the Indians on me."

I guess, looking back, that could be considered a racially insensitive comment in the politically correct environment we have today, because it affirmed Gordon's one-sided characterization of the Native American experience in this country. It didn't strike me that way when I said it, but I acknowledge it now.

She cocked her head. "What?"

"You know how kids get depressed and threaten to kill themselves and I have to talk them out of it?"

"Yes."

"Well, Gordon was trying to talk me into it. He was doing a good job of it, too. He has some counseling skills I didn't know he had."

45

"How did you know where to find me?" I asked Helen. We were in my outer office. I had retrieved Randy Galphin's pistol from my desk.

"Steve Hall told me. He came to the funeral home."

"In Elmwood? I wonder how he managed that."

"It wasn't easy. He looked like the devil was chasing him. My guess is they ran him out of Brownville. He was so weak I could hardly make out what he said. He seemed to be in excruciating pain. He managed to tell me Gordon had you in your office. He ran out in the yard. When I ran after him, he was gone. I think he went over right on the spot."

I pulled out my handkerchief and wiped my brow. I felt my knees begin to tremble.

"I tried to talk him into going over with Freddy. I guess it's a good thing for me he didn't."

"You can say that again."

"Steve wanted to do something heroic. This qualifies him for a Medal of Honor in my book," I said.

Helen must have noticed me trembling. "What's wrong, Bill?"

I looked at the door to my inner office. I had closed it behind me. "I came very close to shooting myself in there."

She put her arms around me, and I held her in a very tight embrace.

I buried my mother the next day. It was a simple graveside service. Mom had already made plans for my cousin, who is a Baptist minister in Conway, to preach the eulogy. She hadn't planned for the mid-morning thundershower, but somehow it fit my mood.

After the funeral, I went about rebuilding my life.

It was a lonely afternoon. I drove to Brownville and ended up on Cemetery Drive. I wanted to say goodbye to them one last time. I visited all of their graves and remembered something about each one. The way Randy Galphin's face lit up when he told about his mother fanning through her mail and finding the envelope with Warfield's drug money. Johnny Brown stepping out of my closet the day I introduced Helen to George and Linda Sue. Little Melissa King scolding Scuttles in the back seat of my car at the cemetery. Freddy Seaton with his hand on Legrand Warfield's shirt in the Li'l Cricket parking lot. The anger in Barbara Fields's eyes during our first session, the first time she called me "Moses." Will Masters and Charlie Green drunkenly butchering "Crocodile Rock" as they were leaving Ira Cavandish's bash. Sally Brock hugging me in her dormer studio. Sammy Tribble's body jerking as he pounded away on the Steinway at the Levitt mansion before I removed the wires. Laval Crenshaw's quivering lip when I chided him for wrecking the semi. Sometimes I wish I'd never laid eyes on Laval. Thanks to him, I can't pass an abandoned mutt on the side of the road without picking it up. Steve Hall trying to harness Legrand Warfield's mule in the swamp. Steve saved my life, and to my way of thinking, every good thing I do in the future is a credit to him, despite what Chad Corley would have you believe.

On my way out of town, I met a hitchhiker by the Dempsey Dumpster at the town limit. I usually don't stop, but this one looked like somebody I knew. It also looked like my work might not be finished.

I pulled over.

"Mr. Fellars, you got a minute?" the hitchhiker said.

"Are you Todd Grant?"

"Yeah."

"Get in."

He was big, over six-foot-four, and very muscular. His size made you wonder why he should kowtow to Gordon Wallace. His hair was long and tied in a ponytail with a red-and-white bandanna. His eyes were scrunched into a scowl and had bags under them. Unlike Gordon Wallace, he had a death scar that didn't show unless he had his shirt off. He had been knifed in the chest during a barroom brawl.

He produced a CD from his shirt pocket. "Do you mind if I play this?"

I looked at it. It was *Last Night in Town* by metalcore band Every Time I Die from the early 2000s.

"I don't mind," I said.

He placed it in my CD player and turned up the volume. The music seemed to relax him. He leaned back in my seat.

I turned around and headed back into Brownville.

He turned to me. "Mr. Fellars—"

I looked at my CD player. "Todd, you're going to have to turn that down if we're going to talk."

He turned down the volume.

"Mr. Fellars, I'm sorry for what Gordon and me did last night."

I looked at him. "Exactly what was your part in it, Todd?"

"Gordon wanted to lure you to Brownville so he could do you in. We knew Steve Hall would warn you, so we trapped him in the Levitt house. Then Gordon went to meet you at your office. The two of us could hold Steve, but I couldn't do it by myself. He got out. I managed to get between him and the school. He ran into three or four houses to try to use a cell phone, but I kept knocking them out of his hand. When he saw I wasn't going to let him connect, he started running. I chased him as far as I could, but he ran out Highway 21 toward Elmwood. The farther I got from Brownville, the weaker I got and the more it burned. Steve was still running when I turned around. I almost didn't make it back. I don't know how far Steve went."

I maneuvered onto a side street and made my way onto one of the dirt roads that circled around the outskirts of town. "He went all the way."

Todd's eyes widened. "To Elmwood?"

"To Elmwood. My guess is he never looked back to see that you'd stopped chasing him."

Todd was clearly impressed. "Man!"

I let him concentrate on Every Time I Die for a long moment.

"So where do we go from here?" I asked.

"I want to cross over."

"What's stopping you?"

"Same as the others. I'm scared."

"Why didn't you come to me with the others?"

"I let Gordon do my thinking. Now I see that hasn't gotten me anywhere."

I studied his face to see if it betrayed any signs of insincerity. I saw none.

"Does Gordon want to cross over too?"

"Gordon knows he's a lost soul. He's not in any hurry to start shoveling coal."

"What about you?"

"If I go to hell, at least I'll belong there. I can't stand it the way it is anymore."

"How is Gordon treating you?"

"He's furious with me. He's scared too. He's begging me not to go. When I go, he'll be stuck here by himself. He won't get any comfort from the living or the dead."

As we passed over Lover's Lane, I noticed the county coroner had painted a fresh white cross on the road where Julie Summer died on prom night.

"How can I help you?" I asked.

He considered. "I don't know."

"We've got to start somewhere."

He shrugged. "I have no idea where to start."

"Is there something you feel you need to do before you go over?"

He shook his head. "Not really."

"Then you should be ready to go."

He turned and looked me in the eye. "Will you sit by my grave if I go over tonight?"

"Yes."

"Don't leave until sunrise," he said, with a pleading edge to his voice.

"I'll stay all night," I promised.

"Thanks." He took Every Time I Die out of my CD player. "You can let me out here."

I pulled over and let him out in the middle of nowhere.

"I'll meet you at the cemetery at sundown," I promised. "If you run into Gordon, tell him to call me if he needs me."

I had debated over whether to make that offer to help Gordon Wallace, and professional dedication won out over prudence. I told myself that, true to Steve Hall's prophetic insight, Gordon had indeed approached me in the moment of my greatest weakness, while I was grieving over the loss of my mother. He had sniffed out all of my personal baggage and woven it into a death shroud of gloom and despair. "Gordon's good at getting somebody else to do his dirty work," Steve had warned. In my case, that someone had been me. I told myself I would be prepared for him next time. I would help him, but on my terms.

I kept my promise to Todd Grant that night. He didn't cross over until just before sunrise. I heard his life story, a depressing earful of selfishness, bitterness, wrong choices, and people not caring. Like the kids I counseled at school, he just seemed to want to get it off his chest.

Gordon Wallace never showed up to say goodbye.

46

I came out of grieving to attend graduation ceremonies two nights later. It was Brownville High's last graduation, and the tears flowed like beer at Butch's Bar during happy hour.

I had kept my promise to the wasted, dead youth of Brownville, but it ended up costing me my good name. Nobody came right out and told me to my face that I was crazy, but I'd noticed that conversation sometimes stopped when I walked into the teacher's lounge those last couple of months. And at graduation, people would poke each other and stare at me when they thought I wasn't looking. I know the town couldn't help but notice the way Legrand Warfield and Bubba Wilson were quick to step out of my way when they met me on the street.

I walked out of the hell of my long night with Gordon Wallace with an insatiable thirst for life. That was their gift to me. When you've got something somebody else wants very badly, you appreciate it. They taught me to appreciate being alive—"they" including Gordon Wallace.

Helen and I went to Myrtle Beach, where I came close to overdosing on laughter and sunshine and fresh air. I gave Helen a one-karat diamond on the boardwalk in the ocean breeze. I can still hear the refrains from Alabama's "Give Me One More Shot" and Travis Tritt's

"It's a Great Day to Be Alive" in my head from endless replays on my CD player during those days.

Now that I think about it, they also taught me another lesson. You never know how much time you've got left to mend your fences or go for your dreams. When Helen and I returned from the beach, I wrote my daughter a long letter. I took my mother's novel that Hiram Thompson had rejected to Aaron Brock and told him I wanted to have it edited and published. Aaron understood, and he promised to help in any way he could. It eventually became a print-on-demand novel put out by an internet publisher. I sell about fifty copies a year.

I never did connect with Gordon Wallace. Sometimes you have to cut your losses in my business. You don't reach all the kids. Just like I was never able to reach Bennie Norris, the tire slasher. Or Bennie's brother, who is still on death row. Or Larry Ringer, who fancied himself ahead of his time. Or Randy Galphin the first time around. The troubled kids leave, and you never know what happened to them.

Gordon was there at graduation night, staring across the football field, where now only the ghosts of yesterday's teams will play.

When I left Brownville High for the last time in early June, carrying the last of my belongings in a box, the halls were empty. Gordon was standing at the east wing corner where I had first seen Randy Galphin. He had his foot propped up on a locker like he owned the place. Which now he did.

THE END

ACKNOWLEDGMENT

Thanks to Wendy, Jennifer, Donna, and Eddie for reading an early version of this work and offering suggestions.

Thanks to Lara Kennedy, my editor, for her eagle eye. Because of the two decades between drafts, the manuscript I sent her had many anachronisms and timeline inconsistencies. Working with Lara was like being a murder suspect lying to a master detective, who found all kind of holes in my story.

Thanks to teachers Pat Schroder and Susan Helfrich for allowing their students to read the original manuscript and provide feedback.

Thanks to the late Donald Hamilton, author of the Matt Helm adventure series, and to romance novelist Elizabeth Graham for their professional encouragement. Thanks also to C. Hope Clark, author of the *Edisto Island Mysteries* and the *Carolina Slade Mysteries* for her kind words.

Thanks to the following models who posed for photos in the photo section:

Mike Sanders . . . Perry Ellison

Bill Fellars . . . Larry Rothman

Helen Noble . . . Roberta Lairson

Melissa King . . . Megan Floyd

Freddy Seaton . . . yours truly

Photos for the following characters in the photo spread were licensed from Adobe Stock: *https://stock.adobe.com*. All rights reserved.

Legrand Warfield

Sally Brock

Sammy Tribble

Tony Cunningham

Steve Hall

Laval Crenshaw

Johnny Brown

Gordon Wallace

Randy Galphin

Will Masters and Charlie Green

The Summer Sisters

Todd Grant

Barbara Fields

Chadwick Corley

Photo of Crybaby Bridge was licensed from Adobe Stock: *https://stock.adobe.com*. All rights reserved.

Photos for the following characters in the photo spread were licensed from iStock: *www.istockphoto.com*. All rights reserved.

Bubba Wilson

Tim Boyle

George Baucom and Linda Sue Boyle

Cover photo was licensed from iStock: *www.istockphoto.com*. All rights reserved.

The Story Behind
the Novel

Lost on the Edge of Eternity is an expansion of an unpublished short story I wrote in 1984. The story was entitled "New Student," and it grew out of my grief over the deaths of several students over the years at the high school where I served as guidance counselor. The story was written years before the television show *Ghost Whisperer* and the movie *Casper*, which capitalized on a similar theme.

In 1995, I decided to expand my short story into a novel, and the first draft of *Lost on the Edge of Eternity* was born. Despite going through two agents, I was never able to get the novel published. In 2001, I decided to self-publish the novel under a pseudonym in newspaper format, complete with a photo spread of the characters. In order to publicize my novel, I offered to send free copies to teachers, with the understanding that they would have their students critique the novel and provide feedback. This was in the fall of 2001, right after the September 11 terrorist attacks.

I ended up getting one teacher at Coconino High School in Flagstaff, Arizona, in trouble. Here is the way her letter explained the situation to me:

After she assigned the novel for her English 12 classes to read, one parent became uncomfortable with the novel. The parent considered the novel inappropriate for high school seniors because of the terrorist attack on America (this was in the fall of 2001) and a recent suicide at the school. The parent never read the novel but formed her opinion based on the front cover and the photo spread. She complained to the school's principal and was not satisfied with his explanation. She proceeded to contact district administration officials and convinced them to "ban" the novel. English teachers at Coconino High were outraged that one parent could censor reading materials, especially without ever reading them. Each member of the English department took home a copy of the novel and read it over Thanksgiving vacation. Satisfied that the novel was appropriate, they fought the administration and, "after the endless meetings came to an end," the students finished reading the novel.

I sent copies of the novel to several authors, requesting their feedback. Two writers who responded were the late Donald Hamilton, creator of the Matt Helm adventure series, and romance novelist Elizabeth Graham, author of *Jacintha Point*. I will always be grateful for their encouragement.

With self-publishing made easy by IngramSpark and Amazon's KDP program, I decided to revisit my novel this past year. Using suggestions made by Coconino High students twenty years previously, I updated the novel and fleshed out the characters (if you can "flesh out" ghosts).

Hopefully the reader will enjoy the experience as much as the writer did.

"AIN'T TOO PROUD TO BEG," AS THE TEMPTATIONS WOULD SAY

It's no secret that the key to book sales is word-of-mouth praise. So if you enjoyed *Lost on the Edge of Eternity*, please consider going on Amazon and/or Goodreads and leaving a review. I wish I could promise you eternal happiness if you do so, but I can promise you my eternal gratitude.

Jonathan Floyd

278

"A small-town tale simmering with interpersonal
squabbles yet imbedded with heart and soul."
— Kirkus Reviews

From the author of Lost on the Edge of Eternity

Urbanicide
Murder of a Town

A Novel

Jonathan Floyd

Stories from the Attic by Jonathan Floyd available from Amazon.com

www.ingramcontent.com/pod-product-compliance
Lightning Source LLC
Chambersburg PA
CBHW072350110726
47909CB00003B/658